A Certain Magical **Index**

10

KAZUMA KAMACHI

ILLUSTRATION BY
KIYOTAKA HAIMURA

[CROCE DI PIETRO]

Also known as the Cross of Peter. The cross is from the grave of Saint Peter, one of the twelve apostles who received the keys to Heaven from the Lord. Anyplace the Croce di Pietro is planted becomes the domain of the Roman Orthodox Church, including the surrounding space. The Croce di Pietro forcibly exerts control over all things, both physical and mental, then it allows only events beneficial to the Roman Orthodox Church to occur. No one thinks the changes are strange because the Croce di Pietro convinces them that what they see and feel is "happiness."

contents

[DAIHASEI FESTIVAL]
A massive athletic meet held in Academy
City, the supernatural-ability development
organization with just under 2.3 million
people. All of the city's schools compete
against one another over the course of seven
days, from September 19 to September 25.

"Allow me to say one last thing: It is over.
I will re-create this world into a better one, and
that includes all of you."

Honored Roman Orthodox disciple also known as the Mardi Gras (Shrove Tuesday) **Lidvia Lorenzetti**

VOLUME 10

KAZUMA KAMACHI

ILLUSTRATION BY: KIYOTAKA HAIMURA

NEW YORK

A CERTAIN MAGICAL INDEX, Volume 10
KAZUMA KAMACHI

Translation by Andrew Prowse
Cover art by Kiyotaka Haimura

TOARU MAJYUTSU NO INDEX
©KAZUMA KAMACHI 2006
All rights reserved.
Edited by ASCII MEDIA WORKS
First published in Japan in 2006 by KADOKAWA CORPORATION, Tokyo.
English translation rights arranged with KADOKAWA CORPORATION, Tokyo,
through Tuttle-Mori Agency, Inc., Tokyo.

English translation © 2017 by Yen Press, LLC

Yen On
1290 Avenue of the Americas
New York, NY 10104

Visit us at yenpress.com
facebook.com/yenpress
twitter.com/yenpress
yenpress.tumblr.com
instagram.com/yenpress

First Yen On Edition: February 2017

Yen On is an imprint of Yen Press, LLC.
The Yen On name and logo are trademarks of Yen Press, LLC.

The publisher is not responsible for websites (or their content) that are not owned by the publisher.

Library of Congress Cataloging-in-Publication Data

Names: Kamachi, Kazuma, author. | Haimura, Kiyotaka, 1973– illustrator. |
    Prowse, Andrew (Andrew R.), translator. | Hinton, Yoshito, translator.
Title: A certain magical index / Kazuma Kamachi ; illustration by Kiyotaka Haimura.
Other titles: To aru majyutsu no kinsho mokuroku. (Light novel). English
Description: First Yen On edition. | New York : Yen On, 2014–
Identifiers: LCCN 2014031047 (print) | ISBN 9780316339124 (v. 1 : pbk.) |
    ISBN 9780316259422 (v. 2 : pbk.) | ISBN 9780316340540 (v. 3 : pbk.) |
    ISBN 9780316340564 (v. 4 : pbk.) | ISBN 9780316340595 (v. 5 : pbk.) |
    ISBN 9780316340601 (v. 6 : pbk.) | ISBN 9780316272230 (v. 7 : pbk.) |
    ISBN 9780316359924 (v. 8 : pbk.) | ISBN 9780316359962 (v. 9 : pbk.) |
    ISBN 9780316359986 (v. 10: pbk.)
Subjects: | CYAC: Magic—Fiction. | Ability—Fiction. | Nuns—Fiction. |
    Japan—Fiction. | Science fiction. | BISAC: FICTION / Fantasy / General. |
    FICTION / Science Fiction / Adventure.
Classification: LCC PZ7.1.K215 Ce 2014 (print) | LCC PZ7.1.K215 (ebook) | DDC [Fic]—dc23
LC record available at https://lccn.loc.gov/2014031047

ISBNs: 978-0-316-35998-6 (paperback)
    978-0-316-35999-3 (ebook)

1 3 5 7 9 10 8 6 4 2

LSC-C

Printed in the United States of America

CHAPTER 5

Restful Moment on Strings of Tension
Resumption_of_Hostilities.

1

"*Sorcerers have snuck into Academy City,*" Stiyl Magnus, a member of the English Puritan Church, had said.

"*Right now, we have a lead on the Route Disturber, Oriana Thomson, and the Mardi Gras, Lidvia Lorenzetti. Apparently, they're trying to make a deal for a real important Soul Arm somewhere in the city, nya~,*" Motoharu Tsuchimikado, the sorcerer, had continued.

As Touma Kamijou, the high school student, walked through Academy City that afternoon, he thought back to what they'd told him. The city was bustling with people due to a special citywide athletic meet called the Daihasei Festival.

"*Security here is usually far too strict, but with the Daihasei Festival going on, they must have at least a few clerks helping them out. They took advantage of that to slip into the city.*"

"*And you know how it goes, nya~. If Anti-Skill or Judgment gets ahold of anyone related to sorcery, there's going to be some problems. But we can't let a bunch of sorcerers inside to chase down Oriana and Lidvia, either. Not all sorcerers are friends of Academy City, nya~. Both the science side and the magic side have noticed what the two of them are doing, but their hands are tied.*"

There were a lot of adults around today, which was unusual for a city made up of 80 percent students. Parents and guardians had come here in droves to watch their children compete. They were all gazing at the power-generating wind turbines, autonomous cleaning robots, and other things they looked upon in curiosity. Espers like Kamijou were included in that list.

"*Which means we're the only ones who can act right now.*"

"*If we can't stop their deal with the Stab Sword, it might be everything the world of sorcery needs to go to war, nya~.*"

Kamijou wove through the crowds as he strolled along. Around him were parents and children walking with helium-filled balloons and elderly people with their Daihasei Festival pamphlets, which had inflated to the size of overseas travel guidebooks, checking on the event schedules.

"*The moment the group of magicians waiting outside the city detects any mana flows inside Academy City, they'll use it as an excuse to barge in. They would have searching spells spanning a big area.*"

"*Still, none of their spells will be able to cover the entire city. They're probably using Index as a focal point and searching from there for about one or two kilometers. After all, most of the sorcery-related incidents in the city have been around her, nya~.*"

"*Which means that if she gets close to the situation, they might detect mana from me or Oriana and Lidvia. But if we get her farther away from things, there's a much lower chance their search will spot us.*"

"*Welp, that's up to you, Kammy. If you could just lead Index far away from the incident, it would help us out a whole lot.*"

Everything around Kamijou was peaceful. Nobody knew anything about the strange occurrences…

…including what was about to take place in Academy City…

…or how there were people working to stop it.

"*Damn! The Soul Arm they've got wasn't the Stab Sword—it was the Croce di Pietro! It has the power to dominate everything, physical and mental, in the space around where it's planted into the ground, making it all Roman Orthodox territory. Everything in the affected area will start to go the Church's way, and nobody will even think anything* is up. If they used it in a city directly opposed to the religious world...If the best thing for the Roman Orthodox Church is Academy City falling under its control, **then it'll just happen!**"

"This deal Oriana mentioned wasn't for the Soul Arm itself—it was a deal to gain control of Academy City. It's the leader of the science faction. Gaining control of it means they'll scoop up half the world, nya~. If the strongest member of the Church takes the biggest member of the scientific side...then the Roman Orthodox Church will conquer the whole planet!"

"That's why we knew Oriana's and Lidvia's names and that they'd be handing it over, but never who they were going to trade it to. They never planned on giving away the Croce di Pietro in the first place. The deal is between Lidvia and Oriana and the entire Roman Orthodox Church they belong to!"

Touma Kamijou walked through Academy City—

—where, on the surface, espers clashed. Where, below the surface, sorcerers lurked.

2

The Daihasei Festival.

This unique athletic festival held over seven days in Academy City, the facility for supernatural-ability development taking up all of western Tokyo, was already nearing the halfway point of its first day. All events were suspended right now from noon till two for lunch break. The swarms of students who had just been participating in the games and cheering on their classmates were now loose in the streets. The presence of general attendees from outside the city drove the current population density through the roof.

"Indeeex?"

Touma Kamijou walked through the utterly crowded city streets.

He had changed clothes temporarily, and now he was just a regular boy sporting the regular short sleeves and shorts of his gym uniform. Certain circumstances had left him with scrapes on his arms and legs, some gauze plastered on his cheek, topped off with rips and mud stains on his clothing. But with every esper in the city participating in the Daihasei Festival's fierce battles, he didn't stand out very much.

Also, due to said circumstances, he hadn't eaten anything even though lunch break was coming to an end. He plodded along, rather hungry, continuing his search for an equally hungry girl.

She should be around here somewhere...I made sure to give her a zero-yen cell phone, but its battery is dead, so she can't use it. Tsuchimikado told me to keep her away from the incident, too, so I need to find her and keep an eye on her.

Kamijou's eyes darted around, wondering why he was so relaxed while the likes of the sorcerer Oriana Thomson and the Roman Orthodox disciple Lidvia Lorenzetti were plotting who knows what behind the scenes. But Tsuchimikado and Stiyl had strictly warned him about this, too.

"If their goal is to use the Croce di Pietro to gain control of Academy City, then why didn't they use it right away? There must be a reason they couldn't. It's a damn powerful Soul Arm, after all. Activating, controlling, and stabilizing it would take more than a mere incantation. For example...the caster might need to purify herself with fire and holy oil for a long period of time. Or she might need to put up a special barrier so the cross itself doesn't pick up any stray thoughts of passersby and confuse the caster's orders...In any case, they must not be able to use the Croce di Pietro without first doing some sort of complex preparations."

"If we could just figure out what its usage conditions are, we might be able to get a leg up on 'em, nya~. Either way, investigating Soul Arms is a sorcerer's job. Nothing you can help us with here, Kammy."

That was the gist of it. With everything going on, the top priority for Kamijou at the moment was to stay with a certain girl.

The person he was looking for, named Index, was a small, fair-skinned girl with green eyes. Her hair was silver and went down to her waist. Plus, she was wearing a white habit embroidered with gold thread that made her look like a teacup.

A foreign girl wasn't that unusual, considering how much international visibility there was for Academy City and the Daihasei Festival. Every once in a while, he'd pass a girl with silver hair and green eyes, but even he wasn't going to mistake one of them for her and strike up a conversation. However many silver-haired, green-eyed girls were here, Index was the only one wearing that ridiculously outlandish habit. He would never miss her.

…But he still couldn't find her. He tilted his head, confused. What had happened?

"Toumaaa…"

Then his ears heard a familiar cute voice.

He looked in that direction, but all he saw were people, people, and some more people. They were completely blocking the view, and he didn't have the time to stop and look at every single one of their faces. He caught silver out of the corner of his eye, but when he looked, it was a girl in a cheerleading uniform, with a white pleated skirt and a pale-green tank top. Index would never wear something like that.

"Toumaaa…"

He heard it again. He turned around, but he still couldn't find any sign of that ostentatious white habit. Just a girl who looked almost exactly like Index, wearing a cheerleading uniform, holding a calico in both arms, with silver hair and green eyes—

"Touma!! Why are you trying not to look at me?!"

"Ack!!"

Kamijou reeled back in surprise—the cheer girl had come right up next to him without his noticing and shouted in his ears. She must have been searching for Kamijou on her own, too.

Oh. Now he remembered. *Right, wasn't Miss Komoe helping Index change into a cheerleading uniform or something this morning…?*

"…Touma, Touma. Did you just think about something lewd? You look really happy to see me right now."

"I…I am not! Ha-ha, of course not!" Kamijou hurriedly shook his head. "Wait, Index, what happened to your usual habit?"

"I left it with Komoe," answered Index, visibly peeved.

Wh-what could she be angry about? He felt uneasy. His eyes met the calico's, but all he received in return was a sleepy yawn. He thought for a few moments, still looking at the cat's peaceful face. "Okay, I get it. You're hungry, right? I was about to meet up with Dad to eat some lunch, so you just need to wait a little longer."

The moment he said that, Index balled her little hands into fists and gave Kamijou a whack on the head. "No, that's not it! Touma, you idiot!"

"Ow, that hurt! Then what is it?!"

"I changed my clothes and learned dance steps from Komoe so I could cheer you on! But where were you the whole time?! I don't think you were at the bread-eating-race thing! Or the rope-pulling thing, either! Were you in *anything*?!"

Oh. That reminded him— He was currently in the middle of a few things. Circumstances had dictated he leave his class for something else, *but of course he couldn't explain any of that to Index.*

She groaned. "I did everything, and I tried really hard, all because I thought I could finally be with you! Then you went off alone, and I didn't know what to do...," she mumbled, her head hanging as low as it could go.

Index wasn't familiar with being in Academy City during such a huge event. It was like he'd left her alone at a party she hadn't been invited to. She must have felt totally helpless. Kamijou scratched his head. "Ahh, I'm sorry, Index! I just thought, you know, you were mad because you were hungry like you always are."

"No, I wasn't! I tried really hard so I could cheer you on, but you wouldn't even look at me! That's why I'm mad!! And besides, I've taken a vow of poverty like all proper sisters. Getting mad because I'm hungry is something I would never do, Touma!!"

"Really, now? Food seems to be the only thing on your mind for three-fourths of the year...Wait, no, I didn't mean it!! See, I just accidentally said what I meant— No, wait, you know, I, uh, I can explain...!!"

Kamijou tried to plead his case, but Index's anger would not be quelled. Her tiny fists pummeled his cheeks and chest over and over. This was cute to see, but he suddenly felt like something was wrong.

"…? Index, what happened to your usual biting?…Wait, no! It's not like you need to force yourself to do it—really!!"

The last part had been added quickly, but contrary to his expectations, Index showed no response. In fact, her pummeling hands suddenly stopped moving.

He looked at her face. And he almost groaned out loud.

Index's head was tilted down as far as it would go, and her face was bright red all the way to her ears. Her shoulders were trembling a little, and her small lips were locking up in an attempt to say something. The calico sensed the strange situation it was in and meowed up at her, but things had gotten so tense he wasn't even sure she could hear it.

Index stood there for a few moments, frozen up and silent. Finally, she muttered, "…You're a pervert."

"What the heck? You were the one who was always biting *me* this whole time, Index! Mr. Kamijou screamed and cried every time for you to stop and get off! If anything, that would make *you* the perv— Gbahh?!"

Before he could finish arguing, a tiny fist shut him up.

And a pretty serious fist, at that.

3

Oriana Thomson had just gotten a two-scoop ice cream cone from a shopkeeper wearing a cute uniform.

Golden locks, curling around and fluffing out behind her. Pale white skin and blue eyes. A tall body and looks that killed—she was the perfect image of a foreigner from a Japanese person's point of view.

She was no longer wearing her earlier work uniform. Now her outfit consisted of a lightly colored camisole and a loose skirt. On her feet, she wore thin mules. Her skirt went down almost to her ankles, but she couldn't exactly be called "neatly dressed." The skirt was split every ten centimeters into strips of vertically hanging fabric, gaps between each of them. They didn't bother to hide her underwear, so she was also wearing a pareo around her waist, the kind someone would wear as part of a swimsuit.

Her skirt was basically no more than a see-through bamboo screen. With every step she took, her legs would stick out, expose more and more until her thighs appeared, then sink back inside again. The sight of her bare skin going in and out of clothing meant to hide her underwear made it look like she was offering a fundamental rejection of how skirts were supposed to function.

In Crossist society, clothing was an item that displayed one's position and status. From an archbishop's vestments to a prisoner's uniform, no matter what you were, there was an outfit specifically for you.

Among them, destroyed clothing—especially a torn-up woman's skirt—meant that the person had been divested of all authority. Those who were subjected to this were labeled as shameful and unworthy of protection, and society as a whole would hold them in contempt. It was done, of course, to sinners.

"Sinners…," muttered Oriana, gliding her brightly colored tongue over her ice cream. "Sinners, hmm? Heh-heh-heh," she giggled.

"What might you be laughing about?"

She heard someone else's voice.

It had a clear timbre, belonging to a woman.

Oriana had a thick note card tucked behind her right ear like a ballpoint pen. The paper vibrated to create this "voice."

"What? I was just thinking how surprising it is that I've come this far, Lidvia Lorenzetti."

"I believe I advised you three times now not to call me by my true name. I also believe it is too early to indulge in such displays of emotion. In my opinion, this is where the important part begins."

"I hear you. I haven't forgotten my duty in this. If I score some points out here, even a *sinner* like me might be able to be a decoy for this tightly closed faction. Maybe you'll get something out of it, too?"

"…I don't need…"

"Oh, just accept my goodwill, okay?"

"*I simply believe* you *should be prioritized right now, not me. I wonder if you are all right—you haven't taken a rest. Perhaps I should let—*"

"Let me take a rest? That's funny! Anyway, Lidvia, nobody's found you, right? I'm the one out in the open, and you're supporting from behind the scenes. If we both find ourselves unable to move, the plan will fail."

"*Rest assured. While you are running about outside, I am staying put in the lobby.*"

"How very luxurious. I wish I could lounge around in the hotel, too! Or get some exercise in one."

"*...I believe I already asked you to refrain from such indecent comments.*"

"Oh my. I think you're reading too much into this. Don't you know hotels these days come with all sorts of amazing facilities like pools and gyms? Eww, Lidvia, you're so lewd!"

"*...*"

"Oh? Wait, don't clam up on me just for that! Lidvy?"

As Oriana spoke, she happened to spot a balloon stuck in a tree branch on the roadside in front of her. An average Japanese person's height might not have been enough to reach it, but she had no difficulty snagging it. She needed to stretch only a little to grab the balloon's string. She looked around and found a little boy right nearby, staring up at her face.

Oriana crouched down and held out the balloon to him. Without a word, he clutched the string and ran away at full speed.

"*...I believe I instructed you to avoid contact with civilians as much as possible.*"

"I am! As much as possible. That just now was unavoidable."

She heard an exasperated sigh over the communication spell.

Without particularly minding it, she licked the ice cream again with the tip of her tongue. "Still, though," she said, watching the blimps in the blue sky. "I knew *waiting* would be a pain, but man, this is boring."

4

"Gwaaah! Touma, I think my tummy is completely empty…"

"…You've been saying that, but why are you pretending not to notice the smell of sauce and mayonnaise on you, Index?"

Touma had brought Index to a snug little café. Everything, from the recommendations menu to the OPEN and CLOSED sign, seemed purposely hard to discern, as though it was a hobby of the owner. Anyway, it wasn't one of those places that guests naturally radiated toward.

But even in here, every seat was taken. The reason was simple—it was currently before two in the afternoon, still lunch break for the Daihasei Festival. With the 2.3 million people who lived here and the spectators from out of town storming every eatery in the city right now, even places like this would be crowded.

"Hey, Touma. Over here!"

"Oh my, oh my. You mustn't shout so loudly."

He spotted familiar faces at a table for four near the window—his parents, Touya and Shiina. Touya was wearing slacks and a dress shirt, his sleeves rolled up, while Shiina was wearing a thin cardigan and an ankle-length dress. They looked less like a married couple and more like a noble lady and her chauffeur.

Touya began talking before Kamijou and Index sat down. "Every single year I'm surprised by how amazing the Daihasei Festival is—or at least by how hard it is to reserve seats. It makes me feel like I'm right in the thick of the competition with all the kids."

Unlike normal athletic meets, you couldn't just reserve one seat at the Daihasei Festival and be set for everything. Each event was held in a different stadium, so parents and children needed to run around requisitioning seats at one place after another. Lunchtime worked the same way. Once the events were over, competitors and spectators alike would be barred from entering the stadiums, so they would need to find seats for lunch, too.

After hitting each point in his mind, Kamijou said, "Well, you know. The whole city is basically cafeterias and shops at this point."

"Hmm. 'Academy City,' indeed. Whoops, need to scoot in so you can fit."

"Oh my. Then maybe it would be fun to try diving into the crowds for a pork fillet cutlet sandwich. Maybe I'll do that tomorrow. Oh my, you can sit right here, young lady."

Touya and Shiina, facing each other, moved in to make room for them, so Kamijou sat next to Touya and Index next to Shiina. Index's stomach immediately rumbled and she collapsed over the table. Shiina watched them with a pleasant smile as she moved the wicker basket from her lap to the table.

It was impolite to bring your own food into an eating establishment, but during the Daihasei Festival, it was more important to find a place to sit down to eat than procuring food. Either the shopkeeper at the counter was aware of the unique circumstances or just didn't care, because he didn't say anything to them. Index had even brought the cat inside the place, but he didn't seem to notice that, either.

Yikes. Why's Dad accepting Index like nothing's wrong, anyway? Oh, right. They met before at the beach house. Despite his initial confusion, he realized nobody present seemed to mind. Of course, he was pretty sure this crowd would accept just about anyone.

"Ta-daa! Our meal for today will be rice sandwiches. Oh, it looks like they got a little squished," Shiina said, cracking open the basket's lid.

Sounds and smells of an imminent meal provoked Index and the calico into swift action, their heads rising up quickly. Kamijou looked at them, unamused...and then noticed something wrong out of the corner of his eye.

He looked around the shop.

Its furnishings were a bit on the old-fashioned side, and not every single chair or the wallpaper looked like it belonged to a strictly uniform collection. But it also wasn't as *stiff* as a decades-old shop that wanted to retain its own unique style. If someone said *café*, you'd easily be able to imagine the kind of place it was. Basically, there were one-person counter seats and a smattering of booths for four, like the one Kamijou's family was using. There wasn't much space between the tables to walk. At the table on the other side of the small path was a girl who looked college-aged, wearing a light gray button-down shirt and a thin pair of slacks. She sat across from a female middle school student in the normal tank top and shorts worn for track-and-field events—and she was a Level Five.

Mikoto Misaka glared at him, legs crossed.

He blinked in surprise a couple of times. "Well, leaving all that aside...Whoa, look at this menu! The coffee here is dirt cheap compared to other places!"

"Hey! Why am I the only one your brain always returns zero search results for?! And don't start thinking the cheaper price means it doesn't taste as good, you idiot!!" Mikoto pounded the table and almost stood up.

Kamijou took his eyes off the menu with an exasperated look. "Well, I mean, I thought I was just going with the flow."

"Wha...? Is that all?! There's never any natural, sane *flow* when you're involved! And also, who the heck is that kid who's always following you around? Where does she even *live*?!"

Index made a grunt and looked up to see a finger pointing at her.

"Who is she? Wait, you...," Kamijou began, but then he quickly closed his mouth. Confessing before his parents that a girl was actually staying in the male dorm—in his room—was a pretty high hurdle for him. Instead, the pure-hearted Touma Kamijou started to worry. How would he trick them?

"That's right, Touma," his father said. "Come to think of it, who *is* this girl? She was with you when we stayed over at the beach, too, but whenever we asked at the house, you avoided the subject."

Pfft?! Kamijou almost sputtered. Mikoto cut in from the side. "Th-the beach?! Y-y-y-y-you *stayed over* at the beach?!"

Her piercing shout hammered his eardrums. He checked what the other lady, the one who looked like she was in college, was doing, to find her shaking her head and sighing. *No, I didn't mean that in any strange way, and why do I have to explain all the details to Misaka anyway?!* Kamijou thought before opening his mouth.

Index, the genuine westerner, cut in. "I should say the same for you, Short Hair. Where do you live and who are you? Are you Touma's girlfriend or something?"

She probably just meant *friend who is a girl*, but the bona fide Japanese person she asked, Mikoto Misaka, gave a jolt of surprise.

"What?! N-no, we're not like that. I don't…"

"You came to cheer for Touma's school, too. The time when they were pushing over the poles."

"Wait, no, be quiet!!"

Mikoto's hands began to scramble in midair, but Index, for her part, didn't seem too interested in any of this. Petting with both hands the calico sitting in her lap, she stared excitedly at the lunch Shiina had put on the table. "Touma, Touma. I think my tummy is empty now. Do you mean you didn't make a lunch today?"

"Oh my. Today? What do you do on other days, Touma?" Shiina asked with a smile, looking at him curiously.

Kamijou felt sweat forming on his back. "No, that's not it, Mother! She lives in the neighborhood and she's really bad at cooking, and there's some stuff going on—"

"Huh? Touma, when you say neighborhood, it's more like—"

"I'm doing the explaining here, so you be quiet! Anyway, why are you arguing about *that* when I said you're bad at cooking even though you're a girl?!"

"But it's true. I can't cook."

"Damn it! You're seriously only an expert at eating, huh, Index?! On the other hand, I wonder how Mikoto is with chores and stuff!"

"Huh? I, well, I can do a little, since I'm still learning. I mean, even I haven't *perfectly* memorized how to fix frayed spots on Persian rugs or how to repair damaged leaves on traditional metal dishes or anything."

"Mikoto," began the other lady, "normal Japanese people don't have Persian rugs or traditional metal dishes in their homes in the first place. I think you're mistaking housework with artistry," she said gently.

Mikoto grunted in surprise. "Huh?! B-but I remember it being in home-ec class at Tokiwadai...!!" she cried.

It seemed like part of the "proper young lady" world was being able to breathe new life into antiques with the same ease as fixing a few loose strands on a shirt. Whichever the case was, Kamijou was relieved. *Okay, managed to get the conversation off* that *topic.*

His father, Touya, checked the clock on the store wall and said, "Well, anyway, let's get to eating, shall we? Touma, make sure to thank them. They waited for you to get here this whole time without eating."

Really? Kamijou looked over to see Mikoto flinch and press her back against the back of the seat.

On the other hand, directly across from Mikoto was the college-age lady—the only one he'd never met before—sitting and weakly smiling. "Not at all. You eventually got here, so let's dig in. So your name is Touma Kamijou, right?"

"Huh? Yes, but, um, are you Misaka's older sister, or...?"

"No, no. I'm Misuzu Misaka, Mikoto's mother. Pleased to meet you!"

....*Mother?*

All four people at the Kamijou table froze for a moment.

Then they all shouted "*MOTHER?!*" at the same time.

Touya looked particularly more flurried than the rest of them. "B-but weren't you saying all those things about going to university?!"

"Yes. I recently decided to go back to school. It's quite stimulating to be able to encounter at this age all sorts of things I don't understand!"

Hearing that made everything seem to fit together for some reason, and that made it strange to Kamijou. Father and son looked over to Shiina then, sitting at the same table in her prim-and-proper ladies' outfit.

"…Well, I mean, don't things like this seem too strange to be real? What do you think, Touma?"

"Now that you mention it, we've got kind of the same thing going on, so maybe it's not really enough to start shouting about how strange it is…is it?"

"It *is* strange! Touma, you have all these unnaturally young-looking adults around you like that *Komoe* and this *Shiina*! If you thought about it normally it would be impossible!! How is this world so filled with youth? Is this like Neverland? Did Peter Pan guide me here somehow?!" Index cried out with the retort of her life, but she, too, had a body that could reasonably be called mini-sized. That one aspect made the cheerleader's words not very convincing.

Of course, the Misakas didn't seem to care much about it, and neither of them paid it any mind. Mikoto took a menu from the corner of the table. "Umm, it's really late at this point, but what do you want, Mom?"

"I don't need anything. See? I came today with my own lunch packed, too. Check it out, Mikoto. It's just like I'm a real mom, isn't it?"

"…Just like it? I certainly *hope* you're trying to be an actual mother! And what's in that bag you have?"

"Heh-heh-heh! Don't be too surprised when I show you!" Misuzu rummaged around in her bag for a moment, then pulled out a huge hunk of cheese, a bottle of white wine, a silver stock pot, and a portable gas stove. "Ta-daa!! Today we'll be having cheese fondue!!"

"You can't bring propane gas into Academy City! It's dangerous!!"

Whack! Mikoto gave her mother a slap on the head. It was obviously not the time for her *biri biri*. Misuzu Misaka, for her part, showed what an adult woman capable of controlling her tear ducts through acting could do, and began purposely looking at Mikoto with wide, moist eyes. "Nooo! My own daughter hit me! But, you know…girls who eat so much that they need a pot like this to prepare their food grow up splendidly well-figured. Exercise may be important, too, but you won't get any bigger if you just nibble away at a tiny little lunch every day. If you do that, the nutrients might not go to the places you want to grow. Sheesh, why do you think I brought in so much cheese? It was for you!"

"No, er, I…Growing, getting bigger…What are you on about?"

"Hmmm? Well, what *am* I talking about? I was only saying that your bones need calcium to be healthy…Could you have been thinking about something *else* that you *actually* want to get bigger? And why did you suddenly start thinking about wanting to get bigger, anyway?"

"Sh-shut up, you stupid mom! And you! Don't give me that blank look of amazement!!" After the red-faced Mikoto finished yelling at Misuzu, she snapped at Kamijou for some reason.

Misuzu smirked, her smile not looking very refined. "Well, leaving aside the need for dairy products, it's common knowledge that biologically, eating more will make you grow more. Whether you grow horizontally or vertically is another problem, though. Getting fat from eating just means your body can't manage it. If you balance your calories and your exercise, the places you want to grow will grow just fine. Western dietary culture is amazing, isn't it? If you eat buckets of food like this, you'd have a better body than Japanese people. A huge chest means huge life benefits!" As she spoke, she purposely stretched out her arms. She stretched as she tilted back, like a tense bow, emphasizing her swells.

The still-developing Mikoto winced slightly. "Y-you don't need to worry. Eating more to grow more is basically just superstition, isn't it?…Hey, you! Get your eyes off my mother!!" she cried, implicating Kamijou.

Whoosh!! He pulled his gaze away at the speed of sound. Now in his forcibly changed vision was a rather mad Index in a cheerleading uniform, whether because of being hungry or because of the topic of breasts.

"…What is it, Touma? Why are you looking at my face so closely?"

"Nothing," he said with an extremely pained grin. "Eating a lot to grow a lot, huh? Just thinking how nice that would be."

"!!" His words got an instant reaction from Index. Her mouth opened wide as if to devour his head, but once again, she stopped halfway through the act. She seemed to be starting to be conscious about her mouth on someone else's body. Her face grew bright red at the thought, and with slow motions, she sat back in her seat and shrank down.

Right…She's so hard to deal with. He didn't like being bitten because it hurt, so why was he feeling somehow uncomfortable from not being bitten?

As for the people sitting around him…

"T-Touma, I'm sure it's not true, but did you do something to *this* girl, too? You already told *that* girl that you were making a bet and whoever lost had to do what the other said…Did you do it again?!"

"Oh my, oh my. The girl is mad, and yet you still brought it into the conversation. I'm feeling an extremely strong sense of déjà vu."

"…I…I see. Something happened between you. Ah, I see how it is."

"Ahh! My little Mikoto is so into him, but she's acting like she doesn't care! You're so cute! You can only get this kind of thing from an unconsciously ill-starred girl!"

"…Touma, you're…stupid."

Urgh! They're all so hard to deal with!!

As everyone present started saying whatever they wanted, Kamijou couldn't help but cradle his head in his hands.

5

She's so hard to deal with.

The sorcerer Stiyl Magnus was listening closely to his cell phone.

He was sitting on a park bench. No one sat next to him. In the empty space beside him were a sandwich and a bottle of iced tea he'd bought at the convenience store. Of course, his first sip of the latter had ended with him swearing to never pick up a bottle of iced tea again. Though imperfect, he was still a citizen of England, the tea capital of the world.

That, however, wasn't the cause of the bitterness on his face.

It was the friendly voice on the other end of the phone.

"I did make sure to look into the British Library's records. But the Roman Orthodox Church has always been a stubborn ass about showing the Soul Arm to anyone. And even if there *were* public records, or if they actually *did* unveil it, that doesn't mean it'd be the real thing, you know?"

The rough but sonorous voice belonged to Sherry Cromwell. She was the go-to decryption specialist of the English Puritan Church but simultaneously an enemy to Index. She was in an extremely complicated position because of the relationships between different factions. On one hand, she would attack even other members of the English Church, and yet when it came to problems affecting all of England, she would cooperate in a heartbeat.

On the first day of September, she had launched an attack on Academy City. As a result, she was now subject to religious deliberations. The fact that she, a combat specialist, was doing clerical duties basically meant she was under house arrest. Stiyl had predicted that Archbishop Laura Stuart would give one of her "lenient decisions," since the whole incident had happened only because of the complex background of England. And besides, he knew she wouldn't let go of someone with Sherry's skills at decryption—and combat. The incident must have caused injuries, but he figured that they had come to terms by now, probably after a series of deathly tense meetings with Aleister, head of the science-ruled part of the world.

For Stiyl's part, leaving aside all those circumstances, Sherry had tried to hurt Index. He had half a mind to catch her at a good time and have a nice long talk with her *after ramming a flame sword into her once or twice.*

"After all, not even I, another Roman Catholic disciple, have actually been allowed to see the Croce di Pietro. That must mean it's a very important trick up their sleeves. It seems like it will be quite difficult to find a weakness in it."

The second voice, speaking in a relaxed tone, was Orsola Aquinas. Like Sherry, she specialized in magic-related decryption. After she "deciphered" the grimoire called the *Book of the Law*, the sister had converted from Roman Orthodoxy to English Puritanism.

At the moment, Stiyl was trying to ferret out the usage requirements of the Croce di Pietro by plumbing the vast records of the British National Library, a distinct entity from the British Museum.

And the administration of the British Library, which collected information from throughout all time periods and locations, was entrusted to those skilled at encryption because of its unique qualities. That circumstance led Sherry and Orsola into the same department. But...

"*Munch, munch.* Oh, wait just one moment. Miss Sherry, Miss Sherry! This notebook has scribbled notes from a Vatican Preserver."

"Hey! How many times do I need to tell you not to eat your damn muffins in the library?!"

"Now, now. Look at the time. Why not have a light snack?"

"Don't give me that! I just told you not to eat it! Stop stuffing your damn face!!"

"But this is a specially made muffin with food rites integrated into it. Everyone from Amakusa made them for me. They help replenish my stamina and heal external wounds. I am still not at one hundred percent, you see."

"Now you're just avoiding the subject— Wait, you moron! Is letting crumbs fall out of your mouth really needed for that stupid Amakusa spell to work?!"

Stiyl sighed. Their personalities and levels of excitement didn't meld well at all. He began to hear through the phone the sounds of struggling, and by some chance, it hung up a moment later.

Man. He folded up the cell phone and put it back into his pocket. *When did Necessarius start getting so soft?* Until not long ago, he always felt a nervous tension with them, like he was tiptoeing across spider threads. Despair always on the heels of hope, having to kill enemies to save allies, shedding blood to stop another's tears—that was the kind of group he *thought* they were.

Once again, the only cause for this change he could conceive of was that one boy. Meeting *him* and being influenced by him had caused a good many sorcerers to rethink their lives. Stiyl himself included.

"...Too annoying to admit it, though," he spat, dropping his now-short cigarette to his feet. As it hit the ground, the butt burst into an ember and vanished without a trace. He pulled out a new one and stuck it in his mouth, then produced a weak flame on the end without touching it.

He exhaled. *Tsuchimikado was talking about trying to get into Academy City's security or something, but I don't think I can rely on him too much. Let's see what's next...*

Stiyl leaned back up against the bench and stared at the sky. It was so blue he hated it. He blew the smoke from his cigarette straight up like a chimney, when...

"?"

He suddenly felt eyes on him. He brought his face back down to see a woman standing there, about 135 centimeters tall.

Komoe Tsukuyomi, was it?

At the end of July, when the girl named Index had first snuck into Academy City, this woman was the one who had sheltered her in her personal apartment after she'd been slashed in the back. She looked no older than twelve, but apparently, she was a schoolteacher. For some reason, today she was wearing a cheerleader-like uniform, with a light-green tank top and white pleated skirt.

She stared at him.

Hmm. Even in a peace-drunken nation like this, I suppose some people have some danger-management abilities. Komoe Tsukuyomi shouldn't have reached the core of that incident, but he grinned sardonically. She must have at least gotten a glimpse of the strange man known as Stiyl Magnus during that time.

"I'm sorry. Is there something you need?" he said slowly, cigarette wiggling at the corner of his mouth. He recalled what Necessarius was like as he sensed the first clear rejection and dread he'd felt in a long time.

Miss Komoe, however, stuck her index finger right at Stiyl's face and shouted something completely outside his expectations.

"Hey! There is a total ban on smoking in public places in Academy City!!"

Stiyl blinked in silent surprise for a second, then gave an audible sigh.

"Wh-why are you looking away like you're so tired?! Miss Komoe is giving you a serious warning here! I'm actually trying to give you a stern talking-to!!"

He frowned a little; she was already on the verge of tears. Without a care for his expression, she continued to carefully observe his face. "Mgh! Excuse me for asking, but how old are you? You look like a minor to me!"

"So what if I am?"

"If you were, I'd scold you, of course! Come on! Listen to what I'm saying! Don't turn the other cheek—look at me!!" cried Miss Komoe in full angry mode, snatching the cigarette from his mouth and then casually shoving her hand into his pocket. Her small fingers fished around in there before coming out with a box of cigarettes.

"..." Stiyl's expression tightened a bit, but his moral code fundamentally prevented him from attacking people unrelated to the world of sorcery. (Though there were exceptions, such as a certain boy with a special right hand.)

After Miss Komoe looked at the name of the cigarettes she'd confiscated, her eyebrows shot up. "And you picked ones with such a pretentious name, too. Are you the sort who started smoking because he wanted to be an actor or something?!"

"No, it's just that brand is the most famous kind where I come from..."

"Jeez! Anyway, I'm keeping this! You shouldn't smoke cigarettes anymore. Nicotine and tar are bad for growing children!!" she finished, looking him straight in the eyes.

Stiyl couldn't help but avert his gaze. *She's so hard to deal with.* That's what he honestly thought.

This Komoe Tsukuyomi reminded him very much of a certain girl.

The one who'd ignore all size differences and come right up to you...

...the one who was brash, but always for the sake of others...

...the one who'd tell a person off as much as necessary to keep them safe—

——and the one who had, just a few years ago, yelled at him every time he put a cigarette in his mouth.

"Man..."

"Huh?! Why do you look like you're utterly exhausted?! M-Miss Komoe is very, very angry, for real today! Wait, you had more?! I'm taking those, too— Ah, ah! Stop using that box like a beanbag and give it to me right this instant!!"

Stiyl looked to the side and away from the shouting Komoe Tsukuyomi. Whatever she said was going in one ear and out the other, but she wouldn't stop shouting at him and never tried to leave.

Yes, telling him off as much as needed.

6

Lidvia Lorenzetti was in a hotel lounge.

Her habit, not only old but riddled with little cuts and patches of fading color, stood out like a sore thumb among the modern scenery around her. Her hair and skin had lost their sheen along with the habit, looking damaged and faint of color. From her face one could guess that she was, at one time, a beauty to behold. But now her whole body, from head to toe, resembled more what one might see in an aged movie.

The habit was from one generation before the ones the Roman Orthodox Church currently used. Habits from then had different color variations available. Lidvia wore one with white fabric with a red cross design: the symbol of Saint George. At the time, the habit had caused discord in the Church, since the Puritans wore the same symbol. Lidvia had purposely kept it as her habit of choice. She had inherited it from her grandmother's generation, yes—but more important, she firmly believed that the blessed and talented had a duty to extend a helping hand to everyone, even sinners.

On an international scale, the hotel she was in wouldn't be rated as very famous. It was still young from a historical viewpoint. Inferior in every way to the huge buildings in Italy, which all had an antique value in the building itself to match...but crammed to the brim with more people than any other in the world.

Lidvia speculated the congestion was due to the Daihasei Festival, a sporting fair with a global scope. At all other times, Academy City was a closed-off environment. Aside from housing academic conferences and VIP invitees, hotels weren't necessary. During big events like this, what few hotels *did* exist would immediately be filled to capacity. Every room in Academy City would be taken right now, and hotels outside the city would be doing great business because of those who couldn't get in.

As the people hurriedly rushed around her, Lidvia began to walk, the only one calm.

It seemed like the little portion of time and space around her had been separated from reality.

Well, then... Lidvia Lorenzetti left the lounge and passed through a large glass revolving door. Harsh sunlight poured down on her. She squinted. *Oriana is doing her best. I must start soon as well.*

As she thought this, a Daihasei Festival commentator's voice reached her from afar. When she looked up, she saw a blimp off in the distance, floating along. The big screen affixed to its side displayed weather forecasts, its broadcast stating that the nice, cloudless weather would continue for a while longer. *Good weather indeed*, thought Lidvia, looking away from the sunlight.

The city was completely at peace.

She disappeared into the crowds—as if to slip through that widening gap.

7

2:20 PM.

Lunch break had ended, but there was still time before the next event for Kamijou's school. The fight over seats in the cheering section would begin before the game started, though, so Touya and Shiina Kamijou along with Misuzu Misaka each set out for the next stadiums their respective children would be playing at.

As the adults walked up the road to the station, this left the three of them: Kamijou, Index, and Mikoto. Mikoto went to a different school, of course, and she needed to get to the rest of her classmates.

*Well, anyway...*Kamijou walked behind the two girls, secretly breathing a sigh of relief.

Neither of them had seemed to realize what was slowly happening in Academy City right now. He had already accidentally gotten Seiri Fukiyose involved, and he didn't want to wrap up anyone else in this incident. No matter how much strength Index or Mikoto could bring to the table.

Mikoto didn't notice Kamijou's relief. "...Wait. I've been thinking this since the time before last, but why are you two always together?" she asked, casting a dubious glance at Index and Kamijou.

He gulped. This was actually something Touma Kamijou himself didn't understand. He had amnesia. The only thing he knew was that the first thing he remembered was Index already freeloading in his dorm room. To top it off, he'd been keeping secret the fact that he had amnesia.

He could only deflect the topic by giving an immediate, vague answer that she could take in several different ways—or by forcibly changing the topic. Before he could, though...

"Then why are you always with Touma, Short Hair?"

...Index retaliated with a question of her own.

"Huh?" Mikoto grunted, a little daunted. "Always? There's no way I could spend every waking hour with this *thing*! Th-that's idiotic. And impossible. I don't have that much free time."

"…Wow. This thing? Idiotic? Nice combo attack…," he muttered exhaustedly, but neither of them seemed to mind.

Index tilted her head and for a moment said, "Hmm…" in thought. Then: "Well, it isn't like I'm with Touma all the time, either."

"What? Is that right???"

"Yep. Whenever something happens, Touma leaves me behind and goes off somewhere. And every time he gets near a really important life event, he always, *always* runs off alone and solves it by himself. He's stupid…I thought you would be involved in all that, but I guess I was wrong?"

"I…I don't know what you're talking about!"

There had actually been a few incidents involving Mikoto, but it wasn't enough to be called "always, *always*." So what on earth could he be doing all those times? Index and Mikoto both started to wonder this simultaneously, and then they whipped around to look at Kamijou at the same time.

"…Touma, you always get sent to the hospital and then apologize after the fact. What's going on?"

"…You mean you've been doing stuff like that every single time? Come to think of it, you didn't waste a second helping *those girls* or Kuroko…"

Kamijou flinched away from them with a panicked groan and stepped back. What they were saying did, in a way, cut straight to the heart of the matter. But considering what was happening right now in Academy City, he couldn't just answer them, so…

"O-oh, come on, everyone! You're just seeing that especially charming part of Mr. Kamijou's yearly routine! I'm not like this all year round or anything. Come on, everyone wants to look cool for no good reason at least two or three times a year, right?!"

His immediate, shouted reply earned him only cold answers like, "…Only twice, now?" and "I don't think three is a high enough number…"

After that, they continued to nag and complain to him for a while. But after venting every bit of their mental haze and murk, they seemed to brighten up a bit and started walking at a normal pace again.

"The next event's in a few minutes...," Mikoto said as she walked. "Argh! After all that, I don't feel like I rested enough. And I'm super cold now that I was in the air-conditioning for so long. I hope my muscles haven't tightened up." She pretended to stretch out her arms.

Kamijou, next to her, watched and said, "...You're oddly gung-ho about this. Did you find a rival in your school for young ladies or something?"

"..." She paused mid-stretch. "You...You couldn't have forgotten about our bet, could you?"

"Huh? The one where whoever's school gets a lower score has to listen to whatever the other says, right? The punishment game? Oh, I'm fine. Hey, did you see the points? Tokiwadai isn't *that* far in the lead right now."

"D-don't seem so relaxed! Hmph. Our school is known for the pressure we put on in the second half. That attitude of yours won't last...Hey, wait! Listen to me! You're just gonna speed-walk away from me?!"

Zip zap!! Electricity lanced out of Mikoto's bangs several times, but despite being at point-blank range, Kamijou's right hand blew them all away.

He was shouting in his head, *Holy crap! What the heck is she doing?!* and trembling head to toe with tears in his eyes, but he *was* completely unscathed after one of the city's seven Level Five's direct attacks. In the end, with her esper pride in tatters, without even the opportunity to tell him off, she yelled, "Why doesn't at least *one* hit you?!" and ran off at a blistering speed. Kamijou worried a little about whether she warmed up properly before doing that.

Then Index, who had been silently holding the calico until then, spoke up. "...Listen to whatever the other says?"

"No!! Not *everything*, Index! There are limits, of course! Please refrain from any crazy delusions of an erotic persuasion that you might have in your head right now, ma'am, and rest assured!!"

"I-I wasn't thinking anything like that!!" *Gwoarrr!!* Her mouth opened wide, but once again, she froze mid-motion. She had stopped in a weird position, one where he wasn't sure whether she'd grab him or not. Her mouth opened and closed a few times.

Kamijou shivered, thinking, *Gahhh!! I don't want her to bite me, but it's really hard on me when she's this weird about it! This unresolved situation is suffocating me!! How am I supposed to turn it around?!*

Using this chance to properly tell her to stop biting him from now on was one choice, but if he slipped up when he did it, he was scared he'd just prolong the awkwardness. *What the hell is this "one step before getting confessed to by a childhood friend" dilemma, anyway?!* he thought in terror.

Meanwhile, Index, still locked up stiff, decided to avert the topic from the biting. "T-Touma. I think my throat is a little itchy. I want some of the fruit juice they were selling over there."

"...Another forced course correction..."

"It doesn't matter! I want something to drink, okay?!" she cried, grabbing Kamijou's hand and pulling it. *No biting, but she's totally fine with grabbing my hand?* he thought. He couldn't quite get a handle on her decision-making process.

"Err, wait, wait a minute, Index! You just ate lunch a few minutes ago. If you keep wolfing down every food and drink you see, you'll get fat."

"Wha...?" The calico fell to the ground from the arms of the cheerleader uniform–wearing Index. After it nimbly plopped down, it did a kitty jump to get back into her arms.

Index was so red in the face, she could have started steaming. "N-no I won't! I may eat just a little bit more food than other people, but I'll never get fat, and then you'll be totally wrong about me!!"

"Really? You know about body weight, body fat, your waist...Are you making sure to measure all that? Maybe your defensive power is going up and you just don't know it." Kamijou stared at Index's belly.

Unlike her normal thick habit, the extremely thin cheerleading uniform stuck tightly to her skin, openly displaying the outline of her body. She wore a tank top as well, so he could see her belly button clearly.

"I-if you don't believe me, just measure my stomach! I'm ready anytime!"

"Yeah, but I'm not! Do I look like I go around everywhere with a tape measure, Index?!"

"You don't need one of those! Just put your arms around my waist and you'll see!!"

Huh? Kamijou's eyes became pinpoints.

"Come on! Do it, Touma!!"

The cheer girl's slender hands latched onto the frozen boy's arms.

Darn it...How could I forget the announcement? I must have been really losing it...

After leaving Kamijou, Mikoto was running double-time back down the road they'd walked through.

The event schedule was listed in the Daihasei Festival pamphlet printed by Academy City. But it was a schedule that had been made *in advance*. Several factors had already caused changes to be made for the day.

They decided before lunch break to change the time of the bread-eating race Tokiwadai Middle School would be taking part in. She needed to inform her mother, Misuzu, or she'd end up waiting for Mikoto in a stadium that had nothing to do with her school.

Mikoto's cell phone was in the bag she'd given to the Garden of Learning's storage officer, and there were no public phones around, either. So now, just to say one or two words, she had to run full speed through the city.

Misuzu was already heading to the next field and probably wasn't at the café where they'd eaten lunch. Still, it would be easier to go back along the road they'd taken partway if she wanted to follow her mother.

Then someone began moving alongside her with beautiful form as Mikoto continued her running.

It was a girl covered in bandages riding a wheelchair with its wheels adjusted for sports use—Kuroko Shirai.

She was wounded and a visitor, so she was wearing Tokiwadai Middle School's summer uniform, with the short-sleeve blouse under a beige summer sweater and a gray pleated skirt. Her brown hair was tied back with ribbons in twin tails, and it flew up and behind her in the wind.

"Big Sisteeeer! Where are you off to in such a hurry? Would you like to use my teleportation? I can use my ability even if my limbs are hurt, so there isn't a single problem here!"

"...As soon as I say yes, you're going to hug me, so I'll pass."

"Damn!! I should have expected that from you, Big Sister! You see right through me! I was only trying to refill some of my Big Sister energy, since I haven't had enough of it in the hospital!!"

A tingling chill went down Mikoto's spine. She put an extra few steps between her and Shirai. After a long, sparkling smile, Shirai suddenly seemed to come out of it.

"But Big Sister, where are you hurrying to...? N-no! You're not going to that gentleman—I mean that *rotten ape-man* and asking him to come cheer for you...?!"

"N-no, I'm not, stupid! In fact, we're enemies right now!!"

"Oh? But that gentleman would appear to be in front of us right now."

Mikoto sighed—at least she'd made it that far now. She casually looked away from Shirai and in front of her.

And there...

A boy and a silver-haired, green-eyed cheer girl were facing each other.

He was squatting down, arms wrapped around her waist, and he was pressing his cheek to her belly.

Mikoto tried to shout, "What?!" but it came out as only a dumbfounded groan.

Despite the Daihasei Festival, this road held no other human presence but theirs. It was a good thing, too, because that boy was shamelessly hugging the green-eyed girl's waist, who was one or two times slenderer than Mikoto. A boy hugging a girl was already a completely out-of-the-ordinary situation, but what the heck did he have to squat down and get his face on her stomach for? Mikoto was speechless.

As she stood there agape, Shirai spoke with an exaggerated, theatrical voice as she sat in her sports wheelchair. "Ho-ho—I wonder how many months pregnant she is. Maybe they can feel kicking in her belly...pfft."

Though she was clearly joking, Mikoto was shivering madly all over. Pale-blue sparks snapped and crackled from her bangs, going every which way.

She could fire a spear of lightning, but it wouldn't get past the boy's right hand.

In all likelihood, he would have no trouble emerging unharmed even if she hit him with Railgun.

But still, Mikoto tightened her right hand into a fist and shouted, "Youuu...Eat this, you freaking pervert!!"

She charged at the boy, swung her fist up, and punched him with as much force as she could muster.

"Gohhaaaaaaahhhhh?!"

Unexpectedly launched away from the side, Kamijou found himself torn from Index before rolling onto the road. The back of his head, which had been struck, and his limbs, which scraped across the road, stung with pain.

The strangely soft sensation of the girl's stomach under his cheek, the slight sense of sweat moisture, the sweet scent and warmth, and other various factors had all overlapped to put Kamijou in a state of dizziness, and then Mikoto's blow finally snapped him out of it. Which also meant he gained physical distance from Index. He wondered why he wasn't happy at all for killing two birds with one stone.

"Huh...? That hit him?"

But it was Mikoto, the one who punched him, who murmured dumbly.

Kamijou lay on the ground and started to twitch. *Ooh...No, this time, it was for the better. That strange pinkish air surrounding Index and me...It wasn't possible for me to get out of there with my own power. But no, well...Why didn't the world give me a resolution that was a little gentler?!*

Half crying like a little kid, he rubbed his eyes. But what he felt wasn't his familiar hand—it was the sensation of thin cloth. Satin, perhaps—a smooth, slightly slick fabric. *Wait, what is this?* he thought, reassessing the situation. It was a white cloth, folded several times like one of those paper fans used in comedy routines.

It was a pleated skirt.

The one Index had been wearing.

"..."

The skirt had become just a wide piece of cloth, its side zipper torn vertically.

When he put his hands around Index's waist, he must have been grabbing her skirt. He'd been punched away, which meant he must have torn it off as he went.

But that means...

Kamijou looked up from his hands very, very slowly.

There he saw Index, motionless, her face bright red. She was still in a cheerleading outfit, but the outfit had been reduced to the light-green tank top. The skirt below that was absent—because Kamijou was holding it.

Not only was the silver-haired, green-eyed girl's navel visible now, but her underwear and the tips of her thighs as well. Actually, strictly speaking, it was *under-clothing*, like a tennis player's skort. He could see the glossy light-green satin cloth sticking tightly to her skin. And though it was obviously an illusion on his part, he kind of thought he could see certain things being outlined by the wrinkles in her underwear, so he couldn't bear to look closely (after having so elaborately explained it to himself).

"~~~~!!"

Index used the calico in her hands to frantically try and hide her lower section, but that obviously wasn't going to completely guard her. In fact, her desperate, red-faced attempt to remove herself from Kamijou's sight was oddly provocative.

He looked between the view in front of him and the glossy skirt in his hands in turn.

——*I'm dead. In five seconds, my skull will be wide open. Not just by her front teeth but by her canines and molars, too. Look forward to it!...No, wait. Index is being weirdly awkward about biting me right now! That means I might still be able to survive, doesn't it?!*

After discovering the hope at the end of despair, he started to calculate how he'd get out of here, but he was too late.

"...Wait right there, you."

"...It has certainly been a while, good sir. ♪"

Mikoto Misaka's and Kuroko Shirai's cold voices echoed simultaneously.

"..."

Kamijou slowly looked to them. The girl with bluish-white sparks popping from her bangs took a coin out of her pocket that looked like the kind you'd use in an arcade. The girl sitting in the sports wheelchair boldly flicked up her skirt and pulled dangerous-looking metal darts from her thigh.

"Look, it's not like I *need* to stand up for that girl..."

"And Big Sister's enemy is my enemy, too! ♪"

Though they were suggesting they were not enthused, the voltage from them seemed to reach its peak. Index, his last resort, was bright red and immediately hid herself behind Mikoto.

So...I guess it's all over for me...

He slumped tiredly and put a hand to his forehead before saying one last thing, sore loser that he was.

"Wait! Right now we need to do something about Index's skirt, so let's stop the pointless arguing and put our heads together because I think that would be the best thing we could do right now so how does that peaceful resolution sound to you it doesn't sound good does it no it doesn't *I'm so sorry!!*"

He had been trying to excuse himself, but the moment he finished his sentence, the two girls took that as his final will and testament and attacked.

8

Just as he was about to be filled with holes from a railgun and metal darts, Kamijou fled all over the place until finally finding a bench and plopping down onto it, tired.

Index, her clothing lost, went off somewhere with Mikoto and Shirai, deciding her torn skirt had to be fixed (apparently—Kamijou had left her behind when he ran away, and after Mikoto caught him, that was all she told him). He wondered if they were going to use safety pins again.

Blech...

He checked the clock displayed on his cell phone screen to see that it was nearly three o'clock. He'd gotten no messages from either Motoharu Tsuchimikado or Stiyl Magnus.

Considering Oriana and Lidvia's goal was not to give a Soul Arm to someone else in Academy City but to activate the Soul Arm there instead, it was possible they were just hiding out in a single place, like a hotel room, to evade pursuit. Because of that, Stiyl said, their current method of trying to ruin the deal and catching Oriana and Lidvia on the run might be too difficult. Right now they were apparently trying to find the usage conditions for the Soul Arm, the Croce di Pietro. With Oriana no longer anywhere in sight, they had no clues as to their location. This was the only thing they could rely on.

If their enemy, the Roman Orthodox Church, aimed to take control of Academy City by using the Croce di Pietro, then they wouldn't have to wait around like this. They would just have used it right off the bat. They didn't, though, and Tsuchimikado took that as proof of it requiring special conditions.

If they couldn't use the Croce di Pietro without meeting those conditions first, then as long as those prerequisites couldn't be met, Oriana and Lidvia's plan could be prevented. Simple pursuit was hopeless now, and this was the only path left to them to fight back against the two ladies infiltrating the city.

Still…

"…This is taking a while," Kamijou muttered to himself.

It had been hours since they last saw Oriana. He had nothing to do, but he wondered if it was okay for him to be relaxing like this. He couldn't help but feel impatient, not knowing when and where the Croce di Pietro would be used.

What stung his heart the hottest…

…was that he had an instant-win trump card.

Index…

She had perfect recall; she had 103,000 grimoires recorded in her head—a living library of magical tomes. Her vast stores of knowledge would obviously have information on the Croce di Pietro.

It went without saying that the quickest solution was to ask her. Asking Index about anything sorcery-related, whether it was the Croce di Pietro or whatever else, would get him an answer in less than five seconds. In fact, the English Puritan Church's organization, Necessarius, had created the "index of forbidden books" for this exact purpose.

If he asked her, he'd know right away. But at the same time, he wasn't allowed to ask her. *Because of those magicians outside the city…* He'd been told there were many sorcery faction outfits outside the city, both large and small. If they noticed magic being used in Academy City, the lot of them would probably bust right into the place. Unfortunately, not all of them were cooperative toward Academy City. Some would surely use the chance to commit sabotage—they couldn't get into the city under normal circumstances.

The greater part of them seemed to be using spells outside the city, trying to detect any trace of mana. And the idea was that they were centering those searches around Index. Many sorcery-related incidents had occurred near her in the past, so they believed that if something *were* to happen, it would be there.

Which meant…*If I bring Index near the center of this incident, their searching spells might detect Oriana's and Lidvia's mana. So we can't*

*get Index involved in this one. We can't let her get close. Even allowing
her a faint whiff of something happening would be dangerous.*

Index had immense knowledge when it came to sorcery. She
wouldn't let a slight trace of sorcery out of her sight. And if she got
one single hint, given her personality, she would definitely jump
straight into the fray without a second thought even if Kamijou
shouted at her not to come.

"Jeez. Someone who can give me a hint is in front of me and I
can't even ask if it's right or wrong, because as soon as I do, it's over.
Damn it, this is one crazy dilemma," he said, unwittingly sighing,
when—

"What. What kind of. Dilemma?"

Suddenly he heard a voice beside him, and he nearly jumped out
of his skin. Surprised, he turned to see someone had sat down beside
him without his realizing. It was a girl with long black hair in a gym
uniform: Aisa Himegami. She wore the school-designated short
sleeves and shorts, but there would be a silver cross necklace under
her clothing. And indeed, a thin chain looped around her collarbone and neck, hidden by her black hair. The chain went down and
disappeared below her neckline, into her gym clothes.

"H-Himegami? What are you doing here…?"

"I was worried about something. I was looking for you."

I wonder what it is? he thought. Aisa Himegami was never very
expressive, so normally he couldn't really tell if she was angry or
happy or what. Right now, if she said, "I'm hungry," he'd believe her.
And if she said, "I want a cat," he wouldn't doubt her at all.

So he honestly asked, "What are you worried about?"

"Well. Miss Komoe. She was making trouble. She seemed very
mad about something."

"???" Kamijou decided to follow after Himegami for now. She took
his hand and started pulling it off in a different direction.

Suddenly, he looked down to their clasped hands. His long stare
made Himegami frown slightly. "Is something. The matter?"

"Hmm. It's not a big deal or anything, but I was just thinking you
don't really mind stuff like this."

"_____"

As soon as he said that, Himegami jerked her hand. Her face was still impassive, but he could see a slight tinge of red in it. She put the hand to her chest and began to put her other hand on top of it. Apparently she *did* mind it—a lot. She just didn't let it show.

Aisa Himegami ended up bringing him to a relatively large park.

Because lunch break was over, not many people were around. The Daihasei Festival was still the main event right now, and most of the athletes and spectators were on their way toward the stadiums. Most of the people coming and going on the streets were basically either going from one stadium to another or picking out souvenirs for themselves. The spectators in particular had made time to travel all the way to Academy City and stay overnight. They spent a lot of energy watching the events, but they wouldn't just be lazing around.

In one corner of the sparsely populated park, there was a bench. In front of the bench was Miss Komoe, in the same cheerleading uniform as Index, acting mad. She was passionately going on about smoking manners and minors smoking or something.

On the other hand, the second person on the bench—the sorcerer Stiyl Magnus—was barely listening to her. He was smiling, not in a defeated way from the lecture but in more of a "I'm really getting tired of this" sort of way.

Miss Komoe seemed to be trying to confiscate the box of cigarettes from Stiyl, but he was tossing it from one hand to another like a beanbag, and her hands couldn't keep up. From a distance, the leaping and dodging kind of looked like a puppy playing with a gumball.

"There. There. Miss Komoe. And the person who came to save me last time. They're arguing. I don't know what to do."

Himegami looked uncharacteristically lost as she watched. For she owed her life to both Miss Komoe, of course, and Stiyl Magnus, who helped during the Misawa Cram School incident with the scheming alchemist Aureolus. She probably didn't want them to get into a fight with each other.

But as soon as Kamijou saw the perfume-stinking priest's face, he felt utterly exasperated. "Uhh…Himegami, don't feel like you have to stop them. He needs to get a good scolding from Miss Komoe for his own sake. While she's at it, he really needs a lecture on the way he's lived his entire life."

Himegami's face weakened even more at his words. "But. The person with the cigarettes. He seems worried. And he's looking this way."

"That idiot is so happy a little girl is clinging to him that he could die. Just leave him alone. He'll be fine."

"But. Miss Komoe's face is all red. She looks like she's tired. Of being angry."

"Our teacher's smile gets bigger for every bad child she sees. Just leave her alone. She'll be fine." Kamijou sighed, shaking his head.

Miss Komoe noticed them, and without stopping her attempt to grab the cigarette box out of the air, called out, "Oh, Kami!! Don't just stand there watching! Help your teacher! This boy smokes so much, it's scary! Please stop throwing that box and just give it to meee!"

Without any other options, Kamijou started walking over to them. After looking at Miss Komoe, he moved his gaze to Stiyl on the bench and said, "…Good for you. There's still someone in this world who will get mad at you."

"I'll agree with that statement wholeheartedly, Touma Kamijou. But I need to be doing something else right now. She won't leave me alone."

As Stiyl spoke, with the cigarette box moving through the air, he casually realigned his collar to hide his pointing at the cell phone strap in his breast pocket. There was a light in the shape of a skull blinking on and off, the epitome of poor taste. He was getting a call. After indicating it, he caught the cigarette box in the air with a natural motion and began playing beanbag again with Miss Komoe.

If someone was calling this man…then it must have been a member of the English Puritan Church. He obviously couldn't let Miss Komoe hear any information related to the Croce di Pietro.

"Ah! You threw it over there?!"

As Kamijou considered all the pieces of the situation, he noticed something go whooshing past his face out of the corner of his eye as Miss Komoe spoke. He caught it frantically to see that it was a box of cigarettes, of a brand one would see in the movies sometimes.

Ignoring Miss Komoe's words, Stiyl put up his index finger and middle fingers, then brought the balls of his fingers toward his mouth. *And now he's blowing a totally gross kiss?!* thought Kamijou, having readied himself pretty seriously only to realize a moment later that it was a smoking gesture.

Oh. Kamijou pounded his hand with a fist, then stuck the box of cigarettes out to Himegami.

"Himegami, you got a lighter?"

She took a moment, then said, "Huh?"

Miss Komoe whipped herself around at them. "Kami! It's pointless to play the rebel here! And Hime, you need to be more forceful in stopping him!!"

Bam bam bam bam bam!! Miss Komoe stomped over at an incredible speed. When Stiyl saw it, he took the cell phone out of his breast pocket, put it to his ear, and began walking away to who knows where.

I hope it's info on the Croce di Pietro. If it's not, then my being here and getting lectured—in the present tense—is all for nothing. Wait, I have zero intent to smoke a cigarette! How am I supposed to untangle this misunderstanding now?!

Miss Komoe, at this point, had gone beyond the realm of simple anger. Now her eyes were starting to water. Kamijou began to feel seriously panicked, but then he felt his own phone vibrating this time.

Who could that be? he wondered with a tilt of his head, reaching for his shorts pocket.

"Kami! Turn off your cell phone while I'm lecturing you, please!!"

"Yikes!!"

Miss Komoe's snarl made Kamijou flinch away. His hand dropped the box of cigarettes, which she caught in midair. He used the chance to pull his cell phone out of his pocket in one quick motion. A glance at the screen told him it was Motoharu Tsuchimikado.

If he's trying to get in touch with me, does it mean Oriana and Lidvia are on the move...? That's bad. I can't be goofing around like this if that's the case. But I can't let Miss Komoe hear anything about the incident...

As Miss Komoe yelled, "Kami!!" after him, he shuffled behind Aisa Himegami to hide. Then he suddenly grabbed both her shoulders, causing the black-haired girl to flush a bit, but he didn't notice because he was behind her.

He took only a moment to consider how to get out of this situation. "Argh! Himegami, it's up to you! I stopped Miss Komoe and Stiyl from arguing like you wanted to, so you handle the rest!!"

He followed his practically desperate shout by running away. Miss Komoe started running after him. Or at least she tried.

"Wah! What are you doing, Hime?! Please don't hug your teacher out of nowhere like that!!"

She seemed to have politely kept her promise, and he wasn't followed after that. Kamijou, telling himself he'd buy *okonomiyaki* or something at one of the stalls after this, ran all the way out of the park in one burst.

It must have been something important, because the ringtone from Tsuchimikado was still playing, even though quite a bit of time had already passed. A moment before it connected him to the answering machine service, Kamijou pushed the call button on his cell phone.

"Yo, Kammy! Stiyl's line's busy—is he there, nya?! If you know where he is, I need you to tell him something!"

"Eh?" Kamijou thought for a moment. "...Oh. Yeah, someone contacted him, too. You calling about Oriana? They're not trying to do anything crazy and terrible again, are they?!"

"No, it's not really that important...But you should know this, too. I was using...er, special methods to poke around in Academy

City's security systems. The ones Anti-Skill and Judgment use, nya~. Mechanical devices can't deal with sorcery, so I didn't expect much…*but I got a hit.*"

All the hair on Kamijou's body stood on end.

Tsuchimikado continued. "About three minutes ago, in District 5—the one next to us—she was spotted leaving the Seibusan subway station exit. But that's it. Maybe she used magic to block visual information, or maybe she just slipped past the cameras' blind spots. I can't tell."

"Three minutes…That's tough." School District 5 was at the very least more than four kilometers from here. How far would Oriana have moved if he started heading there now?

"We don't need to completely corner Oriana. If she got to Seibusan Station, we can get Stiyl to use a searching spell, nya~. Once we get a precise location, we all rush in. And then it's over."

A searching spell. *The one named Four Ways to Truth, right?* It was originally Tsuchimikado's spell, but Stiyl had been the one using it. It allowed the caster to search about three kilometers out from his current position. It could be used only if they had a magical Soul Arm that the target was using, but they had one of Oriana's note-card pages in their possession already.

"If she goes farther than three kilometers, she'll get outside the search range. We need to go four kilometers before we can even start looking. Are we gonna make it?!"

"That's why we gotta hurry, Kammy. Use a self-driving bus or a train or whatever, just find Stiyl and get to the place as soon as you can!!"

He hung up.

As long as they couldn't really figure out the Croce di Pietro's usage conditions, it was highly probable that this was their last chance. In fact, they needed to go at this under the impression that if they didn't catch her, it would all be over.

"Shit. Stiyl!!" he shouted, taking a detour around where Aisa Himegami and Miss Komoe were and returning to the park. Right now, Stiyl was the only one who could use Four Ways to Truth to track down Oriana.

As he ran, he worked his brain up to full throttle. The one good part about all this was that Oriana might not have realized they'd spotted her. If she was running away as fast as she could, they probably wouldn't make it in time.

She was walking. He was running.

They would just have to make up for the distance and lack of time with speed.

INTERLUDE FOUR

Seiri Fukiyose was sitting on a bench in the waiting room of a hospital.

According to the frog-faced doctor, all the necessary treatment had been finished, and he told her it was okay to walk around freely, if only inside the building. The nurse laughed, saying something about it being a blessing in disguise and how normally it would have been a lot worse. *Thanks a lot*, she thought.

Fukiyose had gotten out of her assigned bed and decided to take a walk around the hospital, partly to check on her condition, but…

"…Ugh."

She put a hand to her temple and lightly shook her head.

Before she made it to the elevator, a mild dizziness had come from the core of her head. This was the reason she'd been assigned a bed—meaning that not only would she undergo a medical examination but that she'd be here for a whole day.

The doctors could cure the intense headaches and strong bodily reactions that stemmed from severe sunstroke, but the stamina she'd lost would just have to recover slowly. Though she had no conspicuous wounds or symptoms on the outside, her body was in a state that was hard to call ideal.

She looked at the small button in her hands. It was a miniature mechanical box, about the size of a box of matches. They told her it was a portable nurse call button, but since radio-wave usage wasn't desirable inside the hospital, it was apparently just a device that made a loud buzzing noise.

It might have been an improved version of the crime prevention buzzers sold in stores, but one could tell from the fact she was given such a thing in the first place that her body wasn't in good shape.

She cast her gaze around. The space also had its own smoking section. It was a small place near the elevator, and though there were no walls setting it apart, there was a kind of ditch running in a straight line along the floor for where you went in. It was the air-cleaning vent; it created a curtain of air. A very small bench looped around inside the square space, and in the middle of it, there was a cylindrical ashtray.

She ignored the smoking facilities and looked over to the wall, her mind still hazy. There were four juice vending machines lined up on it.

"...If I have to recover my stamina, maybe a sports drink is what I need."

Her words didn't have their usual zeal, either. Just standing up from the bench sent a minor wave of pain from her right temple to her left. *I don't think I can return to this afternoon's events*, she thought, frowning and moving slowly to the vending machines.

She held her digital wallet–enabled cell phone to the reader. The buttons all lit up at once. "Which means the ideal option would be… sugar, or amino acids, or minerals, or maybe…*Ah-choo!*"

As she thought about it, she sneezed. As her head wobbled forward, her forehead rammed into one of the buttons on the machine. *Clatter-clatter* came the noise as a type of juice completely unrelated to her own ideas came tumbling out.

As her throbbing headache tormented her, she checked what it was: a strange-looking can with the words *Condensed Milk Cider* written on it.

"...I am the very image of poor health."

She nearly crushed the can in her hand by accident, but she obviously couldn't just throw it away. At a loss as to what to do now, she turned back the way she came, deciding to walk to her own room.

She thought the cold, inorganic hallway she walked down looked like a desert you could find on the Silk Road. If she was feeling this ill inside the hospital, it wasn't hard to imagine what would happen if she tried to run around outside under the blazing heat of summertime.

Jeez. When...will I...? She sighed as she walked, dragging herself...*When can I go back to work? That idiot better not be cutting loose while I'm not around.*

CHAPTER 6

Resumption and End of the Pursuit
Accidental_Firing.

1

"Gosh! Hime, now it's your fault we completely lost sight of Kami!" Miss Komoe called out the girl next to her as she marched down a corner lined with student dormitories.

The black-haired girl wearing a gym uniform following her homeroom teacher, Aisa Himegami, had a clear cup of fruit juice in one hand. She spoke in a relaxed voice. "But Miss Komoe. The next event. It's coming up soon."

"Mgh! I know that. That's why I was trying to quickly scold him and go back to the class!"

They were walking on a road close to the edge of School District 7. Aside from the park Kamijou and Stiyl had fled from earlier, there were shopping districts and dormitories nearby—truly a jumble of unrelated establishments. The buildings varied greatly in height as well, making the skyline look like a comb missing teeth.

This development was a little far away from school—or the stadiums, now—so most of the people walking around seemed to be looking for souvenirs. There were many guests looking curiously at street stalls selling key chains, jigsaw puzzles, and other things city residents wouldn't pick up very often.

Miss Komoe sighed. "I understand. I'll wait for Kami at the stadium. Anyway, Hime, you need to get a move on, too!"

"Okay," answered Aisa Himegami, sipping the cup of juice.

Miss Komoe noticed her reply was reluctant and looked at her askance. "…Hime? Is there something on your mind? Your teacher will listen to whatever you have to say!"

"Not really…" Himegami took the cup from her lips. "Kamijou. He was acting a little strange. It was like. He wasn't really paying attention."

"Hmm. Now that you mention it, he did seem impatient about something. But that's just because the next event is coming up soon, isn't it?"

"…I don't know. It felt like…" Himegami broke off.

This unique chill in the air—she'd felt it personally once before. It was the same as when one boy, with only his fist, had stood up to a murderous alchemist who had power on par with a god. That boy protected others for his own sake, was never picky about how he'd win, and in the end, having his right arm severed served only to spur him on to keep fighting for her.

But…"No. It must be my imagination."

"??? What is?"

Himegami, looking down at the mystified face of Miss Komoe, wondered to herself, her thoughts vague. *But. Just the Daihasei Festival events. I don't think. They'd make him like that.*

As she stood there with a distant expression, Miss Komoe craned her neck up to look at her instead. She tugged on the bottom of Himegami's gym uniform shirt, saying, "The point is, are you interested in Kami?"

"———" Himegami froze in place. The cup with the fruit juice almost fell out of her hand before she uncharacteristically panicked to catch it again. "You aren't wrong. It's true. But that way of saying it. Was very frank. And might cause misunderstandings."

"Am I wrong?"

"…Then, Miss Komoe. Are you interested in Kamijou?"

Slip! Miss Komoe suddenly tripped over her own feet. Her cheerleading miniskirt almost flipped up, but it stopped at just the right point that Himegami couldn't see anything. Her face shot up again. "Wh-what are you saying, Hime?! I have been entrusted with taking responsibility for Kami as his homeroom teacher! The only thing I'm i-i-i-interested in is Kami's future, and if you say it so frankly then people might assume I mean something more complicated!"

"It's the same thing."

"..." Miss Komoe fell silent.

Aisa Himegami held out her free hand then grabbed her homeroom teacher's slender wrist and pulled her back to her feet. After making sure Miss Komoe hadn't hurt herself from the fall, her eyes narrowed just a little bit as if relieved. "But. It might be good. To avoid saying things that way. Kamijou and me. We're not very close. If someone was to misunderstand. He would be the one troubled by it."

"Hmm?" Miss Komoe's expression changed ever so slightly. "Ha-ha. If that's how you feel, that must be why you avoided bringing up the night parade in front of Kami. You were paying such close attention to the flier for it, too! For the students, the night parade might be just as fierce a battle as the daytime events."

During the Daihasei Festival, they would use illumination and laser beams to hold a huge light show after dark. There was even a parade that marched all over Academy City after the events ended, with convertibles covered in electric decorations and stages moving along the road. Television stations sponsored the festival, too, so the parade was extremely big, and many performers as well as celebrities would be participating.

Normally, nighttime travel anywhere in the city was subject to regulations. The last trains and buses of the day even lined up with the last school hours. But even the Academy City General Board would recommend everyone to have fun on this one night. Thanks to that, it was very popular with the students, though it wasn't on the same level as Christmas or Valentine's Day.

But...

"I can't," Himegami said flatly. "Even if I suddenly invite him. He would be confused. We don't go well together. So I don't think. I should bring it up." Her eyes narrowed just a tiny bit, which looked both kind and somehow dark at the same time.

Of course, Miss Komoe didn't like it at all when her pupils made faces like that. "That's not true! Kami might be surprised, but I think it would be because he's happy. I think he'd be happy if you were smiling, and he'd be sad if you were crying. That's the kind of kid he is. Even I understand something that simple." She looked up at her pupil, who stood much taller than she did. "So if you think it will be fun and invite him, I'm sure he'll be happy. And if it's for the night parade, there's no problem at all!"

Himegami blinked several times.

There was a slight hint of surprise in her usually impassive face.

Himegami shook the clear cup with the juice in it a little. Then she narrowed her eyes just a bit as she made a hint of a smile for Miss Komoe. "I won't invite him. It won't happen."

"Mgh! Here I am trying to push forward the shy Hime! Why are you being so stubborn now?!"

"Anyway. I won't invite him."

Grrr!! Miss Komoe's face turned red, and Aisa Himegami secretly relaxed.

2

Touma Kamijou and Stiyl Magnus were running through the city.

In stadiums here and there, a variety of matches had already begun, and they could hear the commentary coming from the speakers and big-screen televisions dotting the roads. Kamijou's own school would be starting the All Boys' Cavalry Battle qualifiers for group A soon, but unfortunately, he didn't think he'd have time for it.

"Touma Kamijou! If we're going to the bus stop, then this way is a shortcut!"

"No, if you look at the service schedules, we definitely want the subway! There are too many bus stops, so we'll stop a bunch of times along the way. We'll have to wait a little bit for the subway at the start, but once we're on we'll race straight past any bus!!"

They shouted back and forth as they turned a corner onto a small street and ran down a staircase to a subway station. They dashed through the station, which was a narrow hallway made of concrete. As they came to the automatic turnstiles blocking the way, Kamijou pressed his cell phone down on one. Nowadays, it wasn't uncommon to see cell phones with ID authentication and payment functions in Academy City.

However, the turnstiles apparently worked only with Academy City–made cell phones. Stiyl cursed and headed for the ticket vending machine. The man probably hadn't jumped the ticket gate because he decided carelessly getting into trouble here wasn't a good idea. He fed a 1,000-yen bill into the machine, possibly because using change would have taken too long, then he snatched the ticket from it and his change and came back. Finally, he made it through the turnstiles.

The subway car was just about to leave the station. An electronic bell was ringing. Kamijou, who had arrived on the platform before Stiyl, dove inside. Stiyl, rushing after him, stuck his arm into the doors right before they closed completely. The doors opened again, their safety functions at work, and he forced his body to twist inside the car. A station attendant had been glaring at him, but it wasn't the time to worry about that.

The doors clicked to a close and the car began to move.

Kamijou rested his back against the car's door. "...That Seibusan Station Tsuchimikado talked about is in two stops...," he said, looking at the electronic sign above the doors.

Stiyl, after putting the change into his wallet, promptly fished around in his clothing and took out a new box of cigarettes.

Kamijou sighed. "How many of them do you sneak around with, anyway?"

"Do you have to know?" he replied, unwilling to give an actual response, before taking out a cigarette with his mouth.

"Gyaah! Don't do it on the train! If it detects smoke, it could just stop the whole thing!"

Stiyl clicked his tongue at the frantic warning, seeming truly bitter about it. Normally he never listened to what Kamijou had to say, but he knew they had to catch up to Oriana as soon as possible. Frowning deeply, he put the cigarette back in the box.

Not a moment later, he pulled another box out of his inside pocket. It was about the same size, but it was made of old wood. He took something out of it and started chewing it like gum. "Chewing tobacco," he said.

"…You must really love tobacco a lot, huh?"

"The world without nicotine and tar is also referred to as *hell*. A virtuous, pious lamb such as myself must never allow himself to fall to hell."

"I wish you'd take a look at your own life before saying stuff like that."

As they were speaking, the car came to its first stop. Some people started to get on. Everyone new stared with surprise at Stiyl's absurd outfit.

The door closed and the car started back up again. *One stop to go.*

"Now, then," Oriana Thomson said in a light tone, standing on the streets of School District 5.

She could feel people's eyes on her as they walked past. Many attendees to the Daihasei Festival were from abroad, so a blond-haired, blue-eyed person wasn't too unusual. However, they likely paid close attention to her attractive body and the clothes that emphasized it. It was said this nation had joined others in clothing designs becoming more liberating over the past ten years, but a long, vertically torn skirt that gave no effort to conceal the bare legs of a beautiful woman still fell into the category of "quite rare." The fact that she needed a pareo as part of the outfit despite its not being a swimsuit already wasn't normal.

But Oriana didn't mind the attention too much.

She was almost unnaturally oblivious, considering she was on the run.

The clock says…it'll probably take a little longer. Well, I'll leave all that to Lidvy. I wonder what I should be doing in the meantime? Hmm.

She walked down the street, dragging the gazes of passersby along with her as she went. Her gait was relaxed—and unaware of the fact that her pursuers had their eyes on her.

The train stopped again. It was the second stop. They'd arrived at Seibusan Station, their goal.

As soon as the doors parted, Kamijou and Stiyl dove out onto the platform and headed straight for the nearby exit. Stiyl spat his chewing tobacco into a garbage can on the way and shouted, "Gah! Where's Tsuchimikado? Without him, we can't set up Four Ways to Truth and search for her!!" As he spoke, he flipped open his cell phone. They were underground, but there must have been an antenna base nearby, because his call got through easily. "Tsuchimikado!!"

"Nya~. Sorry, I'm on a bus, close to the station…But the roads around here are marked off for a 10K course. They changed the schedule and moved it up. The bus is totally stuck."

Stiyl didn't bother to hide his frustration. "How far away are you?!"

"If I get off and run, it's about ten·minutes."

That's not good, thought Kamijou. Three minutes after spotting Oriana, five more minutes to get to this station—if they had to wait another ten minutes before setting up the search spell, who knew how far she would have moved? He remembered Tsuchimikado telling him the range of the spell to find Oriana, Four Ways to Truth, was three kilometers. And if Oriana noticed them, she could get far away enough, too.

Tsuchimikado must have known that. His next words were bitter. "Stiyl. Did you memorize the Four Ways to Truth pattern I made?"

"Nope."

"Do you think you could draw it if I gave you directions over the phone?"

"Don't think so. I could imitate the spell's construction all I want, but I won't understand a bit of the theory behind it. I don't know anything about eastern formulas. And the west and east deal with perceiving the area you used for Four Ways to Truth and the veins flowing through the space. I'm not *her*, after all. Unless you were going to teach me everything about everything, from basic *Onmyou* ideas to its essence, over the phone?"

"…What western-style search spells *do* you have, anyway?"

"If I had any, I wouldn't be relying on *you*. It's completely outside my expertise."

"I see…Should have seen that one coming, nya~."

There was a loud static noise, like he'd sighed bitterly into the microphone.

After just a moment of worry, he said:

"All right. I'll activate Four Ways to Truth from here for ya."

The declaration startled Kamijou.

"What? You're only ten minutes away. That's not enough for a fatal measurement mistake. It's a better plan to do things here instead of taking up the time to get to the station. Oriana could be using a subway or self-driving bus, too, after all, nya~. We should get the search done sooner rather than later."

Before Kamijou could say anything, Tsuchimikado wrapped up the conversation.

"I'll give you the spell results over the phone, nya~. Stiyl, go with Kammy to chase Oriana and apprehend her. The Croce di Pietro might be in Lidvia's hands, not hers. If possible, I'd like you to capture her alive."

"Wa…" After hearing all that, Kamijou couldn't hold it in any longer. "Wait, Tsuchimikado! Are you gonna be all right using more magic?!"

Motoharu Tsuchimikado was unable to use sorcery. More accurately, he *could* use it, but if he did, parts of his body would blow up. The reason was that he was not only a sorcerer but also an esper. Espers had different physical makeup than normal people, so if he used magic—which was created for normal people—his body would respond by rejecting it.

He couldn't possibly not know that. In fact, he'd just gotten bloodied after using one spell earlier today. And yet he still said he would use Four Ways to Truth. Even though triggering it *twice* meant he'd be risking death.

But there was no response to Kamijou's fears. Not from Tsuchimikado, of course, and not from Stiyl.

In fact, Stiyl spoke into the cell phone, as if to bar him from saying any more. **"...You're all right with this?"**

"I dunno why you're asking me, nya? I'm a sorcerer. Say what you like, but that means I'm an expert on magic. Oh, and Kammy, I'll hear your complaints from the hospital bed. Bring me a melon and some apples as a visiting gift, nya~."

Before he could shout *Tsuchimikado*, the phone went silent. Stiyl stowed it back in his breast pocket, saying, "Hmm. The next time we get a call from him will be after Four Ways to Truth is active. If you don't want to let his determination go to waste, then stop thinking about unnecessary things, Touma Kamijou."

"Shit!!" Kamijou couldn't help but slam a fist into the concrete wall.

"And stop *doing* unnecessary things," muttered Stiyl, annoyed, taking a new cigarette out of his inside pocket.

Sure enough, his phone vibrated a minute later. The number was Motoharu Tsuchimikado's. He was calling to tell them he'd gone somewhere deserted and activated Four Ways to Truth.

Suddenly, Oriana's shoulders gave a jump.

Ah...! I see—the exact same pattern as the spell they used before. Maybe they're doing it out of spite, since I can't use any spell more than once, she thought to herself as she walked down the middle of a road in School District 5.

The enemy's spell was trying to trace Oriana's position using one of the flash cards from her ring she'd left behind—or more accurately, one of the world's smallest unstable "original grimoires," which resembled haiku that she wrote down specifically for each situation.

The original copy of a grimoire fundamentally didn't rely on a person's mana. Instead, it was a self-activating magic circle that drew trace amounts of energy leaking from the *chimyaku* (earthlines) and *ryuumyaku* (dragonlines) present in the area.

However, Oriana's were set up so that triggering the unstable grimoires and then self-destructing them could control the spells' activation and deactivation. Oriana needed her own mana for that, and because the pages were endowed with the ability to detect her commands, they could trace that back to her and find her.

Which meant...*My little pages...I wonder what they're calling them? Anyway, the pages and my mana are connected, so if they start fooling around with the pages, I'll notice something strange is going on.*

She slightly quickened her pace. There was sorcery out there that ignored the barriers of distance. Attacks that couldn't be evaded no matter where in the world someone ran were extremely sought-after, especially for assassination purposes.

But...***This one*** *isn't like that, is it?*

When she'd been about to go up in flames with the bus, her pursuers seemed to be extremely afraid of her getting far away from them. If their spell ignored physical distance and could search the entire world, they could take their time in getting to her.

Which means the right plan is to walk far away...But oh my, am I in a bind. What direction should I go in, and how far should I go?

Oriana wondered about it, continuing on her way, ever forward. Until now she'd been blending in to the crowds, but now she seemed to be overtaking them.

Now, let's see...How should I go about this? she thought, looking at the blue sky dotted with blimps.

* * *

Kamijou and Stiyl dashed up the stairs from underground and burst out of the subway station exit.

Unlike School District 7, where Kamijou lived, District 5 had a lot of universities and vocational schools. Many buildings stood side by side, and despite the disorderly impression it gave that closely resembled other districts, the styles of clothing stores and restaurants felt more mature to him. Being a high school student, he felt like there was a slightly inaccessible air about them. It was like he'd suddenly been tossed into an orchestra's concert hall, one that was world-famous but he personally didn't have any interest in.

But it wasn't the time to worry about things like that. Kamijou and Stiyl ran full speed through the chic development as if clipping through the air itself. The cell phone in Stiyl's hands was telling them where they needed to go—in a way that was literally costing someone's life.

"...Oriana...noticed. She started moving differently...Right now she's headed...northwest. She's between three hundred and five hundred meters away...Wait a bit, and I'll narrow it down for ya..."

His voice was going in and out, and it wasn't because of bad reception. On the other side of the phone, Tsuchimikado was probably covered in blood, continuing to cast the spell despite intense pain.

Stiyl, slightly out of breath, said, "Five hundred...seems close, but that's rather far to chase her down then capture her. Just to be sure, you can't use your Red Style artillery attack, can you?"

Red Style referred to the flame sorcery Tsuchimikado used to attack from long distances. He'd used it once before to deliver a precise blast to Kamijou's family's house to blow it to smithereens.

"No good, nya...I'd have to stop Four Ways to Truth and focus on Red Style. But Oriana's gonna keep running, so I won't have her latest position. Gotta be honest here—my accuracy would go way down."

"And we can't make Tsuchimikado go through any more than this anyway!" shouted Kamijou as they ran, but Stiyl just gave him an irritated glance.

With his cigarette wiggling at the corner of his mouth, he said, "Four Ways to Truth is effective out to about three kilometers. Another twenty-five hundred and she's out. At this point we need to get to her no matter what we make *anyone* go through."

"I know that, but...!!" As they shouted at each other, they made their way down the sidewalk of a major road in one spurt. They turned onto a small side street, rounded the corner, then burst out onto another broad street. They darted up a pedestrian bridge staircase and down the other side.

"...Got...a response...From Kammy's position...she's still going northwest...She's between three hundred and nine and four hundred and thirty-three meters away...It looks like...she's trying to go straight and throw off pursuit, nya...Hurry up—only seventeen hundred meters until she's out of range..."

As Kamijou ran, he grabbed—with the intensity of a marathon runner grabbing a bottle of water—one of the thick Daihasei Festival pamphlets Judgment provided for free. He hastily searched for the page with the map of District 5 on it.

"Between three hundred and nine and four hundred and thirty-three meters to the northwest...Ack!"

He'd been running while looking down at the pamphlet, so he nearly crashed into an oil drum–shaped security robot puttering along the sidewalk. Kamijou frantically avoided it, and he heard the robot start making a high-pitched siren noise.

"Could this be it...? About eight hundred meters from here, there's a monorail station. It goes on a loop around District 5. If she gets on here, she'll move three kilometers away no problem!!"

Eight hundred meters from here, which meant there was only four hundred or five hundred meters to go for Oriana, since she was ahead. Given the time to buy a ticket and a monorail to get there, how many minutes did they have left? With all the extra temporary service the monorails had during the Daihasei Festival, there might be even less than two minutes' wait per car.

But suddenly, from the other end of the phone, Tsuchimikado started saying something strange. "No, wait...Oriana suddenly changed direction." He heard the sound of paper flipping. Maybe he was looking at his own technique and the festival pamphlet in turn. "She's gone off at a right angle from the most direct route toward that monorail…That isn't where she's going…!! No, wait—suddenly she's going fast…?!"

What? Kamijou frowned as he ran. Next to him, Stiyl, too, seemed to be listening carefully to the exchange from the cell phone in his hand. The clamor of people was about them, and despite their own rushed footfalls and fairly heavy breathing, Kamijou's ears detected a strange, deathly silence.

The phone was quiet. Then he heard a dry sound, like a finger rubbing the ground. Maybe he was operating the spell. The dull noise persisted for a while, distorting his sense of time.

"Where the hell is she going…Ow! Shit, not now…"

It seemed like the pain in Tsuchimikado's body was mounting as he continued to force himself to use the spell. Kamijou thoughtlessly tried to call out to him, but he was preempted.

"I'm…fine, Kammy…I'll get a read on her…real fast…Wait…no, that can't be…"

There was another dry sound over the phone as Tsuchimikado frantically did something.

"This route…Shit, so that's it! Oriana, you bitch, you're…!!"

As he shouted, a lot of jarring noises suddenly started coming over the phone. It sounded like someone was rubbing a cheese grater against the microphone. The unnatural sounds seemed to force them to lose their connection. As if the electromagnetic waves connecting them had been torn apart.

Kamijou panicked. Without Tsuchimikado's navigation, they couldn't determine where Oriana was going. They had been following her before, but now they could just be creating even *more* distance.

"What the hell? Hey, Stiyl, is your cell phone antenna okay?!"

"It wouldn't just drop the call like that. Stop, Touma Kamijou."

Stiyl suddenly grabbed the collar of Kamijou running next to him and pulled him to a stop. He was essentially being strangled, and his feet ground to a halt. Without much care for the hacking and coughing Kamijou, he said, "...She got us."

Kamijou coughed hard. "Wh-what did she do, you idiot?!"

"Even if Oriana realized we were using the trace spell to follow her, she wouldn't know how far she'd need to run. She can't plan out where to go in this situation. So what should she do? She came up with a very simple answer."

"Hey!"

Kamijou had a bad feeling about this. Tsuchimikado's shout before the phone had abruptly disconnected was strangely ringing in his ears.

"You guessed right, Touma Kamijou. In order to get away from the trace, Oriana Thomson decided not to get farther away but to get in close...*Crushing Tsuchimikado, the center of the spell, is another one of her winning conditions.*"

"Wait, so then she could be...?!"

"*Could be*, nothing. Ten to one Oriana's going straight for Tsuchimikado."

"Then we need to hurry! He's forcing himself to use magic, and his body's probably a mess! Where is he right now?!"

"There's no way for me to know." Stiyl responded to Kamijou's shout with only the truth. And then he added, "That's why we're going to look for him."

3

"Agh...gah...?!"

Motoharu Tsuchimikado hit the marble pathway, bouncing a few times and then falling into a roll. The impact wrenched the cell phone from his hand and it slammed into a nearby pillar.

At the moment, he was in an access passage between two underground shopping centers. It was about eight meters wide and stretched on for one hundred. Currently, another famous mall was connected right to it as a shortcut, so almost nobody, including workers, came through here. There was a line of thick pillars down the middle of the passage to separate one direction of traffic from the other, so he found blind spots in the security cameras in their shadows.

After getting gridlocked at the 10K route while riding the self-driving bus, he had hurried to find somewhere without people and deployed the search spell Four Ways to Truth, but then...

Squash. Someone stepped onto the Four Ways to Truth map he'd made on the ground and crushed it, sending it flying in all directions.

"Don't lose focus just yet! You were using our little connection to find me, right? To think you'd forget I could still feel *you* from over that connection, too. A boy who thinks only of himself is going to irk his partner, you know."

It was a joking tone of voice. She had enough strength to joke.

Oriana Thomson.

She'd changed out of the work uniform they'd seen her in before. Now she wore a deeply colored camisole and a long, lightly colored skirt cut into vertical strips. It meant nothing as a skirt, which was probably why she also had a pareo wrapped around her waist, the sort one would wear as part of a swimsuit. But her buoyant hair, her good looks, and figure that hit you upside the head like the sweetness from sticking a clump of sugar into your mouth—a mere change of clothes couldn't hide those distinctive features.

Her hand played with a bundle of flash cards looped together by a slender metal ring. "Out of everyone I met today, you seem like the calmest. And the one who thinks most dangerously. So I've come to take you out. ♪"

"Shit..." Tsuchimikado stood up and pulled away from the pillars in the middle of the passage. As long as he didn't know whether physical obstacles could protect him from her attacks, the walls and pillars were nothing but hindrances. "...If you would just hand us the Croce di Pietro, let us go find Lidvia, and politely put your hands up and surrender, that would be it. You really want to get your bones crushed and see what it's like to live like a mollusk?"

"Ooh, even though your eyes say you don't like hitting. But I'm okay with being a bit rougher. I'll keep you company until your hips break."

Despite her pleasant reply, she was starting to precisely measure her distance to Tsuchimikado. He mentally gritted his teeth in anger at the skillful position she took. *Kammy and Stiyl...*Beads of blood slowly oozed from spots on his temples, his sides, and his limbs. They weren't from when Oriana hit him. It was his body rejecting the sorcery he'd been casting. *Guess I can't rely on them. They said it'd take ten minutes to get here on foot, but I didn't tell them where I was exactly.* **I'm the one who chose a spot people wouldn't think to come to***, after all.*

He lightly squeezed his fingers and let them go discreetly so Oriana wouldn't notice. It was probably due to the magic causing havoc inside his body—his movements were stiff, like a marionette whose strings were about to break. *You obviously can't always be at full strength during combat...but in this situation, if I lose my grip for a moment, I could just fall over. This is extremely bad,* he thought, showing impatience behind his cold, calculating thoughts.

But even so...

*I...*Wiping the blood trickling from the corner of his mouth with the back of his hand, Tsuchimikado looked ahead. *I can't retreat now.*

His ten fingers, which felt slightly strange, tightened with strength. *I made Stiyl eat the interception spell himself so we could track down Oriana. And I got Kammy involved in an incident he shouldn't have had anything to do with so we could conveniently resolve our English Puritan problems.*

Then, all at once, he clenched both his fists.

So I can't retreat now. I led them onto this battlefield! I can't just let myself go home without a scratch on me! It doesn't matter how disadvantageous this situation is. Or how much blood covers me. Those idiots trusted this traitor and worked with him. Like hell I'm letting their feelings go to waste!!

With a strong glint of light in his eyes behind his sunglasses, he spoke.

"...Fallere825. The backstabbing blade—remember it. It's my magic name."

Oriana's lips twisted up into a smile. She was a sorcerer herself, and so she understood his intent by naming himself.

"My name is Basis104—the one who carries the cornerstone... Now that I've announced myself, I'm going to win, no questions asked. I believe that kind of integrity is the polite response to your intentions."

Tsuchimikado didn't answer.

Oriana didn't comment on his silence, either.

It was as if they were saying to start the fight as soon as possible was the greatest consideration they could show each other as enemies.

A moment later, the sorcerers clashed.

Motoharu Tsuchimikado closed the ten-meter distance all at once.

Oriana Thomson, meanwhile, seized one flash card by her mouth and bit it off the ring.

From thin air, many straw ropes appeared and wrapped themselves around her hand. The ropes looped and coiled around one another, covering her arm in the pattern of a crude cargo net, the kind you might see in an obstacle course.

However, before she could do anything with the net, Tsuchimikado swung his right fist.

He aimed it at her chest, anticipating that she'd block. Then once her arm was locked in place, he would follow with a left uppercut, a move prohibited in most situations, hoping to pulverize the arm she used to block. At the same time, he would slam his shoe soles on her feet as hard he could to break her toes. This tactic would destroy an arm and a foot in one fell swoop, taking away her mobility.

But...

As though she understood all that from the start, she pulled back her foot he had targeted and took Tsuchimikado's first blow with only her arm. She used the fist's impact and her lost balance to widen the distance between them, as though fading backward.

His true attack, his arm-breaking left, caught only air.

As her back continued toward the ground, she waved her netted right arm.

Wind blew.

Air flowed out of all the holes in the net like blown bubbles.

But it hadn't created soap bubbles—each one of the air currents was a blade of explosive fire that could punch a hole in the side of a hill.

"!!"

The blades numbered close to twenty in all, and each one shot straight toward Tsuchimikado.

With the fan-shaped fusillade coming at him like a shotgun round, he dove to the side and pressed himself to the floor, which managed to save him from getting hit. Behind him, a bunch of pillars were smashed, some fluorescent lights in the ceiling were blown away, the building materials in the walls—along with the posters stuck to them—flapped around, and the marble floor began to come apart like it was being plowed.

Without standing up, Tsuchimikado pressed all four limbs to the floor then leaped at Oriana like a wild animal. He did so because they were already so close; getting up and running would have taken longer.

"Ah-ha-ha! Such a wild display of youth! I can't say I hate that sort of thing!!"

Oriana was about to fall on her back onto the floor, so she couldn't evade. Instead she flung out a leg to intercept him, but Tsuchimikado grabbed her ankle with his right hand and her calf with his left. If he wrenched her ankle at a right angle, he'd have only one to go.

"Shhh!!"

The instant Tsuchimikado inhaled before smashing her ankle, a moment before he had a perfect hold on her, Oriana used that ankle as a fulcrum to whip around her body. Her free foot came from the

other direction and slammed into the side of Tsuchimikado's face like a hammer, sending him flying away.

"Gah...ahh!!"

Tsuchimikado's body slammed into the ground and rolled to the left. As Oriana got back up, she tore off another flash-card note with her mouth.

She unleashed from her hand a wall made of invisible force, which drew itself over Tsuchimikado as he rolled along the floor. His momentum changed, and as he expected to bounce back up into the air, his back instead slammed into the wall without bouncing off. He could hear terrible scraping sounds emanating from inside him, and he could taste blood in his mouth.

Damn...it...!

Oriana sent a bullet of light at him next, and he jumped to the side to dodge it. The sphere was white and about the size of a basketball. As it collided with the wall, it exploded, and the overpressure slammed Tsuchimikado to the floor once again.

Slowly, he got up from the floor of the passage.

He wiped the blood pooling on his lips with the back of his hand, thinking, *It's just by one beat, but...my movements are definitely duller...If I was in peak condition, I'd have already broken one or two of her bones by now...!*

"Hmm? Is your personal style using the least amount of magic possible? Well, I don't mean to start commenting on how others live their lives, but...if that's true, you'll die."

After her unamused words, she put her soft lips on the corner of a flash card. At some point, her gaze had frozen over. "If this is your true skill, you can't dodge my next attack. If this is the level of your determination in giving your magic name, then I don't have any obligation to go along with this."

It was like she was complaining that it was too soon to finish him off. It seemed to him as though she felt like she'd done so much studying for a test, only to see the questions were so easy they made all her hard work completely moot.

"...If you were expecting someone to help you after all this, you came ill-prepared. Even I'm capable of planning how to divide your forces. I have a barrier set up over this tunnel at this very moment. Nobody will come near, nobody will find anything strange, and nobody will know what's happening in here. I've hidden the flow of mana and all magical arts, even taking precautions to ward against accidental outbreaks of any sixth sense from leading anyone in—even professional sorcerers can't get close to here very easily."

…At those words, Tsuchimikado looked up.

There was something wrong with what she'd just said. But his mind was weakened, and he couldn't decide what it was. And even if there were contradictions in what she said, she was the enemy. It could just be false information to invite intimidation and chaos on his end.

"So I'd appreciate it if you'd let me break you now. You'll regret having me give my magic name to someone with such weak determination so much, you'll literally die."

After she spoke, she crushed the flash card between her teeth with a single breath. As though she were pulling the pin out of a grenade.

…*What do I do?*

The card began to flutter down to the floor.

With how much damage I've taken, my body's done for with the next spell. But even if I wanted to use Red Style, I don't have the time to chant the spell!

As it touched the floor, a fallen steel pillar next to Oriana burst upward. The one-meter-thick pentagonal beam stabbed up toward the ceiling.

In that case, what would deal the most damage to Oriana…?! Shit, make it in time! Please be in time!!

Tsuchimikado took out a single folded paper from his bloody gym uniform. As he quickly weaved up the crumpled, twisted scrap like a precision instrument, he shouted, "Hey, you maggots drunk on peace! If you don't wanna die, then wake up!! (Bring to me a signal to begin all! Along with twirling lights and piercing sounds!!)"

"You're too late."

As she spoke, the giant steel pillar shattered like an ice sculpture.

A storm of thousands, millions, billions of sharp fragments blanketed the width and height of the entire hallway, hurtling straight toward Motoharu Tsuchimikado. He thought this must be what it would be like to stand inside a giant cannon the moment it fired.

Whump!! The roar reached his ears a second later.

Be in ti——!!

Before he could finish his plea…

…an obliterating wave of steel rushed through the passage behind him.

4

The entire passage had been destroyed.

Every pillar from where Oriana stood to the end of the hallway had been crushed. It seemed like they weren't actually holding up the ceiling; they were no more than just decoration. The only thing the passage had avoided was a total collapse. The walls, ceiling, floor, and everything adorning them had been ripped apart like wrapping paper. Rough ground now showed through the flooring, broken apart as though it had been plowed. There wasn't a flat place in sight. The ceiling tiles had all been ripped off, and water poured out of a broken pipe used for the sprinkler system.

"…"

Oriana's eyes skimmed the disaster she had wrought. *Did I break the surveillance cameras? Security might get a little tougher now.*

The sorcerer she'd been fighting had immediately dove behind a pillar, and he'd apparently crouched down even farther to minimize the damage he took. But, of course, it wasn't enough to protect him. Tsuchimikado lay facedown now, four scraps of metal protruding form his back. Each fragment was only a few centimeters long, but they were sharp as knives. To top it off, several chunks of the fallen pillars rested on top of his body. These were clumps of concrete as big as melons.

"I guess it's over already."

Oriana *had* been careful to keep casualties to a minimum, but that didn't apply to someone who had given his magic name. Magic names were what every sorcerer strove for, and Oriana believed turning aside such a declaration was the most disrespect you could show to those involved with sorcery. To both the one who had been spurned *and* the one who spurned them.

That's why Oriana didn't like it.

She knew she'd eliminated the threat in a minimal amount of time and that she needed to get out of here posthaste, but ignoring her efficiency, she actually felt dissatisfied at having settled things so quickly and easily.

Anyway. Suppose I'll get rid of the barrier around here and quickly escape. I do enjoy basking in the afterglow, but I suppose there's no choice.

After concluding her irritated thoughts and casting them aside, she surveyed her surroundings. To dispel the barrier, she would need to use magic to create a certain type of signal, then send it to her unstable "original grimoire" and cause it to self-destruct.

But...

"...?"

Oriana's expression morphed into one of suspicion. The only change in her face was a slight movement of her eyebrows, but that was all that was needed to express what she was feeling inside.

The barrier was already gone. But she hadn't given the command.

What's...going on here? Sure, it's unstable, but it's still an original grimoire. Pretty sure it can't be broken without any magical interference. Does that mean his little friends are here...?

Oriana slowly checked both the front and back entrances. But there was nothing. Destroying a barrier meant telling the barrier's owner you did so. Nobody could have surprised her from the beginning in this situation, so the usual practice would be to launch a lightning attack as soon as the barrier was destroyed...

The suspicion coloring her face deepened.

Suddenly, her thoughts arrived at another possibility.

"No..." She froze for a moment and then turned around. Her eyes fell to the sorcerer on the ground, pierced by four scraps of metal. At first, she thought he looked no different from before, but then she noticed something.

A single bird-shaped origami, covered in blood, had fallen from his hand.

I think he was trying to construct a spell as a last resort there...Are you telling me it was to destroy the barrier? But why? Why would he do something that futile and not defend against my attack?

It wasn't like destroying the barrier would immediately cause Oriana to lose. It was just a small piece of insurance.

Which meant he was aiming for...

"It looks like...my hand's got its own spell that can break stuff."

The voice startled Oriana. The enemy she thought she'd sent to the grave along with his magic name wasn't dead at all.

"You don't look the type...I didn't know you were into rougher stuff."

Oriana's needless retort made the fallen enemy magician's lips turn up...

...into a smile—and a relaxed one at that.

He...

Motoharu Tsuchimikado moved his bloodstained lips and spoke in an amused way. "You said it yourself, Oriana Thomson. Nobody will know what happens inside the barrier. Y'see, that doesn't quite work for me."

"What are you...?" started Oriana before realizing it.

If you couldn't beat an enemy alone, what was the first thing you'd think of? Calling a friend, obviously. Now that she knew what her enemy was thinking, she felt weary of it all. It was just too pathetic to cling to *that*.

"You're so silly. Your allies—you mean the two who were tailing me before? They're not a big enough threat for me to be afraid. I could take them both at once and not even be out of breath."

"They're not what I'm talking about."

"What?" shot back Oriana reflexively. Right now, she had physically seen only three people.

But...

"What are you, a moron? We're acting on behalf of our national religion, English Puritanism. Do you really think they'd *send only three people here*? Sure must be peaceful up there in that brain of yours. Maybe you should wash your hands of this sorcery business and take up being a florist or something. How many people do you think belong to Necessarius? We were always supposed to stay hidden. You think we'd show ourselves to the security forces of this peace-drunk nation?"

He's bluffing, decided Oriana.

She hadn't come here to sightsee. She and Lidvia had done their research beforehand. Leaving aside the Daihasei Festival's detailed schedule, they had come here knowing that Academy City currently sat in the center, shielded by a delicate power balance between the science faction and sorcery faction.

While the festival was going on in the city, they couldn't call in a bunch of sorcerers from only one particular group. If they did that, it would damage the relationship between the two sides. Their current plan to use the Croce di Pietro had been slipping through the gaps in that fragile equilibrium. Because of that, there could not be any irregularities like what Tsuchimikado was saying—especially if he was talking about the English Puritan Church, which maintained order among the sorcery factions.

That's why Oriana could speak with confidence—though without realizing the tiny hint of unease she showed at listening to everything he was saying. "If that was true, I'd be in a spot, wouldn't I? But that absolutely can't be true. The Puritan Church and Academy City would never allow such a foolish plan."

"Why should I have to ask for permission?"

"..."

"Did you forget my magic name? Thought I told you to remember it. *Who do you think a backstabbing blade would backstab first?* Who gives a shit about the Church's situation? Or what's convenient for Academy City? I'm not drunk on peace like them. No way I'd let *dumb shit like that prevent me from winning.*"

Oriana felt an unsettling silence coming down around them. She took a slow, deep breath.

"I'll do anything to win. I'll use anything that lets me hit a weak spot. If I'm going to stab you in the back, I'll get behind you no matter what you do. Get a grip, Oriana Thomson. If I wanted to, I could have stopped as many of these metal scraps as you wanted to throw at me. But I can't secure a sure victory like that. So I played an even better card. That's all it is, yeah?"

"...Did you think I'd believe that? If you had so many friends, why would you be acting on your own? You should have wanted bodyguards and lookouts for that search spell you used before, too. And even if you didn't, you at least wouldn't be moving in groups of two."

"If small talk's what you're into, then I'll oblige you. But it'll let me buy as much time as I want. As soon as the barrier went down, I sent out the signal. Won't be too long now—she's a serious one, you know. *She took her magic name exactly to stop life-or-death situations like this one.*"

Tsuchimikado slowly reached out with his bloody hand sprawled on the ground.

It came to a simple paper talisman. It was a small sheet of paper, colored and folded up into a shape you might see being sold as a protective charm at shrines. Eastern characters flowed down vertically through the middle. They looked less written in ink than branded on the paper.

"Tsukebumi Tamazusa—it looks like a Shinto protective charm at first glance, but this thing's part of *Onmyoudou*. Originally an item for cursing someone. A Soul Arm for causing distant opponents to hallucinate and kill one another...but if you turn down the power on it, you can use it a little more peacefully."

"Wait...A communication spell?!"

"Correct-a-mundo. Looks like a bag, right? There's a wooden card inside with a person's name on it. Real quaint, eh?" Tsuchimikado smirked. "Now then. Given the situation, who might I have contacted?" he asked slowly. Despite all the blood covering him, it seemed like he was harrying his prey. "You should have just kept on saying you were carrying around the Stab Sword. Now that I know you're not, I can bring *her* into the fray no problem. Actually, without the Stab Sword here, there's no reason *she* needs to be on standby. After all, *her biggest weakness is gone now.*"

Oriana's lips began to dry without her realizing.

She'd heard of this.

There were fewer than twenty saints in the entire world and one stood with the English Puritan Church as a member of Necessarius. She had heard there was a sorcerer, a girl with immense power, who wielded a katana because she didn't want anyone to die. Oriana Thomson was originally a British citizen, and she mainly worked around the London area. So she knew all about that saint. Oriana knew if they had an encounter, she'd lose instantly. She knew that the only things capable of beating that saint would be literal gods or angels.

"That's right. Kaori Kanzaki."

Oriana Thomson's eyes sharpened slightly. She licked her slightly dry lips.

"It's not really all that surprising given what's at stake here, is it? We already know you've got the Croce di Pietro, not the Stab Sword, *and* she was at the center of a battle between the English Puritans, the Roman Orthodoxy, and Amakusa not ten days ago. Didn't it occur to you that she might still be in Japan? Plus, *Kanzaki has a personal acquaintance here in Academy City.* She's no more than a special guest, so even if she *did* get found out, it wouldn't be an issue anyway."

Tsuchimikado went on. "You probably don't get it. Kaori Kanzaki's got a personal debt to me. When she first came over to England, who do you think took care of her? *Another Japanese person was the obvious choice to look after her.* For me it was just a tiny little thing, but she was very attached to those conversations we had. If she knew what was going on, she'd come right away."

*Damn...*Oriana's mind went through several calculations.

Tsuchimikado watched her as though he'd been made fun of. "Whoops. Don't go thinking about destroying Tsukebumi Tamazusa now. Frankly, it's impossible. It's basically an emergency button. Once I activate it and send the signal, its job's over."

As he spoke from his vantage point on the ground, he gave his words weight by taking the communication amulet he made himself and crumpling it up.

"…" Oriana tried to breathe a little more calmly.

She couldn't quite figure out if this Kaori Kanzaki was actually coming here or not. Even if a saint was really on the way, she didn't think she'd necessarily lose to her. If she came up with an effective tactic and went at it prepared to lose a limb or two, she was pretty sure she could kill a few saints at the cost of her own life. But that wouldn't work. She couldn't be preoccupied about winning or losing a simple personal battle—she had something much bigger to accomplish. She couldn't let herself get hurt too badly.

*Then…*For now, she made her first choice: to immediately kill Tsuchimikado, the one using the search spell, and get out of there promptly—however…

"*Shhhn!!*" Tsuchimikado, still on the ground, used the last of his strength to pull a reinforcing bar out of the middle of the pile of rubble. Then he slammed it down onto the destroyed floor, instantly sending up a billowing curtain of gray dust.

She couldn't see anything.

"!!" Oriana immediately launched a heel kick at the spot Tsuchimikado had been.

But the only feeling she got back was that of the hard floor.

He bought time to rally his strength?! It's futile…!!

And now her first choice had been foiled. Her opponent could still fight, and if he was looking for a chance of a certain kill from within the dust screen, it could be a little troubling. Given the situation, she could send Tsuchimikado to his grave for sure, but now it would take a little longer. That meant there were two options.

One: Decide Kaori Kanzaki was not coming, and take down Tsuchimikado slowly and surgically.

Two: Decide Kaori Kanzaki was coming, and make a swift retreat, even if it meant leaving him here.

She could easily blow away the dust around her with a flash card. But if he saw that as a signal that the battle was starting, she would be stuck here until she killed him for good.

It wasn't so much about which to choose...

...but that she regretted being forced into making the choice.

For now, the search spell is gone, along with my page. It would be absurd to get even more badly hurt playing around with a wounded boy...

With a single click of her tongue, Oriana Thomson ran toward the tunnel's exit.

If he was telling the truth, then the English Puritan saint Kaori Kanzaki would be joining the battle. If so, she figured she should have made better use of the Stab Sword cover story. She could prepare a plan or tactics all she wanted, but a saint wasn't something she could run into accidentally and walk away unharmed.

Of course...

...she had no intention of losing.

"Piece of shit...," spat Tsuchimikado in spite of himself in the destroyed tunnel. He knew from the fact that Oriana hadn't left a page spell as a parting gift that she'd left the area.

The dust curtain cleared.

Tsuchimikado had rolled a mere human's width to the side of where Oriana had kicked. With all his wounds, moving that distance had been everything he could do. It meant that he had made a narrow escape, thanks to blocking Oriana's vision, making her impatient, and taking away the calm she needed to discern if he was telling the truth.

"Tsukebumi Tamazusa, a communication spell to call on Kaori Kanzaki in times of need..."

He aimlessly looked up to the ceiling.

Then the sides of his mouth turned up in a self-deprecating grin.

"Wouldn't that be nice, nya..."

Naturally, they didn't have a single person in reserve. The only ones inside Academy City chasing down Oriana and Lidvia were Kamijou, Stiyl, and him.

He looked at the origami amulet he'd crumpled up.

You could look all you wanted—there was no protective amulet or Soul Arm anywhere in the world with such a foolish name, much less in *Onmyoudou*. He had figured Oriana wouldn't know much about eastern magic anyway, so he had just folded the piece of paper arbitrarily. It had no magical properties, of course, nor was Kanzaki's name written on a wooden card inside.

Tsukebumi and tamazusa *both mean "love letter" to begin with... And how would a love letter be a curse? Though I guess a real deep love can be like a curse, nya~.*

Earlier, Stiyl had mentioned tiredly that he had no clue how eastern spells worked, so he couldn't use them alone. Tsuchimikado hadn't thought the notion would help him here. In short, he had made a bet on the possibility that Oriana was ignorant of amulet construction in *Onmyoudou*, then brazenly showed her origami with random Chinese characters written all over it.

Unfortunately...

*She believed it, which means she's gonna be more careful now, nya. I doubt it ended up delaying their plans at all, though. Wish I could have gotten at least a scratch on her...*Still on the ground, he stared down the ravaged tunnel. *The magic circle's broken. The page we had is gone. My cell phone's busted, too. What should I start with, nya...? Don't honestly think I could use Four Ways to Truth again.* He tried to get up, sending a wave of pain through his body.

He mindlessly writhed for a moment, and then finally realized he didn't have the stamina to get up anymore. His body was cold. And heavy. He could inhale, but he wasn't getting enough oxygen.

First things first...

Tsuchimikado thought about the ability his body possessed—not as a sorcerer but as a member of Academy City.

His Level Zero ability, Auto Rebirth: a self-restorative ability that spread a thin membrane over torn blood vessels.

"...Guess I've gotta do something about this body of mine, nya...?"

5

Finally, they got a call from Motoharu Tsuchimikado. It was from a different number, so Stiyl had stared at the screen suspiciously at first. He must have called from a new phone.

After Stiyl heard what he had to say, he learned that Oriana had indeed attacked Tsuchimikado as he'd predicted. In the end, his cell phone—and the tracing spell Four Ways to Truth—had been destroyed beyond repair. He couldn't use the spell a second time with the state his body was in, and more important, the page from Oriana's flash cards that they needed to actually use the spell was gone, too.

"…" Tsuchimikado said he was fine, but if he was *really* okay, his magic circle wouldn't have been absolutely wrecked like that. Above all, his frail voice conveyed his pain just by listening to it.

Stiyl spoke, cigarette wiggling around at the corner of his mouth. "So what do we do now? If we can't use Four Ways to Truth anymore, we basically don't know what direction to go in."

"Yeah, nya…But the one thing I do know is…Oriana's on her guard right now—she has misgivings…but there's a high probability she's getting away from here…For now, at least…it looks like my little bluff worked, nya~. Which means I don't think she's walking… She's probably gonna take a bus, subway, train, or monorail line to its last stop…"

His voice was broken and intermittent, like he wasn't breathing fully.

"Tsuchimikado's in this tunnel now, right?" said Kamijou, opening the Daihasei Festival pamphlet to the page with the map of School District 5 on it. The closest thing to that tunnel was the subway whose line went from District 5 to the neighboring District 7.

"…Without any other guide, we'll just have to follow that. If we can pinpoint which car she got on, we could search for her more efficiently, but…"

"But we don't know that, so we're gonna have to work for it. Anyway, let's get a move on, Stiyl."

"Nya…I'll try…getting into the security again…If she's too impatient to check where the cameras are now…that would be delightful, nya~."

Each of the three spoke, and the phone conversation ended.

They then resumed their battle of pursuit, as though following exceedingly thin threads.

Oriana Thomson was in a subway car.

If I get off this car…

This subway line went from District 5 to the entrance of District 7. It wasn't actually that great of a distance. If she wanted to get farther away, she'd need to transfer to a bus after that.

Oriana came up with a few ideas. *Run as far away as I can? Watch and see what happens? Or lay a trap and see how they react?* She was frustrated, but if Kaori Kanzaki really did enter the battle, then any poorly thought out plans would probably earn her an intense counterattack. *At this point, I'd really like to take a breather and give this some thought.*

She clicked her tongue while looking out at the unchanging underground scenery outside the window. Eventually, the car reached its last stop, the District 7 entrance.

As soon as the automatic doors opened, she leaped out onto the station platform. Then she ran up the stairs and aboveground, slipped past the ticket gates, and rushed outside all in one go.

Her next destination was a self-driving-bus stop not too far from the station. Academy City was still caught up in the festive mood of the events, and large numbers of people milled about the area. The streets were filled with parents with their children waving balloons or seniors come to see their grandchildren, placid faces one and all. But—Oriana wasn't peaceable enough to take this as meaning it was safe.

She needed to follow some specific steps to ensure no assassins were present. *I doubt I'd have to worry about anyone who gets caught by a simple theory like this, though. Whatever. Let's get the annoying stuff out of the way now.*

Looking around carefully, she entered a smaller side road slightly off the beaten path. There were tall buildings surrounding the narrow street, so none of the sun's light got inside despite the cloudless sky, making it feel unpleasantly cold.

Oriana was entering an empty alley to see if any assassins were on her tail. Naturally, if anyone dashed into the alley after her, they would basically be announcing they were assassins. Any pursuers who realized this would have to come up with something really clever then. They could call up their allies and get them to head her off at the alley's exits or use a charm of some sort for remote surveillance. Those were the minute movements she was looking for to see if anyone was tailing her.

We're basically trying to outwit each other, but it really is a pain in the butt to have to think of another plan after your old one was figured out. Like Oriana, the assassins could possibly want to intentionally show her false signs of movement. They could have her think she'd evaded pursuit, then attack when her guard was down and capture her. For a smuggler like her in the sorcery world, these little games of cat-and-mouse were something she was very familiar with.

In any case, if she got any response, no matter how slight, that meant someone was tracking her. If there was no response, then there wasn't. It was that simple.

She exhaled. *The Croce di Pietro will take a little longer to set up. I wonder what I should do in the meantime. Oh, it would be fun to think up anti-Kanzaki spells! That sounds good. What would constitute "winning" against that saint in this case? Successfully running away? Successfully hiding out...? Or maybe just successfully killing her outright?*

As she thought to herself, she overlooked something.

This road was already small, and yet there was another side road branching off.

Suddenly, someone ran out from around that corner.

"Hime, if we don't take a shortcut, we'll never make it to the next event— Eek!!"

"!!"

They collided.

A small girl, about the size of an elementary school kid, ran into Oriana's stomach and bounced off. Then, the back of her head bumped into the girl she had come with, who had black hair and wore a gym uniform. Oriana immediately moved to bite off a flash card, but she stopped herself just barely before doing it. The person who had collided into her was only 135 centimeters tall, dressed in a cheerleading outfit.

The black-haired girl had accidentally dropped her cup of fruit juice from the impact of the short cheerleader in front. She made a tiny grunt as the cup's entire contents spilled all over her gym uniform. The liquid that hit her chest dripped off it onto the smaller girl's head, too.

The black-haired girl looked at her chest impassively and then at the girl who'd run into her. "Miss Komoe. Now you've done it."

"I…I'm so sorry! But I'm soaking wet, too, so that means we're even! Oh, are you okay, Miss?" the drenched girl asked worriedly, looking up at Oriana.

They…don't look like sorcerers following me, decided Oriana, an easy guess based on their clothing and behavior. She gave them the bright smile she always kept on hand. "Yes, I'm perfectly fine. But I think I'm more worried about *her.* That seems a little too stimulating to show on a main road."

"Oh no! Hime, you're all wet and see-through now!"

"So are you, Miss Komoe. Less so in the chest, though."

The cheerleader yelped and hurriedly covered her flat chest with her hands. After seeing her face go bright red, Oriana looked at the black-haired girl's chest once again.

And then she noticed it.

On her chest.

Her short-sleeve T-shirt was completely see-through because of all the juice on it. She could easily see the pink underwear decorated with a green ribbon she had on under it.

But aside from that…

There was another thing visible inside her sheer gym uniform. It was like a necklace, hanging around her neck by a thin chain. The chain went inside her uniform. And attached to the bottom end of the chain was an inappropriately big, metallic—

——*Celtic cross with an English Puritan arrangement on its design.*

Oriana had no idea what that cross was supposed to be for.
And she didn't know what sort of ability the black-haired girl had.
But she was pretty sure about one thing.
A sorcerer from Necessarius?!
They certainly sold plenty of cross-shaped accessories in Academy City. Some children would wear them as earrings or necklaces without knowing the real meaning behind them. That wasn't very unusual by itself.
However...
Roman Orthodox crosses were one thing—they were famous throughout the world. But an English Puritan–style cross? Japan didn't even have a proper Puritan church in it. The very fact that she'd imported such a thing from England was abnormal to begin with. But a *Soul Arm that functioned as a barrier*? No normal person would have something like that. And to put the nail in the coffin, she knew exactly what that barrier's name was.
*English Puritanism's...Walking Church?! She's wearing a Soul Arm in the same vein as the one **that** index of prohibited books uses as protection?! This monster...!!*
Her hand moved immediately.
Oriana brought the ring of flash cards to her mouth. She took one page between her teeth and then ripped it off. On the card's surface were red letters spelling out SOIL SYMBOL in English. An unstable original grimoire came into existence, and with her mana, it activated a spell...

Krsshhh!!
A muffled sound tore through the air.

6

Kamijou and Stiyl exited the subway station and went aboveground. The streets were bustling with people, and the heat showed no signs of receding. Kamijou quickly looked down at the Daihasei Festival pamphlet, wiping the sweat from his brow. "...I think the closest place to transfer is a bus station about three hundred meters north of here!"

"Three hundred...Urgh," Stiyl said bitterly, taking out a new cigarette.

"But there's, like, ten minutes until the next bus comes! We might make it if we hurry!"

As they talked, they broke into another run, weaving through the crowds. A little less than seven minutes separated them from Oriana. It was just barely enough time.

"If we can, we should try and capture Oriana, at least. We don't have any hints as to where Lidvia Lorenzetti's hiding!" shouted Stiyl as he cut through the wind, looking ahead.

The station was three hundred meters north, but in front of them was a large road going to the left and right; a cluster of mixed buildings prevented them from seeing any farther.

The pedestrian signal next to the overpass had just flickered green. Kamijou and Stiyl shot across the street toward the other end. The sidewalk they came to was even more packed than the previous one.

The row of multi-tenant buildings was like a giant wall. To get to their goal, the bus stop, they would need to weave between buildings and run through alleys unless they wanted to take a huge detour on the main road.

They searched for an alley to get past the wall of buildings as they ran down the sidewalk teeming with people.

"Do we seriously have no freaking hints?! Weren't you just talking to someone on the phone before at the park?!"

Kamijou and Stiyl each twisted in a separate direction around an old lady in the middle of the sidewalk.

"Yeah. That was from London! They're checking the British Library, but…"

They looked to and fro but couldn't seem to find an alley to get inside. The actual route seemed longer than they thought, compared to the direct distance there. If Oriana had faced the same difficulties, though, that would help.

"Getting info on the Croce di Pietro?!"

As they went on, Kamijou spotted a crowd in front of them.

"Yeah, but…Doesn't look too good. There's barely any literature on the subject. The most they figured out was that there's a vault specifically for the Croce di Pietro when it's being stored. All the windows closed up, two separate doors to get in, and no light allowed inside…That's all we know." He puffed cigarette smoke.

"That's it?!" Kamijou ran for the crowd.

Beside him, Stiyl answered, "Don't ask me! Now we…Damn it." He coughed a little before he could finish. They were running hard, but maybe it was because he smoked on a regular basis. "Not enough time to explain. Give me your address. I have a text with Orsola's report, so I'll forward it to you. Read it later when you have time."

I didn't know Stiyl and Orsola knew how to text message…, thought Kamijou in veiled admiration, giving Stiyl his contact information. *Actually, maybe Index is the strange one. She's totally useless with anything electronic.*

As Kamijou ran down the road, he decided to give the text a quick skim.

"Vi riporto qua informazioni che ha trovato nella Biblioteca Brittanica…"

Wait…How am I supposed to understand this?! He could tell they were English letters, but the only thing he got out of it was that it wasn't English. He closed his cell phone screen, figuring he'd get Tsuchimikado to read it for him later.

Stiyl sighed as he ran beside him. "Damn. It would be great if you at least knew what the words meant without needing to go through a grammar textbook…But if you can't read it, don't look at it. It's not much to read anyway."

"…Uhh, sure. So basically we're trapped with no way out. Damn it!"

"Yeah. That's why we want to capture Oriana Thomson personally. Then we'll figure out where to go. That's all…Hmm?" Still running, he frowned to himself.

There was a cluster of people in front of them—mostly students, all standing around, blocking their path. No one in the crowd was looking at them. The people had gathered in front of the entrance of a branching small road.

"There's the back road we needed…but I have a bad feeling about this."

"Huh?" said Kamijou dubiously.

The cigarette butt wiggled up and down as Stiyl spoke. "*That smell. It's not a good smell.* When a certain kind of group is in an excited state, they spread their emotions like a scent. This crowd's got the smell of people seeing blood."

The disturbing words startled Kamijou. Meanwhile, they reached the tail end of the crowd. And then he noticed. Everyone here was leaning forward, standing on their tiptoes and even jumping up and down to get a look at something.

But what…? He frowned, but he didn't have time to check. He decided to go straight for the back road and began somewhat forcefully pushing his way through the crowd to get there.

And then he heard an unexpected voice from beyond the wall of people.

"P-please move out of the way! Everyone, open up the path! Hime? Are you okay?! Himeee!!"

"Move it!!" Kamijou instinctively thrust the people near him out of the way and got to the front. The mass of people swayed and split to the left and right. Kamijou felt like some of them wanted to complain about his pushing through, but he ignored them and jumped to the very front row.

Then, without stopping, he dove toward the entrance to the path. And there he saw it.

Blood.

*   *   *

It was a narrow alley. It was midafternoon, but because of the tall buildings overlooking it, there was no sunlight on the ground. The air smelled stagnant, too.

In that dark space...

...was a much darker redness staining the ground.

"K-Kamiii!!"

The familiar voice belonged to Miss Komoe.

But her small hands, her soft cheeks, her cheerleading tank top and miniskirt—it was like dark-red blood had been draped all over them. Teardrops fell from her big eyes, mixing with the splattered blood and dripping down her chin.

The blood wasn't hers.

A single girl lay right at her feet. Her black hair was soaked in the blood on the ground. Aisa Himegami. In contrast, her skin, from her face down to her hands and feet, was pale, devoid of color.

The upper half of her gym uniform had been ripped to shreds. She was covered in bandages from her collarbone to a little above her navel—basically everywhere. It didn't take a doctor to tell she'd been bandaged up properly, but the oozing fluid had already stained them bright red. Her normally smooth features looked somehow uneven.

"...!" Immediately upon considering *why*, Kamijou felt immense regret.

In the puddle of blood, he saw small pieces of flesh, still with skin attached—as if someone had failed to take the shell off a hard-boiled egg.

Himegami didn't move. Kamijou could hear only her shallow breathing. So shallow it might have been his imagination.

He felt a dull impact, like someone had smacked his head. He'd seen this before. When he discovered one of the Sisters whom Accelerator had killed, it felt exactly the same.

"No, why...Why Himegami? Miss Komoe, what happened here?! Who the hell did this?!"

"I...I don't know!" replied Miss Komoe with a very shaky voice, looking at him. "I...I ran into a lady here...And then I said I was sorry, and she smiled, and I thought she forgave me. But then all of a sudden she made a scary face, and...and she...!"

"Oriana...," Stiyl said, grabbing his still-long cigarette and pushing it against the wall in irritation. "With this kind of timing, it would have to be her...She must like messing with us."

"Why?" said Kamijou, his expression bewildered. "Why her? She had no reason to attack Himegami! She doesn't have anything to do with this incident!!"

"That's why." Stiyl pointed at the ground with his cigarette butt.

A bloody cross was on the ground. It was the small, wearable, accessory-shaped barrier the English Puritan Church had made for her to seal her power, Deep Blood.

"That Soul Arm uses the same formula as the Walking Church. Not even Kanzaki, Tsuchimikado, or I was deployed with something so special. If Oriana saw it, she'd naturally think the girl was a sorcerer on the *index*'s level of importance. Academy City is a bastion of science. The presence alone of an English Puritan Soul Arm is strange. Perhaps Oriana thought a powerful pursuer was cutting off her escape route and decided to act first."

When Kamijou realized what he meant by that, his cheek muscles tensed. "By...mistake...?" His throat twitched strangely. "Just... a mistake? She did all this...to Himegami...and it was...by mistake...? That...that...It's a load of fucking bullshit!!"

Without thinking, he slammed a fist into the nearby wall. Miss Komoe, who was still crying, started in fright.

Stiyl sighed, then took rune cards out of his habit's inside pocket. He scattered them about, and they stuck themselves to the ground and walls as if pulled by magnets.

"IHCTPIMTP. (I henceforth change this place into my tranquil place.)"

As he spoke, the people standing around the entrance to the alley began returning to the main road as though a cork had been removed. Kamijou guessed it was Stiyl's Opila spell, which warded off people.

"You've done a perfect job applying first aid. I'm sure you called an ambulance. Just wait at the entrance to the alley. The EMTs won't be able to find either of you if you stay in here now. I think that's better than rubberneckers stopping to stare, anyway."

Stiyl headed deeper into the dark alley to follow Oriana. If she was still trying to get to the bus stop to escape, she would have gone this way as well.

He didn't hesitate at all to venture farther in.

Stepping right across Aisa Himegami and the pool of blood in which she lay.

"Wait, you bastard!"

"What? What on earth do you want? Do you want to stand there yelling or find Oriana Thomson right now and wrap this up?"

"This happened because we got her involved! How the hell can you just leave her here like this?!"

"Kami?" said Miss Komoe, looking up at him. She was related to this, but she hadn't been told anything. She wouldn't know about any of this.

"Then what are you going to do?" Still standing over Himegami, Stiyl looked straight at his face.

And then he reached out with his ring-covered fingers.

"——Don't be so full of yourself, you amateur."

He grabbed Kamijou's hair hard and forced him to look down. There was the girl, barely breathing, bathed in blood.

"Is there something an amateur like you can do for this wounded girl? There's nothing I can do, either, and I'm a professional! Will staying with her heal her wounds? Will holding her hand make the pain go away? If you really believe it, then do it right now! Meanwhile, the cold reality will keep sapping her strength! Right now, the only thing we can do is chase Oriana! If you want to do that, then step over her! If you don't, then stay here like a useless brat!!"

Stiyl jerked his hand violently away from Kamijou's hair.

Kamijou took one unsteady step back, then another.

"...Don't you dare think you're the only one angry about this, Touma Kamijou. Everyone would feel that way if they saw something like *this*. Even Stiyl Magnus does. I risked my life to rescue her from Misawa. You think I can stay calm seeing her torn apart like this?!" Stiyl pointed his index finger, the ring on it glaring in the sunlight, directly below him. "*Step over her*, Touma Kamijou. Step over her and follow Oriana! This is *our* world. And it's a cruel one. We can't heal her wounds, and nothing will ever change that. If you want to protect someone, clench your fist. There was only so much we could ever do. Your right hand can kill only illusions. And now you're trying to protect one? Give me a break."

"...Shit..." Kamijou looked down. His bangs hid his eyes. And, just beneath them, he began to grit his teeth so hard he thought his molars might break. The frustration he felt—was it toward Oriana or toward himself for not being able to offer any argument?

"Fuck...this...!!" he roared, voice trembling, nearly crying. And then he brought up one foot. It, too, shook as he tried to take the first step. Tried to prioritize catching Oriana instead of doing anything for Himegami.

"———" The sorcerer Stiyl Magnus narrowed his eyes and stared at the ceremony Kamijou was performing.

And just before Kamijou's foot went over Aisa Himegami's body...

...the priest saw.

Komoe Tsukuyomi, who had just been a few steps away from the gored Aisa Himegami.

She was sitting there dumbfounded now, her hands, face, and clothing bright red with splattered blood. She sat on her legs, not caring about her skirt or that she sat down with nothing between her skin and the ground.

But that wasn't the crucial thing.

She had begun to slowly gather small rocks and empty cans from nearby. She started lining up the various objects like she was building with toy bricks. And not in a random pattern, either. It appeared to be an unskilled miniature representation of the buildings in this alley and the fallen Aisa Himegami.

"Wait," Stiyl said in spite of himself. Kamijou, about to set down his foot on that first step, lost his timing and pulled back. Stiyl didn't watch, instead staring straight into Komoe Tsukuyomi's eyes.

"What are you doing?"

"The other time…," began the woman, no more than 135 centimeters tall, returning the sorcerer's gaze with bloodred eyes. "…With the sister…This…This worked somehow. So now…this time…it has to work again somehow. Because before, the sister, her back was cut, and there was a lot of blood, but I did what she told me to do, and…"

"I…Wait…" Stiyl Magnus tried to recall. Back to when the index of forbidden books first came to Academy City. Kanzaki had slipped and slashed Index in the back, and Touma Kamijou had fled to Komoe Tsukuyomi's apartment while carrying her on his shoulders.

But…

Neither Index nor Touma Kamijou could use sorcery. Not because they lacked the know-how but because of how their bodies were made. So at the time, who had been the one to use healing magic on Index?

"Was…it you…?" murmured Stiyl in a mix of astonishment and respect.

The small woman didn't notice the change in his tone of voice. "…Before, this worked just fine. I remember it; I remember it exactly. The sister told me what to do, and I did it, and I'm doing it, but…! Why…why won't Hime get any better…?! Hime, she was just talking about the night parade. She wanted to go there with Kami and the others, and she had been constantly checking her pamphlet since yesterday, so why, why did this…!!"

She hadn't directed her cry at anyone.

Nevertheless, Stiyl and Kamijou silently listened to her complain.

Komoe Tsukuyomi was trying to put together a type of spell that linked a fixed area to a sorcerer-made miniature garden. Healing magic generally required extremely fine control to use, but with this system, one could simply repair a wound on a puppet in a rough diorama to "repair" the wound on the body of the linked person.

But it wouldn't produce any effects unless the person actually defined the spell's scope and created a complete link to the miniature garden. It wasn't just a physical thing. You'd need to think about the placement of the magic-related symbols and the flow of telesma as well.

It wasn't easy enough that every sorcerer could do it. Even Stiyl, handy enough to link together runic and Crossist spells, could heal only burns.

Healing magic was a single term, but there were many different kinds that differed depending on religion, rules, and techniques. Not everyone could just repeat an incantation to heal whatever wounds they wanted. Cold medicine couldn't be used to cure broken bones. Unless she put together an appropriate spell based on the situation before her, it wouldn't have any effect on an injured person.

Plus, if they wanted to heal everything—the lacerations, bruises, broken bones, and even her arteries and organs—they'd need an expert caster specializing in all that. Perhaps with the support of someone with as much knowledge of the index, an amateur could do it, but such a major premise was far too unusual.

"..."

And sure enough, Komoe Tsukuyomi's spell was utterly incomplete.

She had caused magic to activate only at Index's instructions before, so it was inevitable. She had learned about the "miniature garden" by pure imitation, and her current one was in complete disarray. Not a single magical symbol was incorporated into it. But of course there wasn't. Komoe Tsukuyomi resided in the realm of science. She had absolutely no idea what underlying theories made the spells work.

But she had called an ambulance...

And she'd done all the first aid she could...

She had used every method she could think of, and none of them had worked. Now, in the end, she clung to "sorcery," of which she understood neither the theories nor the rules.

She didn't even know how terribly far off the mark she was.

She didn't even understand how crude was the spell she was betting everything on.

But she was still doing it…
…all to save the fallen girl in front of her.

"Damn…," Stiyl said, almost unwittingly looking away. This Komoe Tsukuyomi woman was *extremely* like another certain girl.

She was short, naive, and innocent. She could get angry for others. She could cry for others. She couldn't use any magic herself, even though she knew all about it. She was covered in the blood of another and weeping.

Stiyl narrowed his eyes a little. He was, from the bottom of his heart, bitter.

He took a breath, then tossed behind him the cigarette butt in his hand.

"——No. That isn't how it works."

"Huh?" Komoe Tsukuyomi looked up.

Stiyl took several rune cards with complex markings from his black habit's inside pocket. "It's like scooping water out of the ocean with a bucket. First you need to set up the region you're going to delimit with the miniature garden. And you're not thinking about the angle. You have to imagine what direction the angel will come from, and which seat the angel will arrive at. Just imagining it is fine. You're not *actually* calling a winged angel. It's just a cluster of a certain kind of power."

He squatted down.

He faced Himegami, covered in bandages, as she breathed shallowly.

He faced her once again, after having already stepped over her.

"Touma Kamijou. Go on ahead and chase Oriana."

"Huh?"

"I'll give you Tsuchimikado's new cell phone number. If I'm not here, you two had better be able to talk to each other."

"Wait a minute. Are you gonna…"

"Don't expect much. This is out of my field." The sorcerer Stiyl Magnus spoke bitterly. "I can heal only burns. Healing blood loss and broken bones is a completely different family of technique. I've never even tried to do this before, and these wounds are terrible. Not sure even a caster specializing in healing could completely fix all this…" But still, he kept speaking. "…Part of the archive's knowledge must be inside this person. I'll borrow that and reinforce the theory. I can't even commit to memory Tsuchimikado's Four Ways to Truth or Divination Circle, so I'm not sure about this one bit… but I'll buy her time before she gets taken to the hospital. Then we just have to pray there's a good doctor where she's going."

"Ah…Huh…?"

Komoe Tsukuyomi rubbed her eyes.

Stiyl unwittingly averted his own from hers. "When you've finished what I tell you, go to the alley's entrance and lead the EMTs here. Touma Kamijou, you go on ahead and do something about Oriana, will you? This healing spell is going to be really half-assed already. If you stay here, that right hand of yours might just wipe it out completely. When I'm done, I'll follow after you right away…so I'll say it again. If you want to solve everything the right way, *step over her.*"

"…All right." Kamijou looked at Aisa Himegami's face, lying in her own blood.

Then he tightened the five fingers on his right hand.

"I'll do it. If that'll solve everything. I'll leave Himegami to you, Stiyl."

"I already told you not to expect much," Stiyl said, heaving a sigh. And in a seriously bothered tone, he finished. "I'm not used to this, either. With this world of ours…Who would have thought I'd be using magic on someone for a reason other than to attack them?"

INTERLUDE FIVE

Why...?

Aisa Himegami thought as she lay on the cold ground.

I wonder why. It came to this.

The end of September had been wrought with the lingering heat from summer, but this dark side road was cold enough to pierce her skin. Maybe it never felt any sun all year long. The colors of the walls, ground, and street as a whole were a gloomy black.

She could feel her body pounding.

A single slash had ripped her apart, starting above her chest and ending below her stomach.

The feeling of pain had passed the point of saturation, and now it was starting to feel numb instead. Now she had the ability to look around her. But when she saw the splattered blood and pieces of flesh, her mind felt like it was ready to explode.

But...

A fact more painful than that was staring her in the eyes.

Two boys were standing facing each other, one on either side of her fallen body. In her hazed-over vision, she saw them arguing about something.

"——*Don't be so full of yourself, you amateur.*"

An eerily cold voice.

At the same time, there was a strangely piercing clarity to it.

"Is there something an amateur like you can do for this wounded girl?"

There is, Himegami tried to say.

But her voice wouldn't come out. It was like her mouth had shriveled up.

"There's nothing I can do, either, and I'm a professional!"

Those words stung the other boy.

She could see his face twisting a little bit every time he spoke.

"Will staying with her heal her wounds? Will holding her hand make the pain go away?"

That doesn't matter, she wanted to say.

Maybe the wounds wouldn't heal. Maybe the pain wouldn't go away. Something would still happen. She was sure of it.

"If you really believe it, do it right now! Meanwhile, the cold reality will keep sapping her strength!"

Why? she thought.

Why hadn't the world been made to be better?

If the boy could just reject him one time, that would be all he needed. Then the boy wouldn't need to look at him with those tears in his eyes.

But his lips wouldn't open even a little.

His tongue wouldn't move even a little.

His throat wouldn't speak even a little.

The two boys were arguing about something. No, at this point, one of them was doing all the attacking. Violence by using words. Every time the boy heard another word, it hurt him a little more, sapping the emotion from his face.

She didn't want to see him like that.

The honest truth was that she wanted to be with him. And it didn't just have to be the two of them. Being part of the events with everyone else. Cheering for friends with everyone else. Going around the stalls with everyone else. Watching the night parade with everyone else. Making fun memories with everyone else and smiling with everyone else.

That was all she wanted.

"…so I'll say it again. If you want to solve everything the right way, *step over her.*"

No, she tried to say.

"…All right."

No, she wanted to say, but nothing came out.

"I'll do it. If that'll solve everything. I'll leave Himegami to you, Stiyl."

And then the boy stepped over her fallen body, having decided to head farther down the small road. Her words wouldn't reach him. She watched his back retreating, seeming like it would go far, far away.

Why hadn't the world been made to be better?

Why couldn't everything go their way?

None of her fervent wishes had come true. She rallied all the strength she had and still couldn't squeak out a word. From beginning to end, all her hope had been stolen from her…

"Sorry, Himegami."

And yet, she heard just a few words then.

"I'll go back to your hospital before the night parade. Promise me you'll wait for me."

She thought she managed a thin smile then.

This isn't fair.

The world around her was cruel in every way. She couldn't tell him a single thing she wanted. She could desperately summon all the energy she had, but nobody would ever grant her wishes…

…so why did this boy's words have so much strength?

CHAPTER 7

An Enemy to Defeat and a Person to Protect

Parabolic_Antenna.

1

"Damn it…!!" shouted Touma Kamijou at the sight before him.

The bus stop was already empty.

The beating sunlight was starting to grow a little weaker now that it was three thirty PM. The only things at the sidewalk-facing stop were a simple enclosure made of metal pipe pillars and a sheet-iron roof. Nobody was sitting on the bench inside, nor was anyone lined up. He felt like a lost child who had been left behind as those around him passed by without stopping to glance at the bus stop.

He sighed; he couldn't help but grin weakly. For a moment, he stood there in a daze. He didn't know where the bus route started and ended. Not a single hint to help him, either. In fact, not only did he not know which bus Oriana had boarded—he didn't even know if she had used this bus stop to begin with.

They had only three minutes to capture Oriana, and now she'd gotten away by bus.

He had lost a lot of time stopping where Himegami had been attacked. If he'd actually calculated the distance and time, he should have known he'd never be able to catch up to her.

It was the obvious, sensible conclusion. But…

Damn it, where did Oriana go?!

The reality made clear once again, he grew dizzy. He could promise all he wanted. He could feel as strongly as he wanted. Some things just couldn't come true. He knew not everything would go exactly the way he wanted. But he beat down that simple fact as far as it would go in his mind.

He couldn't chase Oriana anymore. Nobody even knew where Lidvia was. At this rate, he couldn't stop them from using the Croce di Pietro.

What do I do?

Kamijou took out his cell phone and punched in Motoharu Tsuchimikado's number. After he pushed the call button and waited for a few seconds, Tsuchimikado picked up right away, as though he'd been waiting all along.

Kamijou didn't waste time. "Sorry, Tsuchimikado, I lost sight of Oriana at the bus stop! Himegami got blasted with sorcery around here, so she's gotta be somewhere close by. Is there any way to figure out where she is?!"

"Well...That would be a little difficult, nya~," Tsuchimikado said in a weak voice. "Four Ways to Truth can get out to only a three-kilometer square. From where I am...I won't be able to get it to work, and Stiyl can't set up the spell by himself...And if Oriana used the bus, then even if I go find Stiyl now...she'll get outside the effective range for sure."

"Then what do we do?!" demanded Kamijou, looking around. Still no hints in sight.

"...So you don't know...which bus line Oriana would be likely to take, nya...?"

"Nope," he said, looking at the Daihasei Festival pamphlet. "...This bus stop looks like it loops around the outside of District 7, but I don't know which stop she'd get off at. With this much time, she'd be about four stops ahead of me. And she could still be on the bus, too."

"Oriana...should be trying to get as far away as she can...So it would be real suspicious if she was still on the bus..."

"But there's a subway station near the second bus stop, and there's a bus terminal for another line at the fourth stop. She could have hopped onto one of those, right?"

"…" Motoharu Tsuchimikado fell quiet.

Around Kamijou, there were all sorts of people: students with free time walking around eating ice cream, spectators hurrying to the next stadium, and children badgering their parents for juice. The hustle and bustle would have been loud with voices and footsteps… but Kamijou felt such a strong silence that his ears were ringing.

They were out of options. They couldn't guess where Oriana would go, whether she'd gotten on a bus or not, what bus stop she'd get off at, which line she'd transfer to.

And most of all, they didn't know where she was even trying to go.

"…Wait a minute, Tsuchimikado," Kamijou said, looking up.

Tsuchimikado answered his murmured words as though he were dragging along his wounded body. "What…is it, Kammy?"

"Why's Oriana walking around the city?"

"Eh? You know why…We're chasing her…and she's trying to get away—"

"*No, before that,*" he interrupted. "This whole game of tag started when Fukiyose and I bumped into Oriana this morning, remember? What was Oriana doing over there?" As he spoke, he organized his thoughts. "We figured out they weren't trying to sell off the Croce di Pietro to anyone, right? She wouldn't have been walking to a meeting with someone. So why was she hanging around the city streets? I mean, it was risky, and now she's been wrapped up in all this trouble."

"…I see what you're saying, nya~." Strength returned to Tsuchimikado's voice. "At the very least…Oriana didn't have the Croce di Pietro this morning. But she was still on the move…She must have had a reason to be moving alone."

"Like what?" Kamijou asked.

Tsuchimikado let out a groan, trying to endure the pain. "Who knows, nya…Don't know that much…But they didn't activate the Croce di Pietro yet. Maybe…it's got something to do with that. Maybe Oriana was looking for something…something they needed to use the Croce di Pietro…"

They needed something, he said. This was what the two sorcerers had been looking into at the beginning, thinking it would give them a hint as to where to look for Oriana. Tsuchimikado had spotted Oriana using Academy City's security system before they figured that out, so they had left that aside to focus on pursuing her...

"Looking for something they needed...? Then does that mean they can use it in only a specific kind of place? And Oriana was moving all over the city to find a place like that?"

"...Seems fishy, nya...They snuck into the city without a destination and *then* started looking for whatever it was?...Man, why is Stiyl's cell phone off in this emergency...? I can't get in touch with him!"

Kamijou remembered that Stiyl had been trading information with allies in London. What had he said again? "Oh, right. He said he learned a bit about the vault they keep the Croce di Pietro in."

"Eh? Kammy, anything...no matter how small, is fine. Could you...explain in detail...nya?"

"Sure, but it doesn't look like they got very much for us. I think we learned only that the vault's windows are all closed up and there're two doors to get in."

"Hmm...Two doors...? Like an air lock in a science lab...?"

"...Er, no. What was it?" He thought for a moment. "Oh yeah. It was to avoid letting light get in."

"Light, huh...It's a really strong Soul Arm, so they probably didn't want to accidentally set the thing off, nya..." Tsuchimikado quieted for a bit. Kamijou could hear only shallow, intermittent breathing, like he was having trouble getting enough air. The short silence was the time he took to think about this.

The silence, punctuated by the muffled breathing, struck Kamijou's nerves more than necessary. He felt sweat rolling down his cheek and grimaced, but he followed Tsuchimikado's lead and thought about it. The vault. The specific usage rules. A room with two doors and no windows. Trying to prevent light from getting in...The light...

"Hey, would it be a problem if the Croce di Pietro or whatever got hit by sunlight?"

"...Probably not, nya...If that was true, place and time wouldn't matter, you know? The sun...It's out right now, and if that made the Croce di Pietro activate...then they'd have done it a long time ago. If it was that easy to use, they could just...force their way into the city...and break out the cross before they got captured...and that would be it. Like a game of kick the can...Except I do think... that the Soul Arm's activation condition...has something to do with light...It's been almost two thousand years, so the Crossist Church...it wasn't yet split up into Roman Orthodox and English Puritanism or anything...There were a lot of spells that took in light. For example, with places they used for baptism...they'd have three windows and three sources of light shining in...to represent the Holy Trinity, nya..."

"Then what *is* the light that has to do with turning it on?" Kamijou immediately asked what he was thinking, but Tsuchimikado didn't answer. He probably didn't know, either.

"Hey, Kammy...Is that really...all the info you've got?"

"All of it...?" Kamijou fell deep into thought, his ear still on his cell phone. Stiyl's sorcery discussions were out of his field. A lot of the time, he'd just keep talking without waiting for Kamijou to understand him, so there were a lot of things Kamijou had trouble remembering as a result. Still, he tried to drag out the few scraps that he remembered.

"!...There was something!"

"What?"

"Stiyl said it would be too much of a pain to explain, and he for-warded an email to my cell phone from Orsola with a report in it."

"...What did it say?" Tsuchimikado's voice was growing cooler.

"Sorry, it was in some other language and I couldn't read any of it. I'll send it over there. Can you read it?"

"If you don't...send it, then I won't know, nya. What do you mean, *some other language*? It wasn't English...?"

After getting Tsuchimikado to tell him his new cell phone number, Kamijou hung up. Then he opened his mailbox and sent over to Tsuchimikado the report he'd gotten from Stiyl.

About two minutes later, his cell phone began to ring again.

"Hey Kammy...I read the report. It's...in Italian...and there's no magical encryption on it, either."

"...So what was inside it?"

"It was basically...a report of some things written in notebooks. Apparently there's a big cleaning...on the Croce di Pietro's vault... twice per year. The record is from...an auditor in a different department...who would go in during the cleanings, nya."

The message stated that there were several rules that had to be followed for the cleaning. The first was that they had to perform it on certain dates. The second was that they needed to finish cleaning by that afternoon.

"I guess...it wasn't really that much, nya~."

"Wait a second. Could you read that message again for me?" Kamijou held the cell phone to his ear for a few moments and finally said, "Afternoon? Not by night? That's weird. They have two layers of doors to keep out all the light. Pretty sure it would be bright out during the day."

"That might...not be all, either."

According to Tsuchimikado, this was what was written next in the report. The actual established routines seemed to be pretty vague. The auditor had written that Preservers who forgot to clean the vault during the day wouldn't do it that night—they'd go home and just do it the next day instead.

"In this auditor's report...there's a bit about how the Preservers... didn't seem to have very good attitudes, nya. Apparently a lot of them...would use horoscopes and do astrology...while on the clock. Damn it, that's...not very helpful, either. Most of this...is just the auditor complaining about shit."

Kamijou felt something about the report tugging at his mind. "...Hey, the Croce di Pietro is, like, a really, *really* important antique to the Roman Orthodox Church, right?"

"You got it, nya…It's supposed to be holy enough to weep over… and kneel at…"

"Then I don't think they would get random lazy guys to care for it."

"Hmm…I don't think…they'd treat it this poorly, either. The Preservers of the Croce di Pietro…they're supposed to be a group of elites recruited from across different departments…But this auditor's saying…the people who left the place…were nothing to write home about…What's that all about?"

"…"

"Orsola Aquinas…She couldn't decipher the *Book of the Law*…but the level of her information analysis skills…posed a threat to…all of Roman Orthodoxy. I guess Stiyl decided it wasn't much…but if Oriana chose this to submit for her report…I feel like there's gotta be *something* in it…"

"Something…," repeated Kamijou halfheartedly, deciding to go over what he knew.

The vault had no windows and two layers of doors to get in and out, which blocked the light from getting in. Despite that, the big cleaning, during which there would be many entering and exiting, was done, as a rule, only during the day, not the night. Plus, he'd think any Preservers who forgot to clean during the day would clean it at night, but they would just shrug and blow it off until the next day, according to the report.

What was important here?

"Tsuchimikado…Maybe this light that has to do with activating the Croce di Pietro is out at night, not in the day? I mean, the Preservers were disregarding the first rule about doing it on a certain date to make sure they followed the second rule about not doing it at night, right?"

Of the two rules, they prioritized one of them and broke the other. There must have been a reason to prioritize the rule to not clean the Croce di Pietro at night.

"Well…I suppose you could say that, b-but…," Tsuchimikado stammered. "What light comes out at night…? It couldn't be…the moonlight. If it had…a specific rule that it could activate only…during the full moon or another moon phase…The lunar cycles don't match up with…our calendar dates. If they always did it…on a certain date, then the moon phase wouldn't align right…and they wouldn't be able to decide on a single date that worked every year."

Tsuchimikado's opinion was that if the moonlight itself, regardless of the moon phase, was the activation requirement, they wouldn't need to set such a strict date to do the cleaning. For example, they didn't just pick the dates for Easter and Christmas at random without thinking about them. But they *did* pick a specific date for the Croce di Pietro, which meant it had to hold some religious meaning, which was probably related to the Soul Arm's usage conditions and conditions under which it might go out of control.

"…A light that comes out at night…" Kamijou sank into deep thought, his cell phone at his ear. *Oriana and Lidvia didn't use the Croce di Pietro because they couldn't, not because they didn't feel like it.* Little by little, he mentally organized all the information he'd gotten until now. *They need some kind of light to use it.* What he'd seen, the info from the British Museum Stiyl had gotten him, the theories Tsuchimikado had suggested…He went over them again in detail. *The light's at night, apparently, not during the day.*

He looked at the wall of a building. An electronic billboard was on it, made up of many small lights. *No, that's not it. If this was, like, a thousand years ago, then they wouldn't have had lightbulbs or luminescent diodes.* He took his eyes off them. *Has to be a natural light.* His thoughts turned even further inward as he held his cell phone. *Plus, the light shines in a way that moves with the calendar…*

Touma Kamijou abruptly looked up at the sky of Academy City.

When Tsuchimikado read Orsola's report, he had said this.

The Croce di Pietro Preservers weren't dedicated to their jobs.

A lot of them would use horoscopes or astrology while on the clock.

But…

What if using astrology was something they absolutely needed to do?

* *. *

"Wait…so, constellations?"

"That could…be it, nya…" Tsuchimikado paused for a moment as though nodding. "In sorcery, Soul Arms…that use constellations… aren't very unusual. Astrology is a basic foundation of a lot of magic, and even angel-summoning…is done in accordance with the constellations of the current season."

He went on to explain. Unlike the moon phases, which changed throughout the month, constellations changed throughout the year. For example, if a constellation out during the spring was the trigger that made the Croce di Pietro go out of control, then they'd just have to decide that the cleanings would take place during the times when autumn constellations came out. That way they could easily decide what dates would be "safe." "Which means the Preservers…weren't just doing a bad job with their work…They could have been getting important job-related information…using their horoscopes…"

Tsuchimikado seemed like he was already convinced, but Kamijou had no idea what he was talking about just from that. So he asked. "So the Croce di Pietro needs the power of constellations to be activated. How do you even *use* constellations, anyway?"

"In general…with a spell that uses one of the eighty-eight constellations…made up of the twelve ecliptic constellations, the twenty-eight northern hemisphere constellations, and the forty-eight southern hemisphere constellations. But when you do…the actual ecliptic constellations, Aries or Scorpio doesn't have any power itself…Stars that make constellations may look like they're lined up all nice…but they're crazy far apart, you know? You really can't…just bunch 'em all together."

"…Is that true?" Kamijou didn't know much about constellations or astrology, but he thought that was what people really believed thousands of years ago. Did they *have* ways to measure distance between stars back then? And did they even have anyone who actually knew how the universe worked?

After he asked, Tsuchimikado said, "*That's exactly what they use, Kammy.*"

"What?"

"A long time ago, the universe...or the sky, as they called it...They thought...the sky was like a big bowl...covering the Earth. Kind of like...a planetarium, I guess, nya?" He continued. "...Constellation sorcery uses this planetarium concept...It has nothing to do with the stars' actual power or distance. They use the regular diagram projected onto the screen of the night sky...to build a magic circle... The diagram itself is simple, but...it's still on an enormous scale, which makes it strong. And the *diagram itself isn't complicated, so it can be applied to many different techniques*...There's probably no other magic circle in existence...as convenient as that, nya~."

Tsuchimikado explained that the magic circle covering the night sky that the Power of God had used at the beach house back then was an even more advanced form of this constellation sorcery, in order to set up the night sky specifically to be beneficial to the caster.

Kamijou couldn't accurately judge how widely spread constellation sorcery was among the entire magic side. But just the fact that this had similarities to *that* angel's spell shocked him. "Then Oriana, she's..."

"The Croce di Pietro's activation mechanism...probably works like this. They need to gather the light from the night sky...down to the earth...so the cross is probably like a big parabolic antenna... It catches the starlight from the night sky then creates a link...to activate the spell. Oriana's still walking around the city...because she's in the middle of looking for the most suitable place...to put that antenna, nya~."

From what he said, these rules didn't apply to every spell utilizing the stars, of course. The Spear of Tlahuizcalpantecuhtli, for example, which Kamijou had seen the Aztecan sorcerer use on the last day of summer break. His spell had used Venus's light—regardless of whether it was day or night. The only important thing was Venus's physical position.

But if the Croce di Pietro worked on the same rules, then Oriana and Lidvia wouldn't need to wait for an opportunity. If they could use any old light that was there all the time, like the sunlight, then they could just activate it right away and Academy City would fall into their hands.

Which meant it was more than likely the Soul Arm used a diagram depicting the appearance of the constellations.

Oriana was moving all over in order to find a sorcery-related point from which they could use the appearance of the constellations. But then why was she still hanging around the city streets? Perhaps the places she'd gone around to check had been unfit for activating the Croce di Pietro, or maybe she was just trying to find a spot more perfect than the others.

"...I mean, you're right; they might be trying to use the Croce di Pietro...with the power of constellations...but still...," he finished, punctuating his own theory.

"But still what?"

"It's...a strong theory, but...there're a few contradictions in it, nya..."

"What contradictions?" said Kamijou with a frown.

As he frowned, Tsuchimikado said his next words. "Listen, Kammy...The Croce di Pietro...it's deeply related to Peter's death... He was one of the twelve apostles and the one who created the first primitive church after the Son of God died. So the first chance they would've had...to create the Roman Papal States by using the cross's power...would have either been when Peter died...or a little bit after."

According to Tsuchimikado, Peter had been executed in the middle of the first century. Emperor Constantine had officially sanctioned Crossism and built St. Peter's Basilica in the early fourth century. The king of the Franks had actually presented territory to them in the eighth century. A large time gap had separated all these events.

Even so, the story was that the initial standing of the cross for Peter, the declaration of intent that the land around it was the legacy of Peter, and the road to the creation of the Roman Papal States, which would become the core of the largest religion in the world with more than two billion followers—all that began after Peter was executed.

"Well, the Croce di Pietro was a cross for his grave, right? It would make more sense that it started when they made it right after he died rather than starting when they made that basilica or whatever. What's wrong there?"

"I agree that the date...and constellations are important for using the Croce di Pietro. But...Peter died...on June 29th. That's...a different season than now, so the stars in the sky would have changed, too...I'm sure you've heard of summer and winter constellations... right? Plus, Japan sees a bunch of different ones...since we're at a different latitude and longitude compared to the Vatican. There's a difference between the Vatican sky on June 29th...and the Japanese one at the end of September. If we can't figure out that part, the constellation theory doesn't hold water, nya..."

So did that mean they couldn't use the Croce di Pietro in this season? Kamijou frowned a little. "Then what would happen if they ignored the constellations this season and used the Croce di Pietro anyway?"

"Kammy...what do you think if you took an electric razor...that worked on direct current...and gave it alternating current?"

"..."

"It might not...get destroyed like that, but...it would malfunction, at least. If not, they wouldn't need...to spend so much time... figuring out usage conditions for the thing, nya~."

"...Then why would they bring into the city a Soul Arm they couldn't use?"

"I dunno, nya...There might be something...that lets them get around that, but...Shit. There's no...time to think about it."

Time. The word made Kamijou realize that once again, they had a time limit. "If we assume Oriana and Lidvia are waiting for the stars in the night sky to come out so they can use the Croce di Pietro, then our time's gonna run out at sunset when they activate the cross, huh?"

"It might not be right after it goes down. Depends on the constellations they want, too, but they might need to have a full view of all the stars in it, nya~. Right now, it's..."

The conversation had taken so long that it was almost four in the afternoon. It was late in September, so sunset would probably be before seven. The first star to appear would be shining before the sun went down, so even six o'clock might be cutting it close.

That meant they needed to find Oriana after another two to three hours. Actually, it wasn't a sure thing that she had the Croce di Pietro. In that case, they'd have to get her to tell them where Lidvia Lorenzetti was and capture her, too.

They didn't have time.

He wasn't sure he could catch Oriana alone, but finding Lidvia on top of that?

"Don't think we have enough to deal a decisive blow...but we gotta get moving. I'll go back along the paths Oriana took...and try to find astrological similarities in those places...If all goes well...I might find out where she's going next..."

"W-wait a minute! Can you even move around with your body like that?"

"With my body like...? Hah...Kammy, with my body like *what*, nya~?" said Tsuchimikado, feigning calm.

Kamijou imagined the idiot on the other end grimacing, his body still covered in wounds. Aside from sorcery, he had an ability called Auto Rebirth, but it was still just Level Zero. Not having it would have been better, but Kamijou was pretty sure it wasn't convenient enough to get rid of all his wounds like an eraser on pencil marks.

He tried to say something but then thought better of it. Anything he said at this point would just be rude. "...All right. What should I do in the meantime?"

"Well," began Tsuchimikado, to advise him...

...when another voice chirped up from behind him.

"...Touma, what are you doing all the way out here?"

2

The self-driving bus sat motionless at the stop.

Oriana Thomson, like the other passengers, glanced around. This wasn't the short pause to let some out and others in. The AI controlling the bus had brought it to an emergency stop because it had gone over the weight limit. The vehicle was already crammed tight, and even more passengers had just gotten on. That must have pushed it over.

A woman's voice began to come through the loudspeaker. Her inflections lacked emotion; it was probably an audio clip recorded in advance. "We truly apologize for the inconvenience. Due to safety concerns, this bus has come to an emergency stop. Once again, we are terribly sorry…"

She wasn't saying what exactly needed to happen to resolve the problem. But in any case, the weight limit issue wouldn't go away until someone got off the bus. Unless someone was willing to toss out their luggage.

Oriana decided to obediently disembark here; she could either wait in a bus for its hopefully eventual departure or find another means of transportation. She stepped down from the air-conditioned bus onto the asphalt baking under the hot sun.

Then she walked down the street. The area was bustling with people—maybe a big stadium was nearby. The stalls lined up around her were all selling cheering-related products like megaphones and handheld fans with school names on them.

Once the bus stop was completely out of sight, Oriana thought, *Well, well. It looks like Kaori Kanzaki isn't coming after all.* She quietly sighed. *I checked a few times for people tailing me but never saw a thing. Damn. That anti-saint page I thought up is totally useless. The thing won't do much against regular sorcerers, after all…Now what? I feel so frustrated, so dissatisfied. Ah well, life is long. Maybe I'll bump into a saint sometime down the road.*

She remembered the black-haired girl whose upper body she'd

destroyed. The female student whose hidden cross had been broken along with her shaved-off flesh.

"..." Oriana looked at the flash cards in her hand. She bit one off, scrunching her face as though it was bitter, and crushed it to activate a communication spell. The spell would allow her to talk to a person she visualized in her mind.

She *sent the scene in her mind*, then said, "Lidvia?"

"*I know what you want to say.*"

She had called Lidvia Lorenzetti, whose voice now rang directly in her brain. But it wasn't her usual way of talking, where she trailed off all the time.

It was a firm declaration. "*The girl you met was a mere civilian.*"

Bam!! Oriana kicked the ground. It was a reflex, and she knew it would attract stares from people around her. *Not one but* two *accidental...?!*

Cold words began to pierce her as she gritted her teeth. "*We have her name and photo from the investigation report on the earlier alchemist incident. Her name is Aisa Himegami. Despite having an extremely important power, she is barely a sorcerer. That Celtic cross was to seal her special ability—merely a Soul Arm given to her by another sorcerer. It has absolutely no attack abilities. We've been notified in official writing by the English Puritan Church to avoid further misunderstandings.*"

The info about Kaori Kanzaki was most likely a bluff. On top of that, the girl she'd thought an enemy had absolutely no relation to the English Puritan Church. "...This is the worst."

"*It is indeed. We have sunken our fangs into not one but two entirely unrelated civilians in this matter. The first time is thought to have been due to the intervention of an enemy sorcerer in the middle of a sporting event, but this time the responsibility falls squarely on our shoulders.*"

Her voice was painfully clear.

"*We have raised a hand against someone we should have been protecting.*"

The voice of a nun who had vowed to spread the Word to those with no knowledge of it.

"Those of perfectly noble character are not the ones we must extend a hand to—it is those in doubt, those who have made mistakes, those seeking help. It is the sinners. Those were the words of the Lord as he sat at the same table as the hated tax collector Matthew. We have transgressed those words. Do you know what that means?"

"..." Oriana fell quiet. Lidvia's sentences were no longer trailing off. They weren't even questions anymore. Her voice would not allow interruption—it would simply declare the fixed words of the Bible from start to finish. And above all...

"We must not make another mistake. For the sake of the girl we have wounded, we must take the utmost caution in using the Croce di Pietro and place Academy City under our control."

...there was no hesitation in her voice.

Lidvia Lorenzetti had continued to speak, transforming every negative into a positive.

She felt remorse. She felt regret.

Lidvia was hurting on the inside more than Oriana was—of that there was no doubt.

But she used even that bitterness she felt to press forward. She knew the meaning of the word *ordeal*. No matter how hurt she was, she would use that experience to accelerate ever onward. She would never stop and stand still. Never, from the moment she was born to the moment she died.

Oriana felt a chill crawl down her spine. It wasn't about which of them was stronger or weaker. There was a more fundamental difference between them.

"This will..."

So she asked this nun, who never hesitated.

"...This will really make everything better, won't it? Everyone's problems—by taking Academy City?"

3

"…Touma, what are you doing in a place like this?"

Kamijou started. He whirled around to see Index there in her cheerleading uniform. She was carrying pom-poms in her hands now, too. The calico, wrapped up in the pom-poms, didn't seem to like the bushy feel of the vinyl and was struggling a little.

Her head was tilted to the side. But her eyebrows were bent inward in an angry expression.

Crap…! Was our school gonna have their next event around here?!

Many sorcerers were standing by outside Academy City. They were all from different nations and organizations. And they were constantly casting spells to detect mana flows at least one kilometer out from Index. As soon as their search spells detected mana, they'd use that pretense to flood into the city.

And not all of them would be trying to resolve the situation with Oriana and Lidvia first and foremost. Those hostile toward Academy City might use the chance to conduct all kinds of subversive activities.

"Touma, why aren't you with the others in your 'class'? Everyone was looking for you. They were all walking together toward the next 'stadium.'" Index seemed to be uncomfortable with certain words. "I think you were playing in events this morning, but this afternoon you haven't been in any of them. Why's that?"

Index's tone was condemning but had none of her usual brightness or intensity. Her cherubic face was betraying a hint of emotion: *Could something bad be happening right now?* Maybe it was her experience talking, of Kamijou single-handedly sticking his nose into every incident.

Oriana moved pretty far away. I'm sure she didn't get off the bus nearby. He began to fire up the forge in his brain. He'd been chasing the woman, but now he wanted her as far away as possible. The situation was terrifically absurd, he thought with impatience.

"…" Tsuchimikado was keeping quiet on the other end of the cell phone at his ear, waiting to see how the situation developed. Kamijou looked near and far on the road and made sure there were no self-driving buses around.

"Jeez, Touma. Aisa and Komoe have gone off somewhere, too. I thought you were with them."

His body gave another start and then stiffened. *That's right. Stiyl and Miss Komoe were using sorcery to heal Himegami, weren't they?!* His movements froze. That was only a kilometer away from here, wasn't it?

"Uh, right. The administration committee didn't have enough hands, so I was helping them out. That's weird. I thought I sent a text to the people in my class."

"Text?"

"Hmm…Maybe I was out of range. Did the waves not reach the center? You know, I didn't check to see how many antennae were around…But I mean, you'd think a normal shopping district would at least have a relay station. I wonder what happened? Maybe everyone's using their cell phones at once because of the Daihasei Festival, and the lines are getting congested. I think I saw it on the news. But didn't they say they were gonna turn up the central station's processing power to deal with it…?"

"???" The cheerleader Index bent her head to the side again.

He'd been trying to confuse her with cell phone talk and other things commonplace in the science world, which she was bad at dealing with. It looked like it had worked. Kamijou shook the phone at his ear a little. "I'm kind of on a call at the moment, Index. I'll be right back, so go back to the others. Uhh, you still there? *Anything particular change over there?*"

"Well…Nah, not a thing. *No changes over here at all.* You can… rest assured…"

That was a relief. That meant the place Stiyl was doing the healing was outside the scope of the search spells centered on Index.

Index watched Kamijou and frowned somewhat, but she let it go. "Touma, Touma. They said next is the 'group gymnastics.' Can you come?"

"..." Kamijou paused for a moment. Then he made a promise he'd never be able to keep. "I'll go. I'll finish this errand for them as fast as I can, and then I'll go there. Wait for me, okay, Index?"

"Okay!" Index nodded promptly. She propped the calico back up into her pom-pom-covered arms. "I will. So you come soon, too. I memorized all the dance moves Komoe taught me. You're gonna be really surprised when you see them!" she said with a smile, turning her back to him. She headed off, probably to the next field. She went straight there, without stopping anywhere, not even looking at the food stalls she passed by. She believed everything.

Touma Kamijou didn't move until he couldn't see her anymore. Once she had completely disappeared into the crowd, he finally made a movement: He looked down and hung his head deeply.

From over the cell phone, Tsuchimikado said, "...Sorry, Kammy."

If Oriana and Lidvia hadn't come to the city, he'd be getting his fill of the Daihasei Festival with the rest of his class right now. If Tsuchimikado and Stiyl hadn't asked for his cooperation, he would have been walking around the city with Index and Himegami without a care in the world. He was just a civilian. It wasn't his duty to fight every single sorcerer who made his or her way in.

Kamijou let his thoughts linger on that for only a moment. "*Don't be,*" he said flatly. "People say ignorance is bliss, but that would be hard in its own way. I don't want to be thinking about how you guys are spilling blood all over while Index and I are all smiles."

Surely Tsuchimikado wanted to have a good time at the Daihasei Festival, too. Even Stiyl might have come to Academy City for a reason other than to fight sorcerers. They hadn't brought him misfortune. And even if they had brought it, *there was nothing that required him to run from it.*

"But at the same time, it's like...I don't want to do it, so it would take a lot of nerve to push it all onto Index, you know? I must sound dumb. Here I am, feeling happy, calmly thinking I don't want to get her involved in this."

"..." Motoharu Tsuchimikado had nothing left to say.

Professionals, amateurs, sorcerers, civilians. The man named

Motoharu Tsuchimikado showed his own consideration with an unspoken silence.

Therefore, Touma Kamijou spoke alone—taking for himself the right to make his own conclusion.

"Let's get this errand over with quickly. Then we'll go back to Index. I want to fool around like idiots, eat our hearts out like idiots, take pictures like idiots—and be happy with all the idiotic memories we're making."

4

Four thirty PM.

Touma Kamijou was searching in a circle around the bus stop where he thought he'd lost Oriana.

Of course, the chances were ten to one—or more—that she'd gotten away on the bus. Still, it was possible she purposely hadn't gotten on, trying to use their expectations against them. He couldn't catch her with regular tactics, and with his lack of skill, figuring out the Croce di Pietro's activation conditions would be impossible. So for now, the only thing he could do was eliminate irregular possibilities like this.

Tsuchimikado, the most likely to succeed, was currently trying to infer the Croce di Pietro's usage point from where Oriana had previously appeared. That had to be left entirely up to the knowledge of sorcerers, so Kamijou could only wait for his report.

As he ran, he felt the four-thirty air creeping up on him. The city was shifting from afternoon to evening, and despite the sun's usual glaring heat, it felt like the rays of sunlight stabbing into his skin had their edges blunted slightly.

As always, there were people buying souvenirs and heading to playing fields all over the streets as he ran through them. Sometimes he caught a glance of blond hair in the crowds.

…?! *No, that's not Oriana…*Students with bleached hair and spectators from abroad were all over the place, so blondes weren't very rare.

Kamijou curved toward the edge of the sidewalk and stopped so he wouldn't get in the way of pedestrian traffic. *It doesn't seem like Oriana's hiding out somewhere and waiting for me to leave...unless she's holed up in a building, anyway.*

He looked slightly up from the sidewalk. Concrete buildings with uneven heights stood along the side of the road, their windowpanes reflecting the harsh sunlight. *Seems a little too hard to go around looking in all of them...But it's better than nothing. Okay!* He clapped himself on the cheeks and headed for the closest building, a large electronics store.

On the way, he heard a child's voice.

"Wait up, says Misaka says Misaka, chasing you and stuff. Come on, Misaka was only looking at the souvenirs, please don't leave me behind, says Misaka says Misaka, arguing desperately, but you won't even stop, you dolt!"

Kamijou turned around casually, but he couldn't see the owner of that voice in the crowds. It sounded like it belonged to a young child, so maybe she was caught up in the waves of people. But wait, Misaka...? No, there was something more important he needed to be doing.

Out of all of us, Tsuchimikado's the one most favored to win, after all. He'd better be trying his best, too.

He passed through the automatic doors and took a look around the open, brightly lit store floor. The air-conditioning kept the place at a comfortable temperature, and there was enough light to see everywhere. It was the kind of place that could make someone lose track of time. He slowly walked around the store, checking for anyone who looked like Oriana, occasionally glancing out the big windows.

The stabbing glare of the four-thirty sky was starting to fade. It wasn't red yet, but the warm tones of the sky had started to peek through. It would transition to an evening sky before another hour was up.

Then the first star of the evening would come out. And the brightest constellations would show up before the shroud of night fell completely.

"…If our hypothesis is right, we have a little under two hours to go," he said to himself—when his cell phone rang.

The screen didn't display Tsuchimikado. It was an emergency call.

He picked up and heard Stiyl Magnus… "I got your number from Tsuchimikado. You can bet I won't save it, though." He must have been smoking, because sometimes Kamijou heard a long exhale. "We finished treating the student. Where are you now?"

Kamijou stopped breathing for a moment. Then he frantically cried into the phone, "?! Himegami—how is she doing?!"

"…I'd appreciate it if you didn't seek perfection from me. It was the first time I used that healing spell. It's all foreign to me. It wasn't going to go that well, anyway. Frankly, I don't want to use a spell like that ever again, either. All I had to go on was random scraps of information from an amateur. You know how hard it was to pick up on what parts of all those vague things she told me were related to sorcery? I don't know how I even threw the healing spell together at all. It was an absurd tightrope walk. I was sweating bullets, thinking it was going to blow up in my face and kill me at any moment. I don't even feel alive *now*." Stiyl delivered his answer in a bitter voice.

He was normally one big ball of self-confidence, so the work must have been really dangerous. Kamijou felt like an anvil had just dropped into his stomach.

"Anyway, I shored up the torn vessels and added more blood, then weakened her sense of pain. I think that was enough to get her out of shock. Now it's up to the doctors…but the EMTs were all pretty confident. Seems like there's a mysterious, blustering doctor in a hospital nearby who gets more worked up the worse the situation is." His tone was uncomfortable. It was like a civilian had seen a villain rescuing a cat out of a tree on the side of the road.

"You're…"

"What? Stop mumbling. I'll tell you again. I don't plan on getting all noncommittal buddy-buddy with you…gwaah?!"

There was a terrible *thud* from the phone. Then someone else's voice came in.

"Oww! I haven't thanked you yet! Bwaaahhh!! If you weren't there, Hime…She would have…!!"

"S-stop it! Don't cling to me! Not when you're about to start spraying tears everywhere! Besides, I can't promise they can save her. Unless they can recover her stamina, she'll just go down again…and are you even listening?!"

For Kamijou, who was listening on the phone, it was a little scary. Who knew when the sorcerer would burn Miss Komoe to a crisp for (apparently) clinging to him? Surprisingly, Stiyl didn't appear to be resorting to force. Maybe he would let his guard down for *any* small girl.

He couldn't give Kamijou any details about sorcery battles in front of Miss Komoe, so Kamijou said, "Okay, talk to you later."

Before he hung up, though, from amid the sounds of struggling he heard Stiyl say, "Call Tsuchimikado. I think he found something. I'll go to him as soon as I can tear this person off me."

5

Tsuchimikado was on a street in School District 7.

He was at the place where Kamijou and Fukiyose had first encountered Oriana.

Nearby was a totally inconspicuous main road, lined by big department stores and wind turbine propellers spinning round and round while oil drum–shaped security robots moved up and down the sidewalks. Students in gym uniforms passed by one another as usual, with guests to the city in personal wear stopping every time they saw one of the robots. The street was the kind you could find anywhere else, which also made it easy to get lost here.

He had since changed out of his torn gym uniform into new clothes, and the bandages he wore couldn't be seen outside them. His face was still pale, though, because of the blood loss. He couldn't hide that. Sometimes he would stumble, despite the absence of wind, and his breathing felt shallow, somehow unnatural. All his Level

Zero Auto Rebirth ability could do was hook together broken blood vessels. Even so, without it, he would've been done for long ago.

In spite of his condition, he continued to stand there on the road under the glaring sun. The reason was simple. There was something he had to do.

Now that I've actually used my own feet to visit these places, he thought, looking up to the blue sky dotted with blimps and advertisement balloons, *I'm starting to figure out a few things, nya. Oriana risked a lot by traipsing around the city like that. Was this why?*

He was a caster skilled at the most predominant among eastern techniques: *Onmyoudou,* the traditional occultism of Japan.

Though it went by a single name, it contained many techniques to be learned and mastered. Geomancy, divination, Chinese alchemy, hexes, the art of worship, calendar creation, the usage of water clocks…It was made up of a myriad of goals and directions, everything from telling time to predicting the fates of entire nations. *Onmyoudou's* true value was in how it governed everything.

Tsuchimikado personally specialized in Chinese-style geomancy, also known as feng shui, but he'd learned more than that. He could tell just by looking up. The dark-green branches and leaves of the trees on the roadside were partially hiding the sky, but not nearly enough to cause an issue.

Given today's date and his current coordinates, he could tell which stars were out and where they were just by looking up at the daytime sky. He didn't have to use any armillary spheres or horoscopes to know; he could accurately envision everything overlaid on the sky with the knowledge he'd worked so hard to acquire.

*Still, if this was Index we were talking about, she could come up with the right answer just by hearing what we had to say. Wouldn't even need to look at the sky at all, nya…*The thoughts came to him involuntarily, and he gave a bitter, inward grin. When it came to Index, the very act of thinking he could take her on in pure knowledge was already a mistake.

But whatever the case was, he focused again and came to a conclusion. *I get it...nyaa...Looks like we were right...She's using the constellations after all. Seems like the autumn constellations are acting as a base, nya...No matter what vantage point I use...the constellations are all aligned in the same magical way...She's gotta be doing it on purpose to read them...Agh.* He summarized his ideas, grimacing and holding his side.

That was what he'd learned from going along the course Oriana had followed. No matter what point from which he looked at the stars, they appeared the same. At first this seemed like obvious logic, but when anything sorcery was involved, things changed.

Constellations were really just fake pictures that people saw from the earth's surface. Seeing them all spread out like on a dome was a mere illusion caused by distance. To give an extreme example, if someone could look at a constellation from the side instead of head-on, they would see something completely different.

But in a stricter sense, observing the stars from but a single step away would be enough to change what the constellations looked like by the slightest of degrees. It was difficult to tell with the naked eye, and many a newbie sorcerer had misread the sky and gotten caught up in a backfiring spell. Practitioners in Greece and Egypt who borrowed the stars' power, for example, had wanted more precise observatories and had begun to build giant temples for that exact reason.

Using the stars themselves was far from unusual. They were a resource, and anyone could use them. The thing about spells that used constellations, though, was that you needed to do a great deal of preparation to actually access that resource. Earlier Tsuchimikado had mentioned that the constellations could be applied to all sorts of different spells. But to actually pull it off, one basically needed to build a separate observatory for each spell one wanted to use. Ancient Greece, in its polytheism, had done just that: They'd separated everything, building a temple to Mars in one spot and a temple to a guardian deity in another. An observatory would have different magical meaning just by moving it slightly.

But despite that, **the exact same "meaning" had appeared in the three or four "observatories" Tsuchimikado had just been to.**

And that can't be a coincidence. So that's settled. Oriana and Lidvia are trying to activate the Croce di Pietro by integrating the autumn constellations...

He looked up at the blue expanse above him.

Behind his sunglasses, his eyes slowly narrowed.

...But then, what do we do about the contradiction, nya?

6

"Oh, is that you, Fuki? Is your body better already?"

After making a phone call, Fukiyose immediately heard Komoe Tsukuyomi's mellifluous voice come back.

Right now, she was in an inner hospital courtyard. Her stamina had begun to return little by little in the time she'd spent resting in bed and wandering around the building. Eventually her range of movement had expanded enough for her to reach here.

It was like a resting place with a roof, with several tables and benches set up. There were also five or six other patients on their cell phones like Fukiyose was. A metal plaque hung on one of the room's support beams, with the words CELL PHONE USAGE AREA. PATIENTS CURRENTLY USING DELICATE MEDICAL DEVICES NOT ALLOWED. It was like a disclaimer for a smoking area or something.

For people who always went on their cell phones when they had free time, the hospital disallowing their usage seemed to stress them out. This area let them do so as long as they met the conditions.

Fukiyose held the cell phone to her ear. "I'm fine. Have there been any problems with the Daihasei Festival? Like those idiots doing crazy things they shouldn't?!"

"Oh! There was, there was! Hime was in a really bad situation!"

"...Don't tell me that idiot saw someone changing again?!"

"No, not that! Somebody attacked Hime, and they brought her to the hospital! Kami and his friend were passing by, so it was okay, but if it had just been me, then...then it would have been terrible..."

Miss Komoe's voice lowered in dejection. But Fukiyose couldn't detect serious despair in it. She was probably relieved at the worst situation, at least, not having come to pass.

Several things caught her attention. *She was attacked...? By who? Why?* Those were the questions that sprang to mind. Maybe Aisa Himegami's transfer to their school hadn't been without reason. Every year people talked about those with hatred toward Academy City using the Daihasei Festival to slip in and make trouble. But if that was the case...

Then what are Anti-Skill and Judgment doing?

Judgment was one thing; they were all participating in the events. Anti-Skill was another thing. They should have been on guard for anything. After all, the Daihasei Festival appearing open and free was just that—*an appearance.*

Were they slacking off? Or was someone who outmatched them in the city?

And more important...

"*If Kami and his friend hadn't been there?* What does that mean?"

"That's right! Hime's wounds were terrible, and I couldn't do anything by myself! But Kami and his friend did a great job of it! Oh, I wonder what happened to that priest who was with Kami? He ran away from me before I could thank him...Oh! I think that was him turning the corner!!"

Tap tap tap tap!! She heard loud footsteps ringing on the other end of the phone.

"..."

She had felt the same way when it happened to her, too, hadn't she? When she collapsed from sunstroke, who was it who reacted immediately and picked her up? The boy who had snuck his way into the other school's event. Upon calm consideration, *that* was obviously strange.

She thought. *In my case, I had sunstroke, and in Himegami's, someone attacked her. Then I guess they don't have anything to do with each other? But Touma Kamijou was involved in both those situations, so...*

What did that mean? Fukiyose frowned. Just what was going on in this city?

7

Kamijou heard the story from Tsuchimikado after he got back. His Auto Rebirth ability had done a little bit, at least, because his voice was regaining its resilience. Still, his face was pale and he was breaking out in a cold sweat. In any other situation, he probably should have just gone to the hospital.

Tsuchimikado told him two things.

One: Oriana and Lidvia were trying to activate the Croce di Pietro by using the autumn constellations. Two: each of the "observatory" points had been set up for those constellations in particular.

But Tsuchimikado seemed skeptical about his own results. "Oriana was definitely walking around because of constellations, so our idea of them being the key to activating Peter's cross was right...but I'm not sure they can actually *do* it. Historically speaking, the Croce di Pietro was used when the *summer* constellations were the main ones in the sky. It's September now, so no matter how you think about it, the autumn constellations are the ones up there. I don't think they could use them...There's something else. I know it. Some gimmick we haven't figured out yet."

Tsuchimikado's face was pale, and his skin was clammy. The gym uniform he'd changed into was brand new, but his fingernails had a little bit of dried blood on them. It looked painful, but Kamijou didn't want to be the kind of person who would happily press the issue. "But Oriana still took the risk of people finding her and following her. That's why she was looking for all those points that had a lot to do with constellations, right? You know where the points she hasn't yet been to are, don't you?"

"Yeah...but this unresolved gimmick is bothering me. Depending on what it is, they might be able to use an observatory besides the ones I found, nya~. Gonna be honest here—it's just a matter of time. We could charge into the observatory we guessed, but if nobody was there and they were about to trigger the spell on the other side of the city, then what? We'd be up the river then, nya~," finished Tsuchimikado, wiping the cold sweat off his jaw.

Kamijou checked the time. Five o'clock PM. He was right—if they had to go from one end of the city to the other, a train or bus wouldn't necessarily get them there in time. They didn't know the exact amount of time they had, either, which made it all the more difficult. In the worst-case scenario, it could all be over an hour from now.

His eyes stayed down on his cell phone's clock as he spoke. "But we don't have any more time to be thinking about it, do we? We're running out of time! I'd rather not end up failing to even get to one spot!!"

Tsuchimikado knew as well as he did how much time they had. "I know that, nya...Damn, what the hell is Stiyl doing at a time like this, anyway?!" he said roughly.

Should they go in with no proof? Should they wait until they had proof? Whichever they chose, they were missing the one factor they needed to be sure. Kamijou's thoughts gave way to silence; the silence gave way to a weight upon him. Finally, just as he was starting to feel choked by the air between them...

...his cell phone rang.

It wasn't Kamijou's. Tsuchimikado dubiously took his out of his pocket, but when he saw the screen, his expression changed. "Kammy, it's from the Church!"

Come to think of it, Stiyl *had* said he was getting people at the British Library to collect information for them. Maybe they figured out something new. Right now Kamijou and Tsuchimikado needed whatever hints they could get. Even Tsuchimikado, usually calm and collected, was a little frantic as he fiddled with his cell phone and turned on the speakerphone. Kamijou got next to him and brought his ear close to the phone anyway.

Finally, they heard the voice come through the phone.

"Oh! Would I happen to be speaking to Mr. Stiyl Magnus?"

""You got the wrong number?!"" they both shouted at the same time.

The woman on the other end apologized in a crestfallen manner. Kamijou was confused, though. It didn't matter, but if she had tried to call Stiyl—a foreigner—why was she speaking in Japanese?

Tsuchimikado heaved a sigh. "Ah, no, this is Motoharu Tsuchimikado. Working with Stiyl at the moment. If you have a report, I'll hear it, nya…You get anything?"

"That is correct! I have a report. We went into the British Library's records and found new information regarding the Croce di Pietro."

Her voice came back to them relaxed. After hearing it again, Kamijou perked up. He'd heard that voice somewhere before. "Huh? Is that Orsola?"

"That voice…Oh my! Why, yes, it is. Thank you very much for the other day. Because of you, I am now thoroughly—"

"Nya~. Let's not get off topic here," interrupted Tsuchimikado, his voice irritated and tired. "Could you kindly get on with it, nya?"

"—acquainted with those of the English Puritan Church. In fact, just the other day Miss Kanzaki introduced me to a wonderful Japanese restaurant that…Oh, that's right! Those of Amakusa have been assigned to Japantown as well."

"Did you just smile away what Tsuchimikado said?! Agh, could you please just tell us what info you got already?!" shouted Kamijou, causing Tsuchimikado's head to wobble anemically.

Finally, Orsola said, "Oh!" and stopped herself. "That's right. I do suppose it would be best that I tell you as soon as possible the information we received from the British Library. Ufu-fu. I'm sure it will be helpful information!"

"…Okay, Orsola, but it better not be helpful info on Japanese restaurants, got it?" said Kamijou lowly.

"Of course. I understand completely," she answered in a bouncing tone. "There is actually a very nice one five minutes away from Waterloo Station with the most delicious—"

"I literally just said not to do that! Stop trying to show off and give us the info on the Croce di Pietro!!"

"Oh, that is truly a shame…Let's discuss the main topic. Please listen closely," she said in an unaffected, gentle voice. Kamijou and

Tsuchimikado, expressions serious, focused on the cell phone. "What we understood from fragmentary records at the British Museum regards the conditions necessary to use the Croce di Pietro."

Kamijou felt his shoulders give a start. Details on the usage conditions. That was exactly the information they needed the most. They forgot to breathe as they waited for Orsola's next words.

"It would appear the Croce di Pietro is a large-scale Soul Arm used by borrowing the power of constellations. Putting the cross up on the land is to precisely collect the night sky's lights. At the right angle, it will accurately get the lights from the sky then use that as part of the spell to activate its magical effects. That appears to be how it works."

"That's what Kammy and I were saying. It's like a big old parabolic antenna. But still…"

"…Yeah. Not the newest of information…" Kamijou couldn't help but sigh. Tsuchimikado's shoulders drooped as well.

"Oh? Do tell what you are so disappointed about."

"Sorry, Orsola. Thanks for doing your best to find that out, but we'd already gotten that far on our own. At this point, we just need one hint to get us there."

"Oh…I see…" Orsola's voice was dejected, but Kamijou wasn't paying attention to her anymore.

He didn't know how much knowledge the British Library had stored away in its archives, but it *had* to have more than he and Tsuchimikado had gleaned so far. But the sweet honey was nowhere to be found—and that was like the nail in the coffin. They were stuck now and wouldn't be getting any hints.

The expressions of both Kamijou and Tsuchimikado, the professional, clouded over.

Meanwhile, Orsola Aquinas continued. "…Then I suppose you have already learned of the constellations corresponding to the Croce di Pietro's usage area that Miss Sherry and I found. It doesn't have anything to do with any specific season's constellations. It uses all eighty-eight constellations. I suppose you have already realized that it can be activated from anywhere in the world…"

"Huh?" said Kamijou and Tsuchimikado at once.

"Wait, Orsola. What are you talking about? We managed to figure out that it could be used only in certain places, but all this stuff about it using every constellation is news to us. Tsuchimikado was just worrying about not being able to use the Croce di Pietro in this season. And that if we figured that out, we'd solve the mystery gimmick. Could you give us a detailed explanation about that?"

"…What a shame. I believe I should be happier for the situation turning out better than I expected, but knowing that all the work we did was for nothing is still somewhat hard to take."

"Listen to me! Stop acting so hopeless and explain! Please, O Beautiful Orsola! And wait, do you mean *that* Sherry?!"

After Kamijou shouted several times, Orsola finally pulled the conversation back onto its original track. "Well. San Pietro, or St. Peter as he is called here, was martyred on June 29th. Of course, it is believed the Croce di Pietro was used in the Vatican directly after that."

Crossism was acknowledged in the fourth century, and the Roman Papal States were actually given the land as territory in the eighth century. But if the Croce di Pietro was used after Peter died, that would have been in the middle of the first century. Tsuchimikado had explained that much to him.

Orsola went on with her speculation. The fact that Emperor Constantine had acknowledged Crossism at the beginning of the fourth century, and the fact that the king of the Franks had given the land to the Papacy after invading Italy…She believed that *those historical events were simply too convenient for the Vatican and Crossism as a whole*—and that it was because of the Croce di Pietro's power.

"???…I'm sorry, Orsola, I'm pretty bad at history lectures."

"The important thing to remember is that the cross was first used in a place called the Vatican somewhere between late June and early July."

Orsola's voice was relaxed, but Tsuchimikado reacted sharply to it. "*…In a place called the Vatican?*"

"Yes. The historical Croce di Pietro was used only that one time, but as we all know, his cross was created to be used in regions other than the Vatican. Now this is the problem..." She paused for a moment, then went on. "On June 29th, it can be used only in the Vatican. It appears that to use it elsewhere, it must be on specific dates set for those places. In other words," she said, continuing on, "in order to use the Croce di Pietro, the user requires a firm grasp of the area's characteristics, features, and traits. Then, it first becomes usable by choosing the constellations from the eighty-eight through which it will be most effective. Because specialized knowledge is needed to choose a location and select constellations, there are various restrictions on its use: For example, it can be used only in a certain place once per year. But with this method, the user can be virtually anywhere on the planet, and they can place that area under the Roman Orthodox Church's control."

According to Orsola, Lidvia Lorenzetti traveled the world frequently in order to spread the Word to sinners. It was possible that meanwhile, she was compiling details on each area's attributes, what constellations applied to them, times for use, and the positions of the observatories, all required to use the Croce di Pietro. When Orsola had still been part of the Roman Orthodox Church, she had seen Lidvia several times, holding an old telescope in her arms as she headed for where she was going to do her next missionary work.

"So then Lidvia already snuck into Academy City once before to figure out the usage location for the Croce di Pietro?"

"That would depend on how she did her measurements...For example, when making maps, you can measure your latitude and longitude from the angle of the North Star as seen from the ground, among other things. But you don't need to perform that at every single location on the planet. You can figure out your main points, and then measure many others from a desk in your study. She may not have needed to enter Academy City at all."

Is that how it works? Kamijou thought about it. And quickly ran into a question. "Wait. Wasn't the cross made when Peter died in the first place? Why could it be used at any time and place besides when and where he died?"

"Well, you see..." Orsola paused to think for a moment. "It appears the Soul Arm itself was created during St. Peter's lifetime..."

"...What does that mean?"

"At the time, St. Peter gave a great amount of thought to where he would have to be martyred. As we know from the fact that the entire Roman Orthodox Church is centered on the site where St. Peter sleeps, he knew that wherever he was martyred would have a significant effect on history. That was one thing he would have been thinking about...But because of that, it is highly likely that the Croce di Pietro was created to have broader usage conditions, just in case there was a place for him other than the Vatican...that would be more suitable for the Roman Orthodox Church."

Kamijou felt his throat dry. Then he said, "So he could choose the place he wanted, but he couldn't change the date, right? He wouldn't just go ahead and use the thing when he was getting really old; he must have planned for an exact date..."

"Yes. And St. Peter was executed on June 29th. The exact date on which the Croce di Pietro is usable."

"...So he got caught on purpose on that day? Prepared to die and everything?"

"It's not...impossible, nya~," answered Tsuchimikado, exhaling quietly as if to expel his fatigue. "At the time, Peter wasn't on good terms with the Roman Empire. He was enemies with an important guest visiting the empire, a sorcerer named Simon Magus, nya~. In the end, he killed Simon himself. Crossism was already persecuted in that era, so you can guess what kind of fate the empire had in store for him."

"There are several anecdotes about when he was executed as well," continued Orsola. "I referred to it earlier, but Quo Vadis is a particularly famous one. When the empire's soldiers caught St. Peter, he was thrown into a prison with his pupil. There, he fervently prayed to escape the city. One time he did make it to the exit of Rome, but in the end, he turned back and let himself be caught by the empire's soldiers again. The story goes that he saw an image of the Son of God at the city's gates, which revealed to him that he must be martyred.

"On the day of his execution, when he was hung on the cross, he made a request. 'I am not worthy to suffer the same way as my Lord, so please, turn the cross upside down.' These, of course, were the words of a pious Crossist disciple, but perhaps there was another reason..."

"...and maybe it meant there was some trick with the cross...," finished Kamijou without really meaning to.

Peter was one of the twelve Apostles. Maybe he knew that he would one day be executed no matter what he did. If that was true, he could have used the exact moment of his death for the greatest effect. Even considering what would happen hundreds of years in the future.

For the creation of the Roman Papal States that followed...

...and for the sake of the people there who must be quietly protected.

It was far from being strictly passive. Where he would die, the time, the effect that would have, his death's results, and the fruits of his labors. Not only had he given careful thought to all those things, but he himself had begun the process toward his own end. Done with the ultimate calmness and the ultimate compassion, all for one spell that had to be described as ultimate. Was that the strongest spell of the Roman Orthodox Church, which used the Croce di Pietro?

"Historically, it's not rare to see people hacking their own graves. Prince Shōtoku placed his grave in a geomantically *horrible* location to purposely eradicate any descendants who would follow him, nya~," Tsuchimikado said, face still pale, with a sigh—half from flat amazement and half from admiration.

Now that Kamijou had heard all that, he returned to the most important question. "So, Orsola...do you know where they have to use the Croce di Pietro today, on September 19th?"

"Yes," came the immediate reply. "But of course I do."

8

Mikoto and Misuzu Misaka, mother and daughter, walked down the street.

The place they were in was complex. The street, lined with big department stores, had an underground section; an aboveground section; and even a gigantic, multilaned pedestrian walkway, as a sort of second floor outside. All three of the floors' paths mixed and mingled with one another. They were currently walking on the second floor, passing by many handmade open-road stalls.

There was still a good amount of time before Tokiwadai Middle School's students would be taking part in the next event, so Mikoto was showing Misuzu around. Most of the places that Misuzu wanted to visit were souvenir shops and open stalls set up specifically for outside spectators.

"Hey! You don't need a quasi-five-dimensional kaleidoscope! You'll get bored of it in three days! Three days!"

"Oh, but Mikoto, Academy City is all about souvenirs filled with technology nobody understands!"

"Right. They'd never let guests take out stuff that's actually cutting-edge. What the heck *is* this kaleidoscope, anyway? 'Reproduces a purely physical vision of a theoretical five-dimensional space using light-refracting technology'? How can you not tell how big a lie that is?! Would you even *know* how to tell if it was really five-dimensional space?!"

"Oh, but the feeling of it being so unproven is fun!"

"If you're gonna get a souvenir, make it something that helps you remember this!"

"Oh, but making sure you remember things? Mikoto, how girlish!"

"Just be quiet, stupid!!"

Mikoto grabbed her mother's hand and dragged her away from the open shop. For a middle school kid going through her rebellious phase, trying to recommend a better souvenir for her mother, at least, went to show how tightly knit their family was.

Both would draw a lot of attention with how they looked, but neither paid any mind to the stares of others.

"Well, souvenirs are all fine and good, but I want to go places you can visit only in Academy City, too! Mikoto, know of any good spots? I want to see a landing dock for a super-giant space battleship or something."

"...What sort of place do you even think this is?"

"Okay, then we'll compromise. I'll let you off if you show me an anthropomorphic pure-hearted maiden who carries lots of weapons on her!"

"We don't have stuff like that here!!" shouted Mikoto in spite of herself.

Then she noticed an intense pair of eyes on her. Not the same kind as the people passing by but more of a clammy, sticky kind of gaze.

She turned around and carefully asked, "K-Kuroko?" The girl with twin tails sat in a sports wheelchair with wheels angled out of the bottom, and she seemed odd. Her eyes were glittering like a Christmas tree in the city, so bright that even the petite girl with all the flowers in her hair grimaced.

Shirai made a loud, clear gulping sound. "Is...Big Sister, is this your family? I say...I say, how beautiful! Truly, truly far too beautiful for one such as I! What is this sudden inflation of Big Sister aura?! D-darn it. It's come down to this, so I must prepare myself! Oh, Kuroko! I don't care if it's sisters or a mother and daughter, you can all come at me at the same time if you please! Ufu-geh-heh-geh-heh-heh-ah-ha-ha-haaa!!"

The nimbus surrounding the Misaka family had been too much for Kuroko to bear, and her thoughts leaped brilliantly ahead of her. Mikoto promised herself not to ever let her know about the existence of any of the Sisters.

"Oh, Mikoto, I didn't know your girlishness went in that direction."

"In what direction?! I've always been on the proper path!!"

"You're right. You've been heading straight for that boy. No time for side trips, I suppose."

"Pfft?! I'll shut you up by force!!"

Mikoto tried again and again to grab her, but Misuzu skillfully dodged them all, blabbering on as she went. Then someone appeared in the corner of Misuzu's vision whom she remembered. *Hmm?* *Wait, that's...Oh, hee-hee. Speak of the devil.*

Misuzu and the others were currently on the third floor of the roads here, which were split into the underground, the aboveground, and the second floor aboveground. A familiar face was down on the surface level, past a railing. That must have been why he hadn't noticed them.

It was a boy with spiky black hair on the short side. Next to him, there was another boy standing a full head above him with blond hair and sunglasses. They were both wearing the same gym uniform, so they seemed like classmates. *But they look really serious about something.* She couldn't make out from here what they were saying, but the looks on their faces were the kind you didn't see often, even during important transactions at the company she worked for. It was the expression a person made when someone had many fates besides one's own riding on one's shoulders. What could it mean? Misuzu couldn't imagine what could be making such young men look like that.

But anyway. "See, Mikoto? That gentleman you long for is right over there."

"I won't fall for that— Wait, no! I'm not longing for anyone, you hear me?!"

Mikoto's face went bright red. Thinking it was a joke, she wouldn't look in the direction Misuzu was pointing. Meanwhile, the two boys went off and disappeared into the crowds.

9

Tsuchimikado hung up.

"So that means the Croce di Pietro they've been carrying can't be used in whatever place they like at whatever time they like."

"Yeah. They must've figured out where the usable 'observatory' point is in Academy City way before they got here. From what Orsola said, while Lidvia goes around the world spreading religion, she's probably looking for these observatory locations or whatever, too."

Orsola Aquinas had said Lidvia had probably been looking around for these observatory locations for a long time, but she may have just been measuring one or two places in a given region and then mathematically calculating where all the rest of them were. That meant she might not have physically seen the observatory inside Academy City.

"That means Lidvia and Oriana have been walking around themselves to make sure there weren't any mismatches in their calculated data and the real stuff...Is that it?"

"That sounds about right. And Oriana's still wandering around, too. Maybe they were having more trouble finding a magically appropriate point than they thought they would. Or maybe there was some other geological factor they needed. Anyway...this is where we settle it."

Of the points Orsola had given them, excluding the ones Oriana Thomson had already gone around to see left only one possible place.

"It's been a long road to get here, but things are finally starting to turn in our favor, nya~. Hope they keep going this well."

Kamijou looked up. It was five twenty PM. The blue sky was steadily shifting to an orange color. "One place left...How long's it been since she found it? Maybe she already checked the place and went somewhere else."

"No, I looked at the other places...Remember, she's *using the visual appearance of the constellations*. That's difficult to do. In two of those places, you couldn't even see the *sunlight*, much less the constellations. Even if you went up on the roof. In three other places, the leaves from the trees along the roads blocked off entire sections of the sky. They've gotta be using this last point. It's *totally wide open to everything*, nya~."

"A wide-open place...Wait, the place you marked on the map?!"

"You got it. Probably can't find anywhere better from which to see the whole sky." As Tsuchimikado spoke, he stuck the pamphlet map, marked with a Magic Marker, toward Kamijou. His fingers were trembling, and even the marking seemed somehow unreliable. He must have taken a lot of damage.

School District 23.

A unique district, the entirety of which was occupied by space and aerospace development–related facilities. Aside from the international airport open to the public because of guests from abroad who came to watch, its whole area on the map was just white—in the sense of no noteworthy places at all.

There, they developed not only civilian aircraft but also jet fighters and unmanned helicopters for the purpose of retaining air supremacy in Academy City. Even during the Daihasei Festival, its security was probably still top-class.

The place Tsuchimikado had labeled with marker was right in the middle of the white on the map. Kamijou couldn't tell, just from looking at it, where exactly that was in the city, either.

Tsuchimikado smirked at Kamijou's perplexed expression. "The place is called the Tetsumi Aeronautical Technology Laboratory Testing Airport…If I remember right, it specializes in developing short-range landing strips, nya~. I know what goes on there, but Oriana's never been there before, so she might have some trouble getting in, nya~."

"…But isn't Oriana a sorcerer? Would Academy City's security even work on her? She doesn't seem like the sort of person who would let herself be caught on the surveillance cameras."

"On the contrary! All the observatory points Oriana's been to have been light on security. You could tell if you went there yourself. She was almost going in order from lowest security risk to highest, nya~. Oriana and Lidvia are more cautious of Academy City than we thought…And I mean, if they were totally unconcerned about security, they wouldn't have been trying to blend in with the crowds. Kammy, think back to the sorcerers you've fought in the past. Did the golem user, Sherry Cromwell, seem to care much about what Anti-Skill was doing?"

Come to think of it…Kamijou got the sense from sorcerers that if they could crash in through the front door, they would actually do it.

Oriana and Lidvia were trying to use to its fullest the current equilibrium of science and magic in the Daihasei Festival. They probably didn't want to ruin that with their own powerful spells and have the situation change into something really extreme.

Countless magicians big and small were standing by in the periphery of Academy City. No matter how crazy they were, Oriana and Lidvia wouldn't want to take on all of them plus Academy City's security forces at the same time.

"In any event, let's pray Oriana gets her feet tangled in the security net and go after her right now. They're headed for virtually the last observatory. We'll catch them there and put an end to all this."

"Eh? Sure, easier said than done. If Oriana has problems with it, wouldn't we lose the same amount of...?"

Kamijou broke off as he saw a conspicuous priest with red hair out of the corner of his eye. He looked that way with a distrusting glance and saw Stiyl Magnus running over to them.

Tsuchimikado gave a suspicious look to his colleague. He was pretty late. "What have you been doing, nya~? You didn't run into Oriana and Lidvia or any of that, yeah?"

"No..."

Stiyl seemed to be having trouble replying, so Kamijou answered instead. "Right, right. Not only did he save a life and move Miss Komoe to tears, I bet she was clinging to him like crazy and he wasn't sure what to do about it."

"Pfft?! E-enough with the absurdities, amateur! I got her off me the moment I hung up on you. But even though I was using Opila, every time I left its area of effect, she found me again. It took me a while to shake her off." Stiyl bitterly spat out his short cigarette and stepped on it.

Tsuchimikado watched, his eyes cold. "...Nya. I see how it is. The Kammy disease. While I was valiantly using Four Ways to Truth at the expense of half the blood in my body, you were having a wonderful time in a rom-com, nya...? And it wasn't even with Index, either, but with Miss Komoe. You two are seriously strange. Staggering into one juicy situation after another. Men are supposed to go straight to their jobs and get them done first!"

"Don't call it the Kammy disease! Also, you have no room to talk about us being strange when you're obsessed with your little stepsister!"

"No! Wh-who are you calling obsessed with his little stepsister, nya?! I, Tsuchimikado, hereby swear that I— *Ow!!*...It hurts when I shout..." Tsuchimikado trembled, holding his side.

Kamijou shook his head and sighed. "Leaving aside Maika, what do we do now? District 23 has a crazy security detail, doesn't it? We don't even know if we'll be able to sneak in!"

"...W-wait, Kammy. This isn't something the elite *Onmyou* practitioner Motoharu Tsuchimikado can simply *leave aside*...But look. We can just use that one-time-only privilege I've got that Oriana doesn't have."

"Eh? A privilege?" Kamijou asked suspiciously, watching as Tsuchimikado smirked and got out his cell phone.

"Yeah. You know the chairperson of the Academy City General Board?"

10

Oriana Thomson was at the terminal in School District 23.

Unlike the other districts, District 23 had only one station: its entrance and also its exit. Every line that connected to the district met there, which made the station extremely large—and about as vast and complicated as an international airport.

Eight train lines, five subway lines, two monorail lines, plus four bus terminals at the front entrance. Other than those, there were even private special freight train lines and VIP-only lines.

That's strange..., thought Oriana amid it all as she casually glanced around. The security had changed.

The terminal had a good amount of Anti-Skill officers stationed there, hidden by so many people with big luggage. However, they'd all been moved quite suddenly. More precisely, it sort of felt like they had raised the security. It didn't mean that she would have to beat a hasty retreat from the station, but she couldn't help noticing that they were all moved to a pretty meaningless spot in terms of security. It had created more blind spots in their net as a whole as well.

Glass panes, mostly white, were on the walls and ceiling, making the inside of the station bright from the sunlight. Inside, Oriana continued to think.

School District 23 was a special district even among those in Academy City. Apart from the international airport and roads connected to the terminal, everything else was completely off-limits. It was actually easy to get to the terminal station, but getting any farther in was absurdly difficult. Which was why she'd been going back and forth between the terminal and airport for a while, waiting for her chance, but...

Here's my chance, but this seems a little too good to be true. She wanted to contact Lidvia, but she wasn't sure if using a communication spell now would be spotted by all the mana-searching going on. After mulling it over for a moment, though, she brought her flash cards to her lips. In her estimation, the enemy's searching abilities weren't that strong to begin with.

She bit off a flash card then quietly said, "Lidvia? Brace yourself. We should get this started soon."

The reply came in the form of letters imprinted directly on her retinas. They appeared at the bottom of her vision like movie subtitles. They read, "*...Is the appointed time not further off?*"

"Look, I'd love to take it easy, too, but our young men seem to be jumping the gun. It would be unsightly for one side to be late to the climax, wouldn't it?" Oriana said, keeping an eye on the Anti-Skill officers changing location, their footsteps silent. "The security detail is acting unnaturally. They probably know we're around. I don't feel any traces of Opila or other awareness-manipulation spells around here, so it was probably Academy City's instructions."

"*Do you mean to say Academy City is breaking the balance and pressing us all at once?*"

"No, just the opposite. It's more like they're purposely retreating to make a spot for us to have a battle. The officers look like they're hesitating about this quite a bit. They probably don't understand why they need to change locations."

"If that troubles you, you needn't press the issue. You have the option of leaving the station and moving to another school district."

"No...," Oriana said, staring at the big clock on the platform. "I've looked all over, but this is definitely the most appropriate place. So I'll tighten up our defenses here...Given how wide-open the spot is, no more civilians will be wrapped up in it, either."

"Are you certain you can buy enough time?"

"It depends on how many they bring, but I can handle myself even when there's a bunch of them on me." Oriana looked away from the electronic sign and headed for the exit stairs going up and off the platform. Her strides were long—and quick.

"Then I will speak to you again soon."

"Yep. You get ready, too, Lidvia. We're bringing down Academy City right here. Like pushing an ignorant, radiant maiden down into the mud."

11

A train roared into the subway platform. The hunk of iron and steel steadily slowed, but Motoharu Tsuchimikado didn't even glance at it.

His eyes were on his allies—Kamijou and Stiyl.

"Talked to the big guys. Got them to change up the security detail in District 23 a bit. Getting them all out of the district was a bit much to ask, though. Basically, we're just slipping through the gap they make while moving from point A to point B..."

Tsuchimikado went on to explain that they'd ordered those in charge of the satellites to change the video processing systems on them. While that switchover was happening, the eyes in the sky would be temporarily blind.

Kamijou thought back to the person Tsuchimikado had been talking to this whole time: the chairperson of the Academy City General Board.

...Aleister, huh?

The conversation had been over the phone, so Kamijou couldn't hear the person's voice. But they were equal, if not higher, than Tsuchimikado, who was fluent in both science and sorcery. Just that fact made it easy to imagine the person would be in a very deep place in the world. Such a deep place that Touma Kamijou, an amateur high school student, wouldn't even be able to peek inside.

"They're using the star chart for the night sky for this, so right after sundown is when they're most likely to activate the Croce di Pietro. Right now, it's five twenty-five PM. It'll take about ten minutes to get to District 23's terminal, nya~. We never figured out a clear time limit, but it'll probably be between six and seven PM. At the shortest...that means we'll have only twenty-five minutes after we get to the station."

"Tsuchimikado, about the whole 'slipping through the gaps as they shuffle around' thing. It'll be ten minutes to get there, right? Is that gap or whatever still going to be there for us?"

"Kammy, the security-detail changes aren't just for one building. They're changing around the whole district's security setup. There's no way they'll be done in ten minutes. Same as an evacuation drill at school, you know? The more people, the slower they all move. It's really common sense, nya~. At the very least, when it's five thirty-five and we arrive at District 23, the setup should still be switching around."

Stiyl took the cigarette out of his mouth and tossed it into an ashtray in the smoking area. "Just so I'm sure, you're going to face Oriana like that?"

"Hah! I'd love it if I could take a nice nap now, nya~. The security might be switching up, but they're not completely gone. District 23 isn't easy enough for just the two of you to bust into."

"That so?" said Stiyl idly. He wasn't asking for a reason—he just wanted to make sure he was willing to do this. "From six to seven. That's our time limit, but it'll also hold down Oriana and Lidvia. If they changed routes and went to another point now, they wouldn't make it there in time. They want to use the Croce di Pietro in District 23 at all costs."

After Kamijou listened to them, he asked, "So this whole game of cat-and-mouse is over, then."

"They're probably thinking the same thing. No objections from me—now we just have to give it everything we've got."

The train completed its gentle deceleration and stopped. The announcement came through the station as the metal doors opened automatically to the left and right. The people in the train started to flood out of the train car. Kamijou's group, however, wouldn't be stopped by the wave. It parted around the three of them so they wouldn't run into one another.

"...Once we get on this train, there's no going back. The only thing waiting for us is a death match with Oriana and Lidvia. Are you fully prepared for this, Touma Kamijou?"

Kamijou stayed quiet for a moment. All sorts of things had happened today. He'd smelled blood, tasted sand, run around the city, fought a sorcerer, fell for several tricks, saw someone injured before his eyes, realized he couldn't do anything for her, gritted his teeth, and kept his fist tightened.

"...Yeah." He nodded, taking all that in. He stepped toward the opened train door. "My mind's made up. We're finishing this. And then..."

"And then what?" Stiyl asked dubiously.

Kamijou didn't turn around. "Remember this. I'm not gonna let this end by killing each other."

The two sorcerers went silent for a bit. Then Tsuchimikado and Stiyl both smiled—Tsuchimikado like a little kid and Stiyl in a sardonic way, each showing their own feelings on the matter.

All three of them boarded the train.

The doors automatically closed, and the train slowly, gently left the platform, proceeding into the subway tunnel.

To invite them to the final battle waiting beyond.

INTERLUDE SIX

Oriana Thomson's family was Crossist.

Every Sunday they'd go to church, where a kind old priest would always be kneeling, looking her in her young eyes, and explaining to her the same things in an easy-to-understand way.

He had told her to do things for the benefit of others.

She had always wondered how.

Oriana, of course, was kind to people no matter who they were. For example, she would pick up empty cans on the road, direct confused people in front of tube maps to where they wanted to go, and deliver things that needed to go somewhere else, even if it would cost her her own life.

But...

Those acts of kindness didn't necessarily turn out for the benefit of others.

Perhaps the empty cans she picked up off the road would cause problems for homeless people who received small change and food from charity for volunteering to clean up.

Perhaps the things she'd been asked to deliver would turn out to be Soul Arms that would curse and kill a person as soon as the box was opened.

Even if she didn't wish it, even if she wanted to help others from the bottom of her heart, tragedies would strike anyway. The world was filled with people, all different, each with their own opinions. They fell into holes in Oriana's personal values, meaning the act of doing something for another person would also hurt that person. In a way she never predicted, in a form she never imagined, she would send the people she wanted to personally protect down to the netherworld.

It was hard. She could never come *close* to predicting whether her actions would backfire. If she knew beforehand that it would happen, she could simply not do that thing. And if she knew her actions were sure to succeed, she'd choose that without hesitation.

Of course...

Oriana's thoughts on the matter were purely selfish, and she understood that as much as anyone else. The logic was like a roulette wheel. Oriana could bet on red a hundred times, but depending on what number the rolling ball stopped on, some other kind of luck or conditions would determine the outcome of each hundred-spin set, regardless of her own wishes or actions. She couldn't choose red and win no matter what. She couldn't gain chips on every hundred-spin set. There was no easy, surefire way to win. That was how reality worked.

But...

What if a person's life was riding on one of those games?

What if they pleaded with her, begging her to win no matter what?

What would she bet on?

Was that choice easy for anyone?

If someone begged her to save them...

Her mind was already scarred. She was afraid. She couldn't even reach out to them. And by not reaching out to them, she was sure to hurt the person who asked her to save them.

She just wanted a standard.

A reference point that fixed everything, so she wouldn't have to anguish over it anymore.

A surefire way to win at a roulette wheel—a single rule would be enough. There were as many principles as there were people, and that created dissent, which would give way to tragedy. Water scooped up with her hands would slowly leak through her fingers, no matter how hard she tried. It was the same thing.

It can be an emperor, she wished. *It can be a king, a pope, a president, a head of state, a prime minister. It doesn't matter what they're called. I don't even care who's sitting in that seat. I can fight for others, too. Science or sorcery—neither of them makes a difference to me...* She clenched her teeth.

...So please, make some rules. Clear points of reference I can use to make everyone happy. So that I don't have to worry about differences of opinions creating tragedy. Please, create a world bound by such an ultimate, surefire victory.

She thought, but she did not speak.

There was a simple reason why.

She kept saying it was for the benefit of others.

But in the end, here she was, once again having hurt another person.

CHAPTER 8
A Reason to Clench Your Right Fist
Light_of_a_Night_Sky.

1

"Touma's missing?" Touya Kamijou asked as the sun was setting on the field.

The game was over, and the students were on their way out. The spectators were shuffling toward the exit as well, a chaos of murmuring filling the air. As several Anti-Skill officers waved their arms at regular intervals to guide the people on, Touya and his wife, Shiina, stood by themselves. Like a branch stuck in the flow of a river of people.

A teacher from Academy City stood in front of them.

She was only 135 centimeters tall, but unbelievably, she was Touma Kamijou's homeroom teacher. They'd met her for a conference for his first semester, so Kamijou's two guardians were not very surprised by the teacher wearing a light-green and white cheerleading outfit. She seemed to have changed once, and the smell of insect repellent wafted from the uniform.

But that wasn't important right now.

"Oh my," Shiina said, a bit worried. "What do you mean our son hasn't been participating? He hasn't withdrawn due to injury or sudden illness, has he?"

She'd been the first one to notice something odd. Earlier, she'd mentioned she didn't see her son anywhere in the team events. The two of them had been depressed, though, thinking it was their fault for not being able to spot him and that they were terrible parents for it.

But after this event, they were sure of it. It was the Spoon Race, when players had to run one hundred meters holding a two-centimeter gumball in a spoon. It had been an extremely heartwarming sight, with students using telekinesis to keep the gumballs in place or pyro-kinesis to blast their opponents' gumballs away from them—but they didn't see Touma Kamijou anywhere this time, either.

In team games, he might have been hidden among everyone. But this was a track-and-field event, so it was impossible to miss anything if they watched it all the way through. Now a little curious, Touya and Shiina had gone to their son's homeroom teacher and asked about it.

Komoe Tsukuyomi, clad in her cheerleading uniform, was in a flurry, her face pale. She hurriedly waved around her pom-pom-covered hands. "Um, well, you see, I put in a request with Anti-Skill to look for him, but…"

Shiina frowned. "Anti-Skill? The…city's police force, right? Did my son get involved in something bad, and now he can't participate?"

"N-no, that's not it. He was running around with a priest earlier, quite energetically. I don't think he's in any kind of dangerous situation, but…"

"??? You mean you've seen him in the city?" Shiina tilted her head in confusion—that didn't have much to do with it.

Her motion was nonchalant, but Miss Komoe's shoulders drooped. "…I'm sorry. You entrusted me with your precious child, and now I don't know where he is or what he's doing."

"Well, no, that's…" Touya and Shiina exchanged worried glances as Miss Komoe bowed to them and held the pose. The couple understood their son's personality and predisposition (though they didn't necessarily agree with either of them), so they hadn't been blaming the teacher—just looking for an explanation of the situation.

"…(And now you're making a woman worry without even being here, Touma? Yeah. That talent of yours is tried and true.)"

"Oh my. Touya, did you say something?"

"No, nothing."

"I do think Touma got it from you, Touya."

"Why are you giving me such a scary look while you say that, dear?" With the negativity pointed at him now, Touya took a quick step away from Shiina. Then he turned back to Miss Komoe, who was still locked in her bow, seeming like she was about to burst into tears. "Err, just one question. Please raise your head."

"Oh, um, yes. What is it?"

"Touma is doing this *of his own accord*, right? Nobody's dragging him around or anything?"

"Y-yes, that's right."

There was a moment's hesitation in her reply.

She'd already mentioned she'd seen their son, so maybe she knew what was going on. Was the reluctance from being unable to tell Touya that whatever it was deeply involved their son or perhaps another student?

What a kind teacher. Touya nodded to himself, and didn't pursue the point any further.

"Then..." Touya Kamijou looked up. As he gazed at the evening sky and at the first star that had just begun to shine, he said, "That means whatever it is, it's more important to Touma than the events."

His voice sounded just a bit like he'd thought of a bitter memory.

"If that's the case, then I suppose I don't see a reason to stop him."

2

The sky was already showing deep-orange colors.

The asphalt ground seemed like someone had taken a blackboard eraser and erased all the nature originally there. There were no signs of plant life, nothing to block the wind, as a calm current of air brushed against her cheek. It smelled slightly of machine oil—one of the unique traits of this country's cities.

Roar!! An explosive sound came from overhead.

She looked up to see the bulk of a passenger aircraft fluttering quite low in the air. Many airplanes were coming and going, most likely due to the Daihasei Festival.

There was nobody around.

The first reason was that this wasn't the sort of place one would invite people to. And the second reason, perhaps, was that the Daihasei Festival, a world-scale sporting event, was currently going on. You could spend your day a hundred times more meaningfully by obediently going to a field or stadium instead of coming to a place like this.

So her shadow was the only one clinging to the asphalt.

It grew ever larger as the sun set in the west, taking the form of a woman bearing a large cross on her shoulders. The one creating the shadow slowly let the cross down from her shoulders, then placed a hand on the white cloth wrapping it.

The fabric came off with a tear.

The cloth looked like thick bandages. It came off like the ribbon on a present, offering no resistance as it left the cross. The cloth rustled as everything completely guarding the cross came away quickly and without resistance. Inside could be seen the true form of the cross.

The Croce di Pietro.

A pure-white marble cross, 150 centimeters tall, 70 wide, and 10 thick. The lower tip of the cross had been sharpened roughly like a shaved pencil.

Simply looking at it made one feel the weight of the heavy stone. In spite of the eighteen hundred years it had spent on this earth, it had retained the look and feel of a brand-new object just taken out of a mold. It was made of marble, but if many human hands had touched it over the centuries, that by itself should have begun shaving away the surface.

Its preservative qualities were not due to a Soul Arm's defensive properties. It was a simpler reason: It had never been opened to the public ever before in history.

Like a noble daughter brought up with tender care, the cross was white and had no blemishes. She checked her grip on it. She slowly lifted the stark and smooth cross once. She felt the marble's particular weight come up her arms and into her back, down to her waist, and then down to her feet.

All of these she ignored, as she quickly swung the cross back down.

Enormous mass, outstanding speed, and a sharpened tip.

The Croce di Pietro had all of these as it effortlessly pierced the asphalt and drove deep into the lands of Japan's principal city.

"Please grant us the protection of the twelve holy apostles—so that the skies in the heavens will be changed to a roof over our heads and create a safe haven in this land!"

As she spoke the unchanging incantation to use the Croce di Pietro, her tone was very different from usual.

The cross sticking in the asphalt ground moved of its own accord. Slowly, like sinking into the mud, it began to change its angle.

She looked up at the sky.

It was not yet entirely night, but the first star of the evening was already there, twinkling.

"Well, all right then."

Alone, a sorcerer spoke on the large experimental airport runway.

No one was allowed into this area, which looked like a flat plain made of asphalt. An endlessly flat and gray land, stretching beyond the horizon.

"I'm all set here. I guess the world's going to change in a handful of minutes."

3

School District 23 was a sight to behold even for someone from Academy City.

This is a lot to take in..., thought Kamijou as he left the terminal station with Stiyl and Tsuchimikado.

He could see the horizon, slightly round, like he might with pastureland in another country. The horizon wasn't green, however, like on a farm. It was black and gray with asphalt and concrete. Runways and rocket launch sites took up the greater part of the plot of land. High fences slashing across its borders cordoned off the endlessly flat land.

The control towers and test facilities were quite large as well, all many times the size of gymnasiums in Academy City. But the runways nearby were so large, the buildings just looked like they were standing in the middle of nowhere, which made it hard to tell how big they were.

Tsuchimikado looked over at the bus stop at the front of the terminal station.

"…It might be one big military secret, but there *are* buses going to the civilian airport. And they need drivers, nya~. People to watch if an industry spy gets off in the middle of the route."

An airplane's engine roar drowned him out. Kamijou looked up on reflex. Three light aircraft were slowly banking through the air.

"The basis of the security here is in the sky. They've gotta watch a lot more than lookouts and guards can see, nya~."

It did seem pretty hard for one person to get a look at everything, considering the area stretched over the horizon. Plus, the entire area was filled with smooth runways, meaning there were no shadows to hide in. No way to escape the eyes in the sky.

"But then she wouldn't be able to get to the Tetsumi-whatever airport, would she?"

"But the fact is, she already did somehow," added Stiyl. "Tsuchimikado, if there's a way, tell us now. We don't have much time."

"Nya~. I've got something we can use," Tsuchimikado said, pointing overhead.

There was a huge *roar* across the air right above them. This time it wasn't a light aircraft but a huge passenger airplane with four engines. As it scattered its roaring noises behind it, it slowly descended to a runway in the civilian international airport.

"When another plane shows up, the surveillance machine patrol routes are programmed to change so they don't run into one another in midair. And..." Tsuchimikado paused as another passenger plane, followed by smaller experimental planes, all tore through the air above them in sequence. "...The sky here is pretty crowded. If we watch the passenger planes and run in at the right time, we can make it past the overhead surveillance. The Tetsumi Aeronautical Technology Laboratory Testing Airport is real close to here, so I'm pretty sure we can get there on foot, nya~."

With all that said and done, Kamijou and the others ran across the gray flatlands.

Tsuchimikado was in the lead, but sometimes he would tilt in a direction like he'd lost his balance. Kind of like when people start to doze off in the middle of class. But even in that state, he'd leave Kamijou behind if he wasn't paying attention. That's how high his physical abilities were.

With Tsuchimikado as the vanguard, they dashed straight underneath the countless planes flying around above them. Maybe they *were* avoiding the surveillance craft, but Kamijou thought it was thrilling in a few different ways, running over the horizon, across this place with no obstacles.

There was nowhere to hide, but Oriana was nowhere in sight. She'd probably already arrived at the point.

Kamijou took out his cell phone as he ran. The screen informed him that it was five forty PM. *Time runs out in...anywhere from twenty minutes to eighty minutes, huh?* That was how much time remained until the Croce di Pietro's activation. After it was used, Academy City would be placed under undeniable control without so much as a peep. And even then, the story went that no matter how unfairly oppressed people were, it would affect their mental processes—they wouldn't feel like anything was wrong.

He was impatient, but that wasn't going to do anything to change the flow of time. Meanwhile, they had approached a fence going straight through the vast gray area. The Tetsumi Aeronautical Technology Laboratory Testing Airport where Oriana waited was probably on the other side.

They charged for the fence—a chain-link one about two meters high. Tsuchimikado jumped onto it with his hands and feet, but the instant he tried to fling himself up and over, something happened.

Something glinted in the corner of Kamijou's eye. Something stuck between the wires of the fence. Something slightly wet with saliva. A flash card.

Normally Tsuchimikado was careful enough not to overlook these things. Was his pain affecting his mind?

"Tsu—" shouted Kamijou in spite of himself. Before he could get out the rest of his name…

Roar!!

…the entire fence in front of them turned orange with heat.

Tsuchimikado's body, attached to the fence by his limbs, jumped as if electricity had shocked him. He frantically removed himself from the fence, then rolled onto the ground to gain distance. He'd let go of the thick Daihasei Festival pamphlet from the shock. No sooner did he see smoke billow from it than it burst into flames.

"Gahhhh!!"

A horrible *shhhhhhh* noise came from Tsuchimikado's hands and feet. An incense-like trail of thin smoke wafted from them. He squeezed his eyes shut behind his sunglasses and clenched his teeth as hard as he could.

Had the fence burned his hands and feet? Tsuchimikado mainly did hand-to-hand combat, so that was like breaking every weapon in his arsenal.

Teeth clenched, he tried to stand, but his wrists and ankles looked like they were locked up tight. He moved once as if struggling in a pit of mud, but despite his spirit, he couldn't get up.

"Kammy, go…," he said, holding his one ruined hand with his other. "…No point wasting time here. Destroy that page, and then take Stiyl in!"

"What are you going to do? Right, Stiyl! Can't you heal him with your magic?!"

"Yes, if it's just burns, I can, but..." Stiyl looked away from Tsuchimikado to what was past the fence. "...They're not going to wait for us! Get your right hand ready, Touma Kamijou!"

"?!" Kamijou whipped around.

Past the fence. More than five hundred meters away. Leaning against the wall of a building facing a small runway—a woman with long blond hair.

Oriana Thomson, her metal ring–bound flash cards sitting in her hands.

She quietly brought them to her mouth as Stiyl shouted, "Touma Kamijou!"

"I got it!!"

Kamijou fired off a punch at the flash-card page stuck in the fence. The red heat shimmer instantly cooled to its original temperature and dimmed. They didn't waste time making sure, though. They both latched onto the fence.

If Oriana gets a head start on us...Tsuchimikado's arms and legs are shot! He won't be able to avoid it! They pulled themselves up in one burst. *That means we have to attack her first! No more victims. No more victims like Fukiyose and Himegami, damn it!!*

They jumped over. At the same moment, Oriana, far in the distance, bit off a flash-card page and crushed it between her teeth.

Her spell activated. Oriana began to shine in a pale-blue light as she raised her arms and twirled in place like she was showing off clothes she'd just bought.

A moment later...

Thud!! An enormous sound came from Oriana, five hundred meters away. The air around her in a sphere had churned. A giant invisible hammer shot toward them in defiance of the distance. It rotated clockwise as it spun toward them, its force utterly destroying the building she'd been leaning against. It plunged toward Kamijou, turning over the asphalt as it went.

"!!"

Kamijou's right hand shot up instantly.

With a *skree*, the high-pressure wall was blown away, still invisible.

Five hundred meters away, the tiny Oriana, clearly irritated, brought her flash cards back up. However, the asphalt was still spraying. The wave of stone in the wake of the hammer closed in on him.

"AFIMH. (A flame in my hand.) ISITOAS. (Its shape is that of a sword.) AIRITC! (And its role is to convict!)"

Rune-engraved cards danced through the air.

At the same time, a red sword of flame burst forth from Stiyl's right hand. He swung it horizontally at the incoming wave of stone. Ignoring Kamijou right next to him, for the most part.

"Agh!!" Kamijou quickly crouched, and a moment later, the tip of the flame sword collided with the stone fragments. Then, the flame lost its form and the whole thing exploded. The explosion had been directed away from them, so it spared Kamijou, who was directly under it. It wiped out the wall of asphalt stretching toward them, blowing it away.

Kamijou almost lost his balance, but he managed to not fall as he began to run forward again.

Stiyl muttered a new incantation under his breath and created a new flame sword in his right hand.

Oriana toyed with the ring of flash cards in her hand.

The three's clash had begun.

The current time was five fifty PM. They would run out of time between ten and seventy minutes from now.

4

As Kamijou and Stiyl closed the distance to Oriana, she stood in an experimental airport. The projects there seemed to be on break for the duration of the Daihasei Festival—nobody was doing work on the runways, and no lights illuminated the buildings on the premises.

It wasn't as large as an international airport. Instead, its small runways were likely used for personal light aircraft to take off and land. Three straight runways, each thirty meters wide and seven hundred long, were lined up next to one another.

In terms of buildings, there were towers on either side of the runways, plus semicylindrical hangars for vehicle maintenance. The place seemed more for runway-related research than aircraft studies; each of the three runways had giant fans, catapults, and other add-on units attached to or embedded in them.

However, with the attack Oriana had just unleashed, the control towers had been crushed from their foundations, the hangars blown away along with the experimental craft within, and the asphalt mangled like plowed earth.

The rubble was like a bombing site's ground zero. Both Kamijou and Stiyl ran through it. They were about three hundred meters away now.

"Mm-hm."

Despite the situation, Oriana Thomson gave a chuckle. Two hundred fifty meters between them now.

"And I was just starting to think going at it with another girl would be fun. I guess the saint isn't coming after all."

She began to bring the ring of flash cards in her hand up to her mouth. Two hundred meters now.

"No more Anti-Skill officers or backup sorcerers, either. Hee-hee. This would be more fun with a bigger audience."

She smiled. No, smirked. A very thin, sideways smirk. One hundred fifty meters.

"Ah-ha-ha! I guess it's just those three! Well, well! They just can't get enough of me!!"

Shouting gleefully, she crushed a flash card in her teeth. One hundred meters exactly now.

"And one of them already retired! I thought he was the smart one…but maybe he put himself in the most dangerous spot so his friends wouldn't get caught in my trap! Ah-ha-ha-ha!!"

Smash!! The sound of glass breaking spread out from Oriana in all directions. The sonic mass bounced back to her after a second like an echo.

A moment after that.

Everything fell silent.

Several passenger aircrafts were coming and going in the sky, but now they were silent, as though something had blocked the sounds. As though someone had just put a TV on mute.

Stiyl took out a rune card as he ran next to Kamijou. "A barrier! The kind that blocks all communication, physical or magical!"

"?!" Kamijou considered looking around to confirm it, but their enemy was *right there*. He didn't ask Stiyl to repeat that, either. Side by side, they charged at Oriana. Without breaking her smile, she, with flash-card ring in hand, accelerated toward them to match.

The one hundred meters closed in an instant.

Kamijou and Stiyl moved to either side of Oriana to attack. Stiyl's flame sword had a longer reach, so his attack would land first even if they started at the same time.

"*Sshhhn!!*" Exhaling sharply, he swung the flame sword straight down on her.

Oriana giggled. "Mm-hm!" Then she crushed another flash card in her mouth.

An orb of water the size of a basketball appeared in her right hand. She used it to catch Stiyl's flame sword as it came down.

There was no explosion. Before it could happen, Oriana's orb twisted and morphed, wrapping itself around the blade.

"!!" Stiyl didn't have time to be surprised as the watery vines quickly crawled down the sword and punished his wrist for his hostility. Then it coiled up his arm to his shoulder and began to envelop his whole body from head to toe. Now covered in a three-centimeter-thick aquatic film, Stiyl fell to the ground, unable to keep his balance. His free hand clutched at his throat.

He's going to suffocate like that!

"Stiyl!!" Kamijou turned away from Oriana and tried to reach out to help him.

"Oh! I'm not sensitive enough for a little side job to satisfy me!"

Her left roundhouse slammed into Kamijou's side. His body screeched to a halt.

"Urgh!!"

When he tried to straighten, Oriana forcefully rammed her shoulder into Kamijou's chest. He managed to hold up both hands, but the impact came from above his guard. Her tackle could have broken down a door, and it sent Kamijou flying right back where he'd come. Every time his body bounced on the jagged asphalt, intense pain shot through him.

Oriana watched him go down, then picked out another flash card with her lips.

Before she could crunch down on it, though...

"BTP!! (Break to pieces!!)"

With a shout, Stiyl, who'd been on the ground right next to Oriana, made his flame sword explode. The watery matter constricting him splashed away.

He created a new flame sword in his right hand, then stabbed upward at Oriana from below. As its tip went toward her chest, Oriana retreated with her left foot. The action made it look like she was turning to give someone room in a narrow passage. That was all she needed to do to dodge Stiyl's thrust.

Instead, Oriana's hand, still holding her ring of flash cards, shot toward Stiyl's jaw. Her hand was only lightly clenched, a move that in another situation might have looked like she wanted to shake hands. Stiyl, however, was already going in that direction from his own attack, and he plunged into the fist with all his weight behind him.

Whack!! came the splitting noise.

Stiyl's upper body careened backward before he slumped to the ground without resistance. The flame sword in his hand vanished as though the gas had been cut off. Oriana looked away from him, then gave Kamijou a comfortable smile. Despite the enemy no longer paying attention to him, Stiyl didn't look about to pull a surprise attack on her. His black clothing and red hair just lay there, fluttering, as though the weak wind were mocking him.

"Shit!" Kamijou hurried to get up, but he staggered.

Oriana watched him and smiled thinly. "Quick to drop to your knees as always, I see. Don't you think it's a little soon for a child such as yourself to exchange blows with me?"

"Shut...up!"

Kamijou opened his hands, then clenched them into fists again. He could make fists. His feet could run. His body could still move.

"I'm stopping you right here. I won't let you use the Croce di Pietro, either. If you're gonna wreck Academy City and ruin the Daihasei Festival, then I'll stop you no matter what."

"Wreck it? How cruel. I think I have the best role here, in fact. I don't know what the English Puritan Church wants you to believe, but the Croce di Pietro doesn't do anything bad. All religions desire individual and world happiness. The Croce di Pietro will change everything so that it will go that religion's way. It'll tear down the walls between sorcery and science. It might lead to world peace and happiness, you know!"

As Oriana spoke, fingering the ring of flash cards in her hand, the corners of Kamijou's mouth turned up. He looked over the destroyed runways, then smiled like a savage. "That'd be nice. Never seen a wall between sorcery and science myself, so I don't get it, but it sure *sounds* nice, anyway…But listen to me."

He stopped there, sparing a glance at the collapsed Stiyl. He tightened five fingers.

Then he clenched that fist even harder.

There were other things he could use his hand for. But right now it was just a weapon.

He spoke. "*I never thought this whole balance between science and magic or the right to control the world was important in the first place.* What bothers me is that you're trying to use the Croce di Pietro here and now. Do you understand what that really means?"

She giggled. "Of course. What do you think I've been trying so hard for this whole time? I want to subjugate Academy City with the Croce di Pietro. But you don't need to worry. I guess *subjugate* is a mean-sounding word, though. When everyone is happy, nobody will doubt why they're happy. It's such a convenient world waiting for us, a wonderful—"

"That's not what I was asking you!" he shouted, anger rich in his voice. It quietly and surely fueled his fist with power. "That isn't what I meant at all. I'm worried about you ruining the Daihasei Festival, you dimwit! Do you get it now?! Science and magic? Sorcerers? The Roman Orthodox Church? The Croce di Pietro? Legendary Soul Arms? They're all bullshit decorations that don't mean anything, so stop lying to me!! You think it's okay to beat people up because your argument happens to make sense?! Anyway, your argument is totally illogical! It doesn't *make* any goddamn sense!!"

He shouted, baring his canines at the enemy he saw before him.

"The stuff I think about might not mean much compared to those crazy dreams you like to spout. But even a total amateur like me has pride, and I've got a few things to say to you." His words flew straight toward Oriana. "Tons of people have been working really hard for the Daihasei Festival. All to commemorate this one day! Tons of people came out to see it. All to enjoy this one day! Tons of people are taking part in it. All to give it everything they've got on this one day! Why do you two assholes have to destroy all that?!"

Every single one of his words served only to rally the boy further. Touma Kamijou had put all his energy into that question.

"Protect yourself with all the great and powerful religion you want! You think you can win against what I just said? You can't! Because that's all your values really are! You're a worse student than I am for not being able to break such a simple, bland argument! You don't have the fucking right to take away what other people really care about!!"

"...Thank you for your tiny little opinions."

The gleeful light disappeared from Oriana's eyes. Her face drained of amusement but retained its smile. A dry smile.

"But did you think such a petty, emotional argument would shake me? If my sense of purpose was weak enough that *that* would hurt it, I wouldn't have done anything to begin with." She rolled her flash cards around in her hand. "I won't be stopped here. I won't stop like you want me to. Understand?"

"...Is that all?"

"What?" Oriana knitted her eyebrows.

"I don't know what you're trying to tell me, and I don't give a shit about what you're trying to do to me, either. None of it's important."

He paused for a moment.

"But could you say the same thing to the people you hurt? To Fukiyose and Himegami?"

Oriana Thomson, for that one moment, was silent. Her cheeks stiffened just slightly—an expression other than a smile this time.

"That's really all I wanted to say. If you promise not to do anything else, I'll stop chasing you. Take your Croce di Pietro and go home."

Kamijou brought up his right fist. And then he continued.

"But if you're still gonna do something to this city…If you're still gonna wave around your stupid magic at the people you hurt, people who can't move anymore…"

There was a light in his eyes—the powerful glint of determination.

"…then I'll take that naive illusion of yours and break it into a million pieces right here."

5

The sky was dyed in red. The current time was six PM. Sometime during the next hour, the Croce di Pietro, wherever it was, would activate. It could be in five minutes, or it could be in exactly an hour.

As the orange in the sky steadily shifted to purple, the first star hung in it, alone. There was only one star out. It wasn't enough to determine where the constellations, made of many lights, were positioned.

In this world, nobody knew when everything would come to an end.

And in this world, Touma Kamijou and Oriana Thomson clashed head-on.

"!!"

About three meters separated them. As Kamijou chased her around with a clenched fist, Oriana moved back to keep just enough distance between them, simultaneously crushing a flash card in her mouth.

A spell activated.

It created an unnatural blue wall of flame, which burst out of the ground between the two of them. But he stepped in anyway, thrusting his right fist at the wall of fire.

Fwooo.

The wall of fire bent inward as though retreating from his fist.

"?!"

Kamijou's fist caught only air as the flaming wall bent around, then rushed out to either side, trying to envelop his body. His weight was already tilted ahead of him, and at this point, he couldn't leap back. But his fist still wasn't going to connect. He didn't even have time to swing his fist to either side. Which meant one thing.

Keep going…

As the flaming barrier threatened to engulf his feet, he urged them on.

Keep going forward!!

Like an arrow, he plunged ahead, his fist shooting toward the deepest part of the wall's corner.

Pop!! With the sound of a balloon popping, the flame wall shattered to pieces.

Oriana Thomson was on the other side. She bit off another flash card, aiming only at Kamijou, ignoring Stiyl, who had collapsed at her feet.

A moment before her spell activated, though, Kamijou made it in close. The blade of asphalt she'd planned to fire shot out of the ground in the wrong direction. It was like a large cannon trying to fire at an enemy outside its maximum angle of inclination.

This time, he tightened his right fist and threw it directly at Oriana's face.

It didn't connect.

Before it could, Oriana used one of her long legs to sweep one of Kamijou's out from underneath him, from inside to out. His body lurched, losing its balance. His fist struck only air. Trying to at least avoid falling down, he dropped to one knee.

"Oh, what a good spot for your head to be. ♪"

Wham!! Oriana delivered a middle kick to the side of his head. Kamijou grunted as it connected and threw him off balance. The roundhouse sent him flying to the side.

It's not...enough...

Kamijou used the force of his roll to spring back to his feet just as Oriana was biting off another flash card. A glass bullet the size of a softball appeared in her hand and fired at him. He grabbed a piece of the asphalt at his feet and hurled it at the incoming attack.

Ksshhhh!! The glass bullet burst apart. Its fragments all aimed inward, piercing through the asphalt he'd thrown, the entire assembly falling straight to the ground.

This...isn't enough.

Kamijou used the opening to run at Oriana.

But with incredible speed, Oriana made it to him first.

"Wha...?!"

There was no time to dodge or defend himself.

She was so close she was practically touching him. She crushed another flash card in her mouth. Her hand gently stroked Kamijou from his gut up to his chest.

A moment later.

He felt a mad rushing of wind. *Fssh!!* With a sharp sound, his body doubled over, then rotated into the air around his solar plexus. A strong urge to vomit made it to his throat. Once his feet floated about forty centimeters off the ground, when he could no longer use his body to move himself...

"There! ♪"

With an idiotic shout, Oriana drove her clenched fist into the pit of his stomach.

"Ack...urgh...!!"

There were cracking noises. Her driving fist slammed his body three meters away.

This...still won't reach her...!!

He rolled, then put a hand on the ground. His mouth tasted bitter, but he clenched his teeth anyway.

Oriana was skilled at both close combat using her body and long-range attacks using magic. Kamijou could swing around his arms and legs all he wanted in response, but she was always one move ahead. His fist always missed its mark at the last second, like there was some kind of thin, slippery film in the way.

His attacks wouldn't land on Oriana like this.

No matter how fast he held to her, no matter how much he chased her, no matter how desperately he swung his fist at her.

"Mm-hm! It's starting to get dark out, isn't it?"

Oriana Thomson turned toward him. The action looked casual— but at the same time, it left no openings to exploit.

Shit...

It was a little late now, but he finally realized that had been her plan all along. She wouldn't go for an instant kill with a big move right off the bat. She'd maintain the balance, and as soon as he made an overeager move, she'd come in with a fierce counter. The techniques were probably things she'd acquired because she naturally wanted to conserve her big moves—she couldn't use a spell more than once, after all.

She wasn't playing with him. This was the ideal setup for her.

"I think it's time for kiddies to scurry on home, don't you? Or were you looking to spend a more stimulating night with me?"

As she made her way toward him, Kamijou, still on the ground, sprang out of his low stance and rushed at her.

The two clashed once again.

Kamijou dodged, parried, but his fist was never able to hit her.

One more...

He clenched his teeth as an attack hammered into him from a blind spot, but he endured the pain.

If I had one more thing...If I had one last move to make... Something...!!

Desperately wishing for something, he swung his fist around.

He continued his attacks, none of them hitting. Like an invisible wall was preventing it.

6

Stiyl Magnus faded in and out of consciousness.

*Urgh...*He saw the world sideways. He felt a creeping pain in his jaw. He felt his balance wavering. It took three whole seconds for him to realize he'd been defeated.

Strength was beginning to return to his limbs, but he couldn't move them with any significant speed.

Contrary to his large physique, he wasn't blessed with the kind of stamina for close combat. Not because he hadn't trained his body—it was a more fundamental reason.

Using his rune cards and casting encrypted spells used up a huge amount of mana. Mana didn't just appear out of nowhere without the need to do anything. It was created only after several internal operations.

Even operations that didn't cause normal sorcerers much difficulty were entirely different when it came to always using Papal-class techniques, such as Stiyl's Innocentius. Simple activities always tired a person out if they did them over and over again. In the same way, the "operation" of refining mana put a considerable burden on him. That meant his stamina ran out quickly: Essentially, he was always doing two different things. One outside his body and one inside.

Stiyl Magnus wasn't a blessed saint like Kaori Kanzaki.

He wasn't a genius sorcerer who had completely mastered one thing, either, like Motoharu Tsuchimikado.

But he still had a reason he needed to fight.

It was for that reason he'd acquired these runic characters, worked them into Crossist culture, and gained the Papal-class spell Innocentius. Even though the price had been an abandonment of all close-combat possibilities and not being able to produce a single flame without a rune card.

Unfortunately, the backlash from that determination was now eating away at him.

Damn…

His consciousness wavered.

Still, he was able to hear the sound of swinging fists and crossing magic. The amateur was still fighting. He was being attacked, pummeled, crushed. And yet he stayed up, didn't admit defeat, clenched his teeth. He just kept his hand tightened into a fist.

He would never be like that amateur.

No matter how many years of work he put in, he would never again be able to stand where he was.

However.

"OOTFECOTW, TGFOTB…(One of the five elemental components of the world, the great fire of the beginning…)"

He had taken hold of many a skill, all to protect a single girl.

Many spells of fire, for which he had suffered pain and blood to gain, all in order to fight those who would trample her smiling face. The result of having recklessly reached further and further, unaware of the faint emotions pushing him forward.

"…IIBOL, AIITAOE…(It is born of life, and it is the arbiter of evil…)"

Stiyl Magnus knew one thing.

This technique no longer held any value. That young girl had someone to walk with her just fine now. All the techniques he had gained were past their usefulness.

"…IIMH, AIITBOD…(It is mild happiness, and it is the bane of death…)"

But his spells could protect someone other than that girl.

Like the one who had been crying wide-eyed. The one bathed in bloody splatters. The small woman who had placed all her hopes into that entirely meaningless, clumsy spell.

Like the one who had been mistaken for a sorcerer because of the cross at her chest. The one girl who had been lying there in a pool of her own blood.

"…IINF, IIMS…(It is named fire, and it is my sword…)"

Doing so probably wouldn't grant Stiyl any comfort. It was much like making a cake for someone he loved, and then a complete stranger eating it and complimenting him on how delicious it was. No matter how much they praised him, it wouldn't fill the holes in his heart. Not ever.

"…ICTIR! (I call thee into reality!)"

But if saving them would keep the smile on that one girl's face as a result…

If protecting Academy City would lead that one to happiness…

Stiyl Magnus would accept that.

He would wield all his power for someone completely different.

He would accept defeating this enemy now, with those faint emotions still within him.

"MMBFGP (Masticate my body for great power)—Innocentius!!"

Whooosh! A flurry of cards burst out of his habit. The massive runes flew like a blizzard of paper, whirling around his body, then sticking to the broken asphalt around him.

Flames exploded.

They shone in crimson light as they closed in on one another, becoming one. At its center was a human-shaped core, black like oil.

And now a flaming titan three thousand degrees Celsius stood next to him.

"...Go, Innocentius...," he said, slowly getting off the ground. He moved unsteadily, his hands and feet both on the ground. And yet his body and mind never broke.

He called into the sky.

His magic name.

Fortis931.

Innocentius, the Witch-Hunter King, created in desperation, branded with his very soul.

And he wanted one thing from it.

"...Prove why my name is the strongest!!"

7

The sky was colored deep purple.

Like ink bleeding onto the back of a page, little sparkles of light were beginning to appear. There were only two or three right now, but within ten minutes, the sky would probably be full with stars. Their light didn't begin to shine during the night. More accurate would be to say that they were already shining, and they simply came into view as a result of the sunlight weakening. So, with the passing of certain intervals of time, those stars rated as first-magnitude, second-magnitude, and then third-magnitude would all make their appearances together.

And now, under that canopy, which looked like the night sky's lights could all scatter at any moment.

Oriana Thomson saw the glint of a flame beginning to cover them, one that would mow down the dusk itself.

"Stiyl!"

Kamijou noticed the same change. Unlike Oriana, however, he grinned madly, shouting the sorcerer's name but not turning around. As if to answer him, the hellfire brightened fantastically.

"!!"

Oriana was currently backing away from Kamijou, who was chasing her from the front. But now a giant human-shaped flame had gotten behind her. As it sucked in oxygen with a loud *roar!!* it swung its phantasmal orange arm over its head.

"Look…I'm not into wax play!!" She dodged Kamijou's fist to the side, then used her momentum to wheel around to his right side—to use him as a shield against the flaming titan attacking from the other side.

"…" Stiyl, a few steps away, frowned. "Die, both of you."

"Whoa!!" Kamijou frantically cowered. A moment later, Innocentius's right arm came sweeping across. The strangely long arm singed the tip of the boy's hair and continued barreling along toward Oriana's upper body.

The boy was too close. If all that firepower exploded, he'd be caught up in it for sure.

"What…?!" Oriana, surprised at that, tried to take a step back.

"Fire's dangerous, you idiot!!"

This time, Kamijou let loose an uppercut at the flaming titan's arm passing overhead. The hellfires didn't dissipate, but the act abruptly and unnaturally altered their trajectory.

That fire was three thousand degrees Celsius. It could melt flesh just by grazing it. It was truly hellfire.

Ugh!! She knew it wouldn't hit her, but the unexpected change in movement made her freeze. During that moment, Kamijou lunged toward her and got in close.

Oh shi—

She crossed her arms in front of her right away. But a moment later, his right fist, with all its weight behind it, struck her guard. *Thwack!!* came a splitting noise. She had no time to escape the impact. Both her arms shook, tingling with pain.

"!!" *I can't stay still*, thought Oriana. Her tactic was to maintain distance and counterattack both magically and physically. She didn't want this to come down to just grappling and boxing. She hated sexual discrimination, but it seemed stupid to her to take on a man whose fighting style revolved around a single fist in a bout of stamina when she used her intelligence to fight.

Instead of moving back in a straight line, she tried to twist backward so Kamijou couldn't gauge her movement.

"Ashes to ashes, dust to dust. Squeamish bloody rood!!"

Whoosh!! Another flame whipped up.

From behind Touma Kamijou came a red flame sword on his right and a blue one on his left as Stiyl rushed forward.

Not good...! Oriana tsked. She could take one or two hits from the boy and survive, but those flame swords probably weren't as forgiving. Their explosive power was more dangerous than any severing they could do. If the flames and bursts from the explosions hit her directly, nothing of hers would be left but bones—or maybe completely incinerated.

I need to deal with the sorcerer first..., thought Oriana, shifting her attention from Kamijou in front of her to Stiyl behind.

But then.

"Urgh...?!"

Blop.

As he ran, Stiyl tripped over a piece of the broken asphalt.

"Just go home already, you klutz of a sorcerer!!" shouted Kamijou, launching his fist again at Oriana's face.

Startled, Oriana looked back at him and flung her hands in front of her face.

"Quiet, you damn amateur!!"

Stiyl, who was falling behind Kamijou, struck the ground with both flame swords. With the sound of a vicious explosion, the air blast traveled forward like a wall. Kamijou lost his balance as it pushed him forward, and his fist missed its mark.

And went right through the opening in her guard.

A little below her face—to the middle of her chest.

Thud!! There was a noise like stomping on a floor plank.

"Guh...agh...!!"

The blast knocked the wind out of Oriana and sent her flying back. She wheezed, struggling to breathe, as she took the back roll and gained distance. Then she tried to bite off a flash card, but her lips were trembling and not moving how she wanted them to.

Then the attack hit.

The reason was simple. Kamijou couldn't tell what Stiyl was going to do next.

If each of them was moving alone, Oriana would be able to predict them. She could juggle them and lure them into counterattacks. A flawless victory probably would have been simple. If they teamed up to come at her as a group, it would be just as easy. In fact, they would need to give each other nonverbal cues, which would be even easier for her to read.

Unfortunately...

"Innocentius!" barked Stiyl.

The towering god of flame plunged straight for her. Oriana rolled to the side to dodge just as Stiyl, behind it, muttered an incantation and leaped at her. "Kenaz! Purisaz Naupiz..."

Those were the words he needed to create his flame swords, his main method of attack. Stiyl moved to graze past Kamijou's side, when...

"Out of the way, idiot!"

"How about *you* move?!"

With zero teamwork, they collided, each knocking the other forward at an angle. Their ridiculous movements, though, were still aimed at Oriana.

I can't tell...?! She barely managed to rip off a flash card with her teeth to parry the flame sword with an ice sword of her own. But behind Stiyl, Kamijou was setting up for a tackle. No mercy for his ally. It was more like he was trying to attack Stiyl. The clashing swords made Oriana lean far back. Then, a moment later, Stiyl's flame sword couldn't handle what he was making it do, and it shattered, disappearing.

If they'd been in sync while they attacked, that would have been one thing. But they were getting in each other's way at every turn. It was like she'd been dragged into a fight other people were having.

But that was exactly why they were so hard to read.

They couldn't focus entirely on Oriana. They were stumbling around. That made the timing of their actual attacks incredibly difficult to see. It was like a bullet ricocheting around a small room.

"Haahhh...!!"

Amid the chaos, Oriana, now leaning far back, still managed to swing her icy sword in a horizontal swipe. She was aiming for Stiyl's waist.

And this wasn't her main attack. If Stiyl avoided the ice sword, she would manipulate the ice particles a moment later and change the form of the sword itself to be ready to launch a pursuit attack along his escape route. Though if she did, she ran the risk of breaking her wrist due to the sudden lurch in the sword's center of gravity.

But I need to hit him! It's time for me to bring you to your knees!!

The sword of ice reached a breakneck speed and whipped toward Stiyl's waist from the side.

And a moment before it hit…

"!!"

Kamijou, who had gone around behind him, stopped the ice sword with his right hand. *Boom!!* Oriana's weapon shattered on the spot.

You always argue with each other…But now you decide to help each other out?!

Before a look of surprise had time to cross Oriana's face, Kamijou and Stiyl had already begun to make their next move.

Touma Kamijou crouched down, his right hand at the ready.

Stiyl Magnus, right behind him, clenched his fist as well.

Then, without any signals between them…

…with their almost magnetically repelling natures in combination…

…they launched their attack at the same time.

Their fists flew at her simultaneously.

Oriana immediately considered which to block, but she didn't make it in time.

Whump!! came a roaring sound.

Struck in both the face and the gut, her body careened backward.

"Ergh…gah…!!"

She slammed into the ground and writhed, aware of how unsightly her dance of pain was. She couldn't breathe. Her balance was wavering, and the strength had fled from her legs.

Her vision faded in and out, but she still saw it.

They were straight ahead, coming right for her.

She didn't need to stop to think what was waiting for her if she lowered her guard against these "enemies." But with all the damage she'd sustained, she couldn't stand back up. Her head was swimming. She could urge her body to do something, but it didn't have the energy to.

Will I...lose...?

She saw her flash cards, bound by their metal ring, sitting in front of her on the ground.

It should have been the symbol of her strength.

I...Am I going...to lose...?

The trivial fact caused her hands to weaken even further. She was barely conscious. The exhaustion came over her like a rippling wave, and she was about to surrender herself to it.

But...what about...my standard...?

Something was still nagging at her in the back of her mind as it slipped into the darkness.

A question. She'd lost count of how many times she'd asked it.

She remembered. She almost groaned out the question, but she swallowed it again.

Once again, she experienced the question's bitterness.

I...I wanted...an absolute reference point...

Everyone would feel differently about a single action Oriana took. Some would thank her, and some would hate her and leave her. Worrying about what was best to do never gave her an answer. If there were as many opinions as there were people, if her actions could mean as many things as there were people, then no matter how firm her internal rules were, the results would always depend completely on the people her actions affected.

Nothing in this world was ever *correct*.

Not as long as everyone had different opinions.

I don't care if it's an emperor, a pope, a president, a head of state, or a prime minister. I'll fight for anyone's sake...

She didn't want to know the answer.

There was no answer. Wasn't that why she'd decided to create one herself?

The kind nobody would wonder about.

The kind everyone would be satisfied with.

That was why she'd been trying so hard. But what in the world was she doing now?

...So somebody, please, make clear-cut rules. Make everyone happy. Make it so nobody is affected by tragedies born from disagreements of opinions. Create the best world possible!!

The wish once again passed her lips.

And her eyes shot open.

Blood rushed to her head, and the recoil made her heart stamp out a single strong beat.

I'll win...

Oriana reached to the ground with a shaky hand. Her legs wouldn't move yet. She hadn't recovered enough stamina for them to support her body. So she decided on a simpler, more efficient course of action.

I'll win, and I'll create my own answer! I am...My name is...

The flash cards, bound by a metal ring, lying on the ground.

Her weapon, once out of her hands—she grabbed it one more time.

"...Basis104!! (The one who carries the cornerstone!!)"

8

Kamijou heard a shout.

It wasn't Japanese, nor was it simply English. He couldn't tell what foreign language it was.

But Stiyl realized what the name meant before Kamijou did.

"Get down, you amateur!"

Stiyl rammed into Kamijou's back. Without watching him stumble and fall to the ground, he called Innocentius, which was standing by. The flame titan moved in front of him to serve as a shield.

Grk.

Oriana Thomson, still on the ground, crushed a flash card in her mouth.

*   *   *

Thud!!
Fresh blood splattered.

Oriana had fired a big sphere of ice, about the size of a soccer ball. It slowly wafted out of her hand, and when it did, it exploded, sending out a rain of sharp fragments in a horizontal fan shape.

The torrent of blades grazed over Kamijou's head as he was on the ground.

And pierced through Stiyl Magnus behind him.

The sound of the sharp blades stabbing flesh was strangely stiff and dull.

Maybe it was because it broke his bones, too.

Stiyl fell limp to his knees, then face-first on the ground. Blood began oozing out from him. Innocentius squirmed in anguish, then burst apart in all directions and vanished.

He didn't speak.

He didn't even groan.

"Sti…"

Kamijou looked up in disbelief.

"Stiiiiiiiyl!!"

"Where are you going?"

As Kamijou tried to run to Stiyl, a voice stopped him.

He turned around. There was Oriana, standing seven meters away. Tightly gripping a flash card in her hand.

"Your opponent…is right here, kid…"

"You…you…"

He didn't do it consciously, but words still spilled from his mouth.

The purple in the sky was shifting to the deep blue of night. There wasn't much time left before the constellations appeared. The amateur's eyes couldn't tell the exact time the sun would set, but the Croce di Pietro could be used in five minutes.

That was what he should have been most worried about now.

"Give it a fucking rest! How many people do you have to hurt, you bastard?!"

That was the first thing Touma Kamijou shouted. The words came out of his mouth before he could think about them. He couldn't just leave Stiyl like that. But Oriana wouldn't give him the time to do any first aid. That meant he needed to eliminate the obstacle.

Oriana smiled at him. "I'm not hurting people because I want to." Her face was somehow unbound, now missing all the relaxation it had before. "That's why I'm fighting. It probably seems ridiculous to you, though. But I still have my own goal in mind. Come on, kid. You're the only playing piece left to defend Academy City. If I get rid of you, my role will be over. Then the Roman Orthodox Church's Croce di Pietro will create the world I wish for..."

"Goal...? Give me a break..." Kamijou clenched the ten fingers of his hands. "You're the one letting someone else decide your future for you. Don't act so high and mighty. Fukiyose collapsed. Himegami almost died. Tsuchimikado's arms and legs are shot. Stiyl was a shield for me! Are you saying none of that was your intent? That you were just doing what the Church said?! And you're letting those shallow ideas take away other people's happiness?!"

"Well, you see...," Oriana said quietly, carefully getting the right distance. Not because she was relaxed, but to conserve what energy she had left. "...It doesn't matter who it is. It doesn't have to be the Roman Orthodox Church. It's not important who I follow. It's like picking a politician. Maybe that's hard for a kid like you to understand. But you know how politicians are different from celebrities, right? You don't pick a politician because you like them. If they were going to make me happy, I wouldn't care where they're from or how high a position they got."

Her breathing was shallow and ragged as she spoke, like she would cough up blood. It wasn't that Oriana Thomson had no personal goals—she just didn't care who she had to follow to accomplish them.

"To be honest, I would have gladly taken Academy City's side. But I have connections to the magic factions, so I just happened to be going along with them...because the Croce di Pietro will supposedly achieve my goals."

As Oriana carefully gauged the distance, Kamijou recklessly took a step toward her. "Your goals? What, you gonna conquer the world and become a freaking empress or something?"

She smiled thinly at the difference in their stances. "That's for those above me to decide. I won't be unhappy no matter who I'm following. If they'll protect my way of life, I don't care who's in control. Listen, kid. On this whole planet, how many principles, positions, faiths, ideals, rights, wrongs, likes, and dislikes do you think there are?"

"…"

"The answer is a lot. A whole lot. So many, you can't even count all of them. Those frameworks for faiths, all based on Crossism… Everyone interprets their denomination in their own way even after that, which means every single person has their own fine-tuned set of values. It's kind of like Oriana Thomson's version of Roman Orthodoxy."

Oriana squeezed her flash cards hard enough to crush them. Then, to match Kamijou, she also took a step forward.

"Kid, there are a lot of results you couldn't even imagine out there. You could give your second-floor bus seat to an old lady, but there might be a spell planted by a terrorist underneath. You could take in a lost child and send her to church, only to realize she was a sorcerer on the run from the English Puritan Church and was dragged by her hair to the Tower of London, only to be told what happened after the fact. Even today. I got a balloon out of a tree branch for someone, but was that really connected to that person's happiness? I can't figure it out anymore."

The words she spoke. She stepped in farther, as though urged on by their strength.

Six meters were between them.

"Can you imagine it, kid? How a person feels when, after everything is over, they learn that there are pitfalls like that in this world? How they feel when they have to take action anyway, and then once again see how people are *still* being hurt right in front of them? Whatever they do, it's wrong. But if they don't do anything, it's wrong. What do you think I should be doing, then?"

Touma Kamijou listened to those words. And he took another step forward.

Five meters were between them.

"Don't you think it's strange? Those who love their neighbor, unable to even protect those standing right next to them. That's why I'm looking for something—someone to stand above me. Someone ruling over somewhere on this planet, someone whose name and face I don't even know."

Oriana found herself clenching her teeth. She stepped forward again as if to discard the bitterness.

Four meters were between them.

"I don't care who it is. What I want is for them to perfectly rule over all the scattered thoughts and values on the planet."

That was Oriana Thomson's goal—to never again be betrayed, after all her kindness had been deceived by a trivial coincidence. To no longer let such a betrayal hurt those standing next to her.

But that goal was too big, and Oriana couldn't do it herself. That was why she tried to entrust everything to someone stronger, higher, and more skilled.

An absolute reference point. So that the misunderstandings, mistakes, and opposing viewpoints created by those coincidences would never again give birth to tragedy.

"I will protect them." She stopped—as if to say she'd gone through all the factors she needed to touch upon. "That's why we'll use the Croce di Pietro to gain control of Academy City. That way, surely all the scattered, disparate feelings will come together as one."

She was implying that there was no way he could advance any further. Her goal was correct, and if it would save a lot of people, then there was no way to argue against it. She stood there like a wall, that idea being conveyed without words.

But…

"Is that all your goal is?"

…Kamijou stepped in even farther.

Three meters were between them.

"Then I guess you really are cheap. You're not a villain, but you're too worthless to call righteous. You want me to give you everyone in Academy City for such a lame 'goal'? That's insane. There's no way I'll accept that."

"What...did you...?" Oriana's brow fell, as if something weighed down on it. The slight motion began to bring her carefully constructed expression to its knees. "Kid, you can say that only because you haven't seen it. It's not a grudge, or a shriek, or an angry yell, or even the voice of someone wanting to be saved...You've never seen an expression of pure frustration before! When a ten-year-old child has no hope! When a hundred-year-old man has no despair! They just stand there, able to only watch as things come crashing down around them! You've never seen it!!"

"Still." Kamijou took another step in, cutting her off.

Two meters were between them.

"That doesn't make it all right to attack Academy City however you want. You can't use it as logic to exploit other people as stepping-stones for someone else's sake. Ever."

——There was a young woman called Orsola Aquinas.

The nun Agnes Sanctis had said in the past that she was especially good at spreading the faith to uncivilized lands. That was probably because she tried hard to make even the slightest connection between everyone's disparate beliefs, principles, faiths, and ideals, so that everyone could live together in peace.

——There was a young man called Motoharu Tsuchimikado.

He probably knew that no matter how hard someone tried, they would never completely connect all of society. That's why he worked in the shadows of Academy City and the English Puritan Church, spending his life to lessen even a little the friction caused by the two societies with different opinions clashing with each other.

Their methods may have been different. But they were all trying to protect the people who lived there.

Thoughts weren't separated along ridiculous lines like religion or national borders. If your values and principles made you who you were, then everyone had them. Sure, they might cause trouble once in a while, but on the other hand, they were important enough to people to cause trouble over. Kamijou thought it was fine for everyone to have one or two things they weren't willing to compromise on.

Orsola and Tsuchimikado didn't try to interfere in the territory of others because they understood that. They could trespass on someone else's territory, wreck the whole thing, then stomp it into a shape more convenient for them to make things equal. But that would mean compromising their wishes, so they faced the opinions and principles of others in their own ways.

So Kamijou spoke. Because those were his own values, his own principles, his own opinions, which he'd arrived at after being hurt.

"Those problems you have are things everyone feels. And everyone has their own way of dealing with them. Just because you have some big goal doesn't mean everything you do is unconditionally okay."

As he spoke, he clenched his fist and moved forward.

Only one meter was between them.

"I don't know much about people's principles and positions and values disagreeing with one another. It's a little complicated for me to wrap my head around. But I don't want Stiyl or Tsuchimikado to get hurt. I want to go to the night parade with Index and Himegami and everyone. I want to have a good time at the Daihasei Festival events with Blue Hair and Miss Komoe. If you're gonna make all those feelings one, then I'll protect them with everything I have."

His fist was already within range.

"Not everything I do always goes the way I want it to, either. My own actions bit me in the ass that time with Agnes, after all. But why the hell would I just stop there?! If I fail, if I fall flat on my face, I can't keep on going with things until I pick myself up off the ground!! So stand up and try protecting something again!! Even if you get a terrible result, even if your feelings bite you in the ass, you're supposed to stand back up and drag everyone out of it!! All that matters is that everyone's smiling and happy in the end, right?! So don't throw other people's lives out the fucking window halfway through!!"

And finally, Touma Kamijou said this:

*   *   *

"...Which will you choose, Oriana Thomson? To leave everything to someone else because you failed once? Or to keep reaching out to the people you failed anyway?!"

Oriana gave a short laugh.

It was a totally normal laugh, without the dangerous, crazed look to it from before.

Then she took a breath.

""‼""

In one motion, she ripped off a flash card with her teeth and crushed it.

A spell activated, but Kamijou swung his right fist before attempting to figure out what it was.

An explosion occurred between them, and the Imagine Breaker's power caused it to disperse. The aftereffect caused pale-blue glints to shine, and Kamijou took a few steps back in spite of himself. Oriana jumped away as well.

The distance between them grew once again to three meters.

Oriana brought her flash cards to her mouth. But this time, she didn't crush only one card. All the pages were now off the metal ring.

She'd unleashed dozens of pages at once. She swung her right hand, holding all the pages, to the side.

"Time to end this."

There was a blizzard of paper.

Above the storm, unleashed like a sword in a straight horizontal line, there were letters.

They were written in black and read ALL OF SYMBOL.

"I command every ability within my body..."

As though answering her, the paper blizzard created a pure-white explosion. All the shining lights then began to be absorbed into Oriana's right arm, like melted candy twisting out of shape. The lights of the explosion tried to stay, fighting against Oriana's strong absorption, creating an effect that looked like a thick sheet of rubber being pulled in.

She swung her right hand behind her.

"...to release mind and body and destroy the enemy before me!!"

Then, with a big motion like she was going to throw something, she fired a fierce white explosion at Kamijou.

Oriana heard a huge *roar!!*

The white lights, stretched out, striating as they swung sideways, retaining their shape. As they went, they didn't keep one clear form—it was constantly changing its outline to keep itself vague. To match that, the air nearby touched by the explosive lights began to rage with amazing speed. Either light or gravity was being distorted—the scenery behind it all, too, was being warped out of shape.

The white lights were actually a huge attractive force. Anything that touched the loop of light was pulled into it without question, then crushed by immense pressure. That was all it was. By compressing with such speed the objects being crushed, it would look like they were being eaten up.

The gases around it raged, as well as the air left behind in pockets of vacuum. Even the lights and gravity present at the beginning were being taken into it. It was a weapon that would surely kill anything.

All right. As she swung around her greatest spell, constructed after using up all her remaining pages, she gave a boisterous smile. The mass of lights was swinging in from the right, about to ram into Kamijou's body from the side. She watched as the asphalt danced into the raging storm to be crushed in the lights. *Now it's over!!*

The boy unflinchingly waved his right hand to the side to block it.

"Raaahhhhhhhhhhhh!!"

He let loose a genuine roar. As soon as it hit his hand, the brilliant white light shattered with the sound of glass breaking.

Then, right after hearing a spray-like noise...

Thud.

Everything the white light had compressed erupted at the same time.

*   *   *

"?!"

The unexpected development overwhelmed Kamijou's mind.

The air, for example. The gases, compressed to one single point, came bursting out in all directions like a hole in a balloon. They were trying to return to normal, and their force hit Kamijou with an explosive wave.

The asphalt, for example. The immense pressure had crushed down the clumps of stone to pea-size pellets, and now, like popcorn, they were inflating back to their original sizes. Having regained their mass so explosively, they became like bullets, riding the wave of heat.

The stones blew and raged in a tempest.

Bam, came a dull noise as a piece of asphalt the size of a fist bounced off Kamijou's right hand. Before he felt the pain, he was then hit in the side, the chest, and the thigh by more of them. Then, when one struck him squarely in the side of the head, even his sense of pain momentarily failed him.

She...She knew Imagine Breaker would erase it...?!

"Gaaahhhhh!!"

Blood sprayed. He felt his skin tearing. He nearly fell over to the side. He could tell his vision was angling, but he was losing the ability to determine how to move his body to fix it. She was pounding away at his thoughts. Then Oriana, all her flash cards used up, jumped straight toward him—to deliver the finishing blow. To crush Kamijou's bones not with magic but with a rock-hard fist.

The strength in his legs started to fall away from him.

Even standing up was becoming difficult.

In this state, he could neither block nor avoid Oriana's attack.

If she completed the attack, it would break Kamijou's body for sure.

God...damn it...

——Seiri Fukiyose had said something.

Can't you put just a *little* effort into making this competition a success?

——Aisa Himegami had said something.

I want you to stop Miss Komoe and Stiyl from fighting.

——Stiyl Magnus had said something.

Don't expect much.

——Motoharu Tsuchimikado had said something.

We'll catch them there and put an end to all this.

They each wanted different things, and they had the smiles of those who, at heart, came to Academy City for the Daihasei Festival. Whatever the scope or degree of their feelings were, everyone was trying to protect this way of life.

Touma Kamijou himself had said something.

He'd told the collapsed, bloody Aisa Himegami that he'd go to the hospital before the night parade started. That was proof of his resolve. Settling things with this sorcerer wasn't everything. He was fighting for someone waiting for him after that.

It was the will of all the people who had told them what they thought during this incident.

I won't...

His consciousness wavering, Kamijou clenched his back teeth.

Firmly.

...I won't let all that go to waste here, damn it!!

"Gah...aaahhhhh!!"

Finally, his legs moved. His vision, sinking to the side, was finally supported by the ground underneath him.

In front of him was Oriana Thomson. With her fist out to get him.

"Wait...What?!"

Her eyes widened in surprise. She probably hadn't even considered the possibility that he'd counterattack. She was completely committed to her attack—which also left her badly defenseless.

His mind hazy, he put everything he had into clenching his right fist. Tightly and firmly enough that it would never open.

One moment later.

Their fists crossed.

Kamijou's attack struck Oriana in the face.

The sorcerer's body sprang away fiercely, then fell to the ground.

9

Oriana Thomson had fallen. She wasn't moving a muscle.

Now that she had been defeated, Kamijou realized that the barrier she had put up had disappeared. The roars of passenger planes flying overhead came back to his ears like a memory. Around him, the experimental airport runways had been torn up like a plow had gone over them, and the control towers and hangars were in tatters as well. A small plane meant for security eventually turned back around hastily. Anti-Skill would probably be landing soon.

"Stiyl!!"

Kamijou forced his beat-up body to move and ran to the rune sorcerer lying on the ground a few meters away. He had taken a deluge of ice splinters, but they seemed to have all melted now. It looked like more blood was coming from his wounds now that they were gone, like a cork out of a bottle.

Stiyl didn't get up.

But his eyes blinked slowly as they looked to the side.

"…I'm…fine. Do something…yourself," he said, moving his bloody lips. "The Croce di Pietro…comes first. Make Oriana…tell us where… Our number one goal…is to stop that Soul Arm…from activating…"

"But!" Kamijou looked around for anything he could use as a bandage.

"I don't believe there is any reason to worry. Everything will be over momentarily."

He heard a voice. It was a woman's. It sounded older than Oriana's.

Kamijou looked around. He didn't see anyone new. The voice was coming from right beside Oriana.

"…Because the barrier…blocking communication…is gone now…,"
Stiyl managed to mutter.

Kamijou wondered if there were spells that acted like radios or cell phones. *If there are, then that means this must be…*

Lidvia Lorenzetti.

One of the people, along with Oriana Thomson, who was given the task of activating the Croce di Pietro inside Academy City, believing that by gaining control of the city, they would have the entire science side of the world in their grasp.

She spoke.

"The Croce di Pietro's effects will activate in a moment. I believe that will alter Academy City into such a form that will be convenient for our Roman Orthodox Church. Hence, it matters not how wounded any of you are. Whatever the case may be, all of Academy City, including where you're standing, will soon be twisted around."

In addition...

The Croce di Pietro was **not in Oriana's hands but in Lidvia's**...

And at the same time...

"So you're just gonna get rid of everyone who stands in your way?!" Kamijou shouted in spite of himself.

Lidvia was unruffled. *"I believe you're misunderstanding something. I simply said we will treat your wounds with kindness and mend them. As long as it is for the utmost benefit of the Roman Orthodox Church, of course."*

"What?" said Kamijou, frowning.

"...You don't need to listen to her, Touma Kamijou," warned Stiyl in a low voice, still on the ground. "She's trying to use the Croce di Pietro, which means Lidvia and the Soul Arm have to be nearby. Your right hand can destroy any Soul Arm's function. So get going. Lidvia is somewhere near these runways—"

"For clarity's sake, I shall say this," interrupted Lidvia.

*"The Croce di Pietro **is not currently in Academy City**."*

"Wh...what?" Kamijou's eyes went to Oriana, who was passed out on the ground.

He then heard Lidvia's voice dispassionately explain the facts.

*"You seem to have investigated the belvederes within Academy City, but that was all simply a result of our guidance. **It would***

seem you haven't gotten to check the belvederes outside Academy City."

Outside it.

It took a few seconds for Kamijou and Stiyl to realize what she meant by that.

"The Croce di Pietro created the Roman Papal States, and at their height, they spanned 47,000 kilometers. I believe Academy City is approximately two hundred square kilometers. Naturally, even if it was activated outside the city limits, calculations would reveal that it could easily cover its entirety."

"Shit," muttered Stiyl. He was collapsed on the ground, unable to move his limbs much at all. "They...got us. Touma Kamijou...Call Tsuchimikado! Oriana was...a decoy to keep us focused inside the city...all along!!"

"Correct. Her role was to investigate the strength of those involved in this incident and to guide their attention to another place. If she wished, I'm sure she could have created a spell like Opila to hide herself. However, fish will not come without bait, so she purposely kept showing herself."

The nun's voice went on.

"It takes time to use the Croce di Pietro, and the points at which one can use it, the belvederes, are set in stone. The problem to be most wary of was that you would send people to intercept all the belvederes beforehand." Lidvia Lorenzetti went on, simply declaring the facts. *"For our part, we focused on how best to prevent such a thing from happening. We decided on a plan: to have Oriana purposely show her movements inside Academy City, thus keeping the attention of those interceptors, or you all, entirely within the city. I am the one who had the Croce di Pietro. I was waiting in a hotel outside the city until the appointed time arrived, and in reality, I stood the cross outside the city as well. I see that you didn't realize any of that."*

Damn it, you...!! Kamijou clenched his teeth, but it wasn't like any concrete countermeasures were coming to mind.

"I had Oriana move while using Opila or Presence Erasing as little as possible. However, the very first Silent Coin being broken happened

during the preparatory phase before the actual operation began, and we were worried at the time. If Oriana was to be captured earlier than anticipated, we wouldn't be able to accomplish our goal."

And now that she was explaining to them the entire plan, they must have already been in checkmate.

Kamijou stood there in a daze, simply listening to Lidvia's voice.

*"It is unfortunate that she was defeated as a result, but I believe the Croce di Pietro will **overwrite even that to be more convenient**. In the end, her defeat is nothing but a trivial matter, one that can be repeated as many times as needed. **Once the Croce di Pietro has placed all of Academy City under our control from the outside**, our stances will be reversed, and everything will have gone according to plan.*"

Lidvia was still speaking flatly. That made Kamijou feel like she was denying everything they'd done so far even more than she already was.

Kamijou grabbed his cell phone in his shorts pocket with a trembling hand. He tried to look up Tsuchimikado's number in its memory.

"There is no use," Lidvia said cheerlessly. Was she getting video in addition to their voices? *"Even if you were to locate me now, I am much too far away for you to reach. Even if you had backup outside the city, I am confident I can end it before they arrive.*"

"...(So that long-range bombardment Red Style...won't work, either.)" Stiyl muttered to himself in such a low voice, Kamijou almost couldn't hear it. "...(Searching and then attacking. Tsuchimikado can't use two spells right now...His body wouldn't hold out. He could give it everything he had and be lucky to even use one...)"

"Shit! What are we supposed to do, then?!" shouted Kamijou. That wasn't going to make Stiyl come up with a decisive countermeasure, though.

Despair hung in the air as Lidvia Lorenzetti's solitary voice echoed around them.

"In what way might you all be reacting to the changes in Academy City to be brought about by the Croce di Pietro?"

Stiyl's lips moved at the voice. "...Like Sodom and Gomorrah...

The only thing you're not doing to it is destroying it. You're doing... the same thing. Anywhere the Roman Orthodox Church doesn't like...You drive them to paralysis, then use its power to show the authority of God...You did the same thing...to the dying Saint George...and to the temples in Rome."

"*That is your biggest misunderstanding,*" Lidvia answered immediately. "*What is important to us is that this rampant science yield to magic, and that's all. I believe the current insolence of science is on the same level as Roman heretics of ages past. And in the same way we dealt with them, we will deny what you believe in, show you our strength, and regain authority for our Lord.*"

Her tone of voice changed. She had been speaking in irregular chunks of words, but now they were all completely connected.

"*Looking at something scientifically. Thinking about something scientifically. Having people offer scientific opinions...The 'science' here is no longer simply an academic subject but a form of paganism. It is exceedingly unfortunate—when a person is told something is scientifically correct, they tend to believe in everything unconditionally. No matter how absurd it may be, and without even seeing it with their own eyes.*"

She was right. Sometimes people used the word *science* the wrong way like that. Just because they said something was scientifically correct, could they state with absolute certainty *why* it was scientifically correct? People should use the word *science* only after thinking it all the way through.

Common scientific knowledge—such a term changed on a daily basis with advancements in the field. Nobody had discovered Pluto until 1930. There was a time everybody had said blue light–emitting diodes couldn't be made, too.

And even if something was scientifically correct, it could still mean that the paradigm of science itself was imperfect. If you couldn't distinguish that, then saying something was scientifically correct was about as valuable as saying something had to be true because your teacher said it.

"*We consider this to be the science side intervening with the religion side. As such, we cannot overlook it. The hands of man have tainted* the Lord's authority. *Naturally we will sanctify it again with those same hands.*"

Kamijou was ignoring Lidvia at this point. It was no longer a conversation. *The time...How much time do we have left?!* He took out his cell phone and checked what time it was. Then he looked up at the sky. It was completely purple now. Twinkling lights dotted the landscape like inkblots seeping through a page.

It was the worst possible situation. Their preparations were complete.

"*Of course, we will welcome all of you as well. We will by no means destroy Academy City. Even this ridiculous festival you call Daihasei will simply be made into a wonderful demonstration of science bending to the Church. After we have made you give up your paganistic science, we will embrace you as beloved brothers and sisters.*"

Stiyl managed to move his wrecked body enough to take a bloody rune card out of his inside pocket. Maybe he wanted to use it for a communication spell like Lidvia was now. "You...call Tsuchimikado," he said, wringing the words from his throat. "...Divination Circle...I think it was. He had a spell...that traced Oriana's... interception spell. We'll use that on Lidvia's communications... and figure out where she is. Then...I'll use my own communication spell...and ask the forces outside to..."

"*That will not work. There are one hundred twelve seconds remaining until the Croce di Pietro changes the world. No, now it is one hundred seven seconds. Allow me to say it clearly: This is checkmate.*"

One hundred and seven seconds.

In that time, even if they found Lidvia, nobody could get to her. Just calling the wounded Tsuchimikado here would use up all that time.

Stiyl sucked in his breath.

Lidvia Lorenzetti probably smiled on the other end of the transmission.

Kamijou clenched his teeth, staring at the purple sky above as it became ever more populated by stars.

There has to be a way...

He couldn't give up. That was the only thing keeping him thinking now.

...There's gotta be a way to solve this! One last card up our sleeves!!

He was frantically grasping at straws. The Croce di Pietro—one of the Roman Orthodox Church's most powerful Soul Arms. When used, it would place a 47,000-kilometer area under their total control. It was a spell that used the constellations. Not the actual positions of the stars. Only what could be seen in the night sky. A spell that used only the appearance of the constellations. They investigated the characteristics, features, and traits of the area to use it in. They chose the most effective of the eighty-eight constellations for it.

They would gather the light of the stars shining down to the ground.

"...!!"

Touma Kamijou grabbed his cell phone. He punched in one number: Motoharu Tsuchimikado's.

"Tsuchimikado! Don't say anything; just answer me. How many points are there outside Academy City that the Croce di Pietro could be used at and still get to it?!"

"What...? Kammy?" His voice was just as ragged as his body now. He probably didn't understand.

But Kamijou didn't have the time or willingness to explain. He shouted again. "Don't sweat the details. What's the farthest point away given what I just said?!"

"...In all, there are five points that could be used from the outside. Of them...the farthest one away is about seventeen hundred meters north of Academy City...Kammy, why did you need this—?"

"Sorry, Tsuchimikado, no time to explain!!" he apologized, ignoring his question and hanging up. Then he opened the application they'd used to communicate. It was like a digital version of the Daihasei Festival pamphlet. *I know how far it is. And we've got...fifty-five seconds. Will this work?!*

"I believe there is nothing you can do at this point. I will crush your hopes just to be sure, but I am not in any of those places you just explained."

He ignored her mocking voice and desperately worked his cell phone. It displayed a map of Academy City on its screen.

That's not it.

He closed the window and called up another one.

Not that one, or that one, or that one, either!

He closed another window and then opened another. This app was just a backup in case you lost the actual pamphlet, and it didn't contain all the information the thick volume did. It was hard to use, too, and Kamijou was having trouble getting the information he wanted.

But he still tried, and kept trying, over and over.

Finally, he looked at the screen one more time and dropped the phone.

Clatter.

The light noise of plastic hitting the ground echoed across the runways in the setting sun. But that was all. Kamijou went to pick it up. But he couldn't. His fingers were shaking too hard. He couldn't move them to do this one simple thing satisfactorily.

Forty seconds until everything was over.

Lidvia wasted away even this final moment with her talking. *"No matter what method you care to use, I believe it is impossible for you to reach me where I am now."* Her tone was polite, as though she was bowing to them as she spoke. *"Allow me to say one last thing: It is over. I will re-create this world into a better one, and that includes all of you."*

"Heh."

Kamijou laughed as though he'd just had an idea.

"You're right. It's all over."

Twenty seconds left.

"Ah, damn it. So much for keeping that promise."

He was looking at something—but not the stars in the sky shining down on them.

"Seriously. I was so confident when I promised Himegami, and now look how things turned out. I'm done for. Totally done for."

He was just looking at his empty cell phone screen as it lay on the ground, shining.

"Don't you agree, Lidvia?"

Five seconds left.

As he watched the screen, he said one last thing.

*   *   *

"Done for, *even though I completely destroyed your stupid illusion.*"

Before Lidvia could make a noise of confusion…
Bang!!
An intense light appeared from the ground, for a moment banishing all the night's darkness.

It was every decorative light in Academy City—from lightbulbs to neon signs, laser art, spotlights, and everything else.

School District 23 didn't have much to do with the Daihasei Festival, but even here, a row of decorative illumination began to shine like a Christmas tree around the civilian international airport. From somewhere far away, a bright, cheerful melody floated to them. It was a song filled with electronic tones, the sort that might play at a children's theme park.

"It's now exactly six thirty PM."

Touma Kamijou picked up his cell phone and looked at the screen.

The simplified digital pamphlet showed a timetable of the festival's nighttime entertainment.

"Didn't you know the night parade was starting now?"

"Wha…?"

A whirlpool of light covered all of Academy City.

The next thing he knew, all those shining stars in the night sky were gone, blotted out by the lights from the ground. Just like how not many stars were visible in the middle of a big city. The utterly weak starlight melted into the stronger lights.

"Man…Before this started, I promised to go back to Himegami's hospital room, but now that's all up in smoke. Shit. I'm a failure." He tsked, truly frustrated. "Oh, right. From what Tsuchimikado said, of all the points outside Academy City that still had the city within range, the farthest one away was seventeen hundred meters out. That's not very far. All this ridiculous light coming from the city's going to cover up the stars just fine."

And then he continued.

"The farthest point away won't be able to see the stars. It doesn't matter where you are—that takes care of all the points, doesn't it, Lidvia Lorenzetti?!"

"…"

The last five seconds had long since passed them by.

And the world still hadn't changed.

"Now that I think about it, we all had some pretty terrible support roles here."

One of the strongest spells that used the shining starlight, unchanging for thousands of years.

In this moment, it was forced to submit to the man-made lights around them.

"I'm not really in a position to talk big, since I couldn't chase you down in the end, but you don't have the right to take the Daihasei Festival lightly, either. You've just lost to the lights everyone here has created. The security setups and the balance between science and magic—none of that even mattered. Before all this started, *you should have tried to figure out who the real main stars of the Daihasei Festival were.*"

They weren't Touma Kamijou, or Stiyl Magnus, or Motoharu Tsuchimikado, or Oriana Thomson, or Lidvia Lorenzetti.

Seiri Fukiyose—she gave it her all to make the festival succeed. Aisa Himegami—she fell into a sea of blood because of a simple coincidence. Komoe Tsukuyomi—she had tried to save her student, crying, covered in blood.

People like that had come together, and they had protected the Daihasei Festival.

They had used a great light to create fun memories for all involved. Their feelings shone through.

"…"

Kamijou got no reply.

What was Lidvia thinking as she stared at the starless night sky now?

"What will you do? Looks like the Daihasei Festival didn't care one bit about your efforts. I don't know much about the power balance between science and magic or whatever. If you break the Croce di Pietro, stay quiet, run away, and never bother Academy City again, that would be enough for me. But what about you?"

"...*Surely you jest.*"

A low tension made its way into Lidvia's voice.

The kind that might explode if a finger so much as plucked it.

"*I am one of the honored Roman Orthodox followers. We will not be rendered inferior to Academy City a second time. I believe there is not much in your request that deserves agreement.*"

"Oh," Kamijou said quietly. He glanced to the side. Tsuchimikado had climbed over the chain-link fence, and he was slowly walking toward him. The only man here who could detect mana from spells being used.

Even if Tsuchimikado pinpointed which point, or belvedere, for the Croce di Pietro Lidvia was at, Lidvia would be able to take the Croce di Pietro and make her escape before they could get there. Their pursuit had been extremely tight just staying within the city. If they went outside, it would take a lot more time and span a lot more distance.

But there were many sorcery factions, small and large, standing by outside the city because of this incident.

Whatever their opinions toward Academy City, they were probably all operating under the same great objective: catch Oriana and Lidvia. Not knowing where the recovered Croce di Pietro would end up was the one point of contention, but that could be solved by having only the groups supportive of the English Puritan Church assist in Lidvia's capture.

And so...

If Stiyl could follow Lidvia's transmission spell to locate the source of her mana using Tsuchimikado's Four Ways to Truth, then they could inform a magic faction close to the English Puritan Church waiting outside the city to get a move on, and it would be over.

There was nothing more for Touma Kamijou to do here.

But he did grin and say one last thing.

"Well then, it looks like you'll get to be a part of the festivities anyway. Up for a game of tag, Lidvia Lorenzetti?"

EPILOGUE

Those Waiting After the End

Those_Who_Hold_Out_a_Hand.

The sun finally set, and amid the flamboyance of the night parade...

Kamijou, Stiyl, and Tsuchimikado were relatively fatigued, and as soon as Anti-Skill ran over and found them, they decided to just bring them to the hospital. Being taken to a hospital with iron bars wouldn't have been odd, but for some reason they just ended up at the same old one as usual. It was in a different school district, too. Maybe that meant some other powers were at work. Kamijou didn't have the time to think about it.

After being contacted, his parents, Touya and Shiina, had been in the hospital waiting room, remaining until he was treated for his injuries. The exhaustion from watching the Daihasei Festival events must have gotten to them, though, because when he was done getting patched up, he found them asleep next to each other on a bench, their shoulders propping each other up. Kamijou got a nurse to bring them a blanket and put it on them.

"...So you didn't say a word to me about anything, selfishly got yourself into a magic battle with the fate of the world and Academy City on the line, and then you got beaten up and sent to the hospital?"

Index, who had changed back into her usual habit, was glaring daggers at him. Kamijou sat up straight in his bed.

"Miss Index, why might you be demanding that my humble self grovel before you on a hospital bed?"

"Touma, Touma. Can I punch you now?"

"I'm sorry!!" Kamijou's head was instantly buried against the soft sheets. That combination of her sweet head-tilted expression and her right hand balled up into a serious fist was truly terrifying.

Her cheeks puffed out in exasperation. Kamijou, on the lookout for danger, glanced up and constructed the best smile he could manage. "B-but you know, Tsuchimikado and Stiyl are all right, too. And please don't jump to conclusions! There is a very good reason you could not take part in the fight, okay?!"

"Then what were all those other times, Touma?"

Now he was digging his own grave. Kamijou groveled as hard as he could.

Index, cheeks puffed in indignant annoyance, said, "Did you really think I wouldn't be able to do anything just because some search spells were looking for mana around me? I could have at least given you advice with these cell phone thingies or something!!"

"I'm sorry, but I find myself having trouble agreeing with you, Index! You don't even know how to charge your zero-yen phone! I don't think you know how to use one, and anyway, if you heard the word *sorcery* one time, you would just shamble right into the middle of the incident no matter *what* I said!!"

"Sh-shamble? Touma, it really sounds like you're making fun of me!"

"Pfft, if you can't tell, that means you're already— Wait, I was joking, joking, jooookiiing!"

Growl!! The ferocious beast girl Index bared her fangs and attacked. His hair stood on end—for a pretty good reason.

"Index, wait! I thought you had graduated from that childish biting thing and were starting to finally spread your wings as a grown woman in her own right!!"

Touma Kamijou, ever the schemer, purposely appealed to Index's self-consciousness by using words like *child* and *woman*. And, already leaning over the bed and about to bite him in the head, the rampaging sister Index stopped. "…Touma, do you understand why I'm this angry now?"

"What? Aren't you just offended because I left you alone the whole day—"

"*Thank you for the food!!*"

What?! That didn't offend her…?! Kamijou swallowed that desperate cry. Index had taken a new step past her suffering and embarrassment. Her teeth dug into his head with even more force.

Kamijou writhed and squirmed on the bed. "You're gonna kill me!! I'm sorry I kept thinking you weren't doing very much! But this is definitely out of bounds!!"

"Maybe you should stop saying strange things and think about what you did! There were people seriously worried about you!!"

As she continued to chomp down on the front of his head, the hospital room door opened and a couple of familiar people strolled through.

It was Mikoto Misaka and Kuroko Shirai.

"W-well…I was visiting Kuroko anyway, and I had extra fruit here, so…Huh?"

"Oh my. It seems we're witnessing yet another delightful scene."

From a few feet away, with a girl biting onto a boy's head on a bed, it probably looked as though the boy was getting his face up close to the girl's chest. Or so he thought, as though it had nothing to do with him.

Shirai, in her sports wheelchair, put a hand to her cheek. "Ah! Their feelings for each other transcend the bounds of time and place! This couple is incredibly advanced…! Big Sister, what do you think the ones who happen across this sort of thing should do? I find myself feeling rather timid, honestly."

Kamijou tried to shout, *Does this look like that "sort of thing" to you?!*

Before he could, Index shouted, "I'm being serious, so stop joking around, Short Hair!"

Miss Index?!

"…" The basket of fruit fell out of Mikoto's hand. Her face went blank for a moment. Then, "Kurokooo…? Judgment is okay with civilians helping with their peacekeeping activities, right? If I put this down as *guarding against illicit sexual activity in advance*, would it be all right for me to throw this man out the window…?"

"Well, actually, the most you could do about that foolish gentleman's nature is— O-oh my?! Big Sister, you're snapping and crackling quite a bit there! We're in a hospital!!"

"Oh, that's right," Mikoto said, withdrawing her *biri biri*. Places like these generally prohibited the usage of electrical equipment such as cell phones. She cursed under her breath not being able to use her strongest card. "Anyway, I'll tell you what you want to hear, nice and slow, once the festival is over. Did you see today's final results? Tokiwadai got just a *little bit* past your stupid school. We're at the top now. Don't forget about the loser having to do whatever the winner wants, got it?"

"W-well, that punishment game, at this point, it's…Hey, Index, get off me already! It hurts!!"

Kamijou waved his hands and managed to tear the sister off his head.

Then he looked at Mikoto again. "A-as you can see, a certain incident has left me somewhat injured. I clearly won't be at full power for the rest of the festival events. How should we decide who wins now?"

"…Hmm, well…"

Mikoto folded her arms, looked at Kamijou half crying, and sighed a little. The anger visible on her face receded a slight amount. Then she slowly relaxed her shoulders, and her lips loosened into a little smile. Kamijou thought he was in the clear now, *but…*

"You'll just have to do it like your life depends on it."

"That's it?! I can't do that! I'm already eighty percent dead! If I try any harder, I'm gonna end up going all the way to the grave!! And besides, we're missing other people, too, like Fukiyose and Himegami and Tsuchimikado!! Maybe canceling the whole thing is too much to ask, but at least give me a handicap— Ah, ahhh! Don't leave without saying anything!"

The two girls left the hospital room hastily. Index, who was waiting for such an opportunity, latched onto Kamijou's head with her teeth again. Once hadn't been enough, which meant this all must have made her *really* angry.

"So, Touma, what happened to all the people outside Academy City?"

"It hurts! Get off! It really hurts!!…What? Tsuchimikado said Stiyl got out a quick message. They should be looking around for Lidvia now. He said it was more the groups who wanted to snatch the precious Croce di Pietro than allies of Academy City and the English Puritan Church, though."

"…Then it doesn't sound like anything's fixed."

"Yeah, but…" He paused. "Stiyl was real beat up, and before he went into ICU, he said it would work itself out. He seemed confident. I wonder why?"

Fourteen hours later…

Lidvia Lorenzetti was eight thousand meters in the sky above France.

She was inside a personal jet aircraft. Black leather sofas lined the interior walls. A large table sat in the middle, bolted down to the floor. It was set up for a party. There were lamps near the walls and a small chandelier light fixture on the ceiling. The furnishings featured polished black wood and luxurious rugs. It was like a floating hotel.

A large cross wrapped in white fabric stood against the sofa next to her.

The craft was quite small compared to the big passenger airliners at international airports. Perhaps they were unusual in Japan. On the other hand, countries like the U.S. and Russia had many times the land as Japan, so long-distance flights were common in those places. In Russia, for example, it could take over two weeks to span the nation on a train.

Lidvia, of course, mainly did her jobs in Europe, but airplanes were still valuable for traveling between member nations of the EU. She hated science as a religion, but she felt no choice but to accept science's technology as a means for achieving an end. For example, it took an immense amount of time and labor to create even a single Bible without the printing press. Even as churches and religious artwork advanced, they couldn't completely discard science. For the religious, it had been a source of conflict ever since the Renaissance. Even later technology helped: The development of trains and airplanes allowed relatively unfit women and children to make pilgrimages to safe sanctuaries, and the popularization of the Internet gave people more chances to spread the Word to those yet unaware of the Lord.

The problem was the way these things were used. Lidvia sighed. *Placing one's faith in science, a mere puppet with no life, is the very image of the heretics during Ancient Rome.* After her light sigh, she abruptly looked somewhere else.

The door leading to the cockpit was open now. Lidvia could see the pilot inside, fiddling with the instruments with calm movements. She wondered what the man believed in. This private jet belonged to Oriana, so it wasn't under the patronage of the Roman Orthodox Church—but the pilot was likely still one of its disciples. On a much lower level, lower than Oriana or Lidvia.

He brought hunks of metal into the skies every day, but before taking off, he'd cross himself and pray for a safe journey. It may have seemed a strange sight, but Lidvia wouldn't laugh at it.

Using tools and believing in God—people had been doing each for different purposes since long ago. Even two thousand years ago, when the Son of God lived, they were at the very least using tools with which to bake bread.

The important thing was this. *Not to reject all scientific tools outright, nor to forget the authority of the Lord by overusing them.* She quietly sighed. She had just failed to demonstrate the Lord's authority. She had just been bowed by a heap of science.

For all intents and purposes, Lidvia was now running backward. However long she waited for more chances to repeat the same attack while keeping the Croce di Pietro out of enemy hands, they now knew where the belvederes needed to use the Soul Arm were located. It couldn't be used if the night sky couldn't be seen. If they constructed simple buildings right on top of the belvederes, it would be much harder to use the cross in or around Academy City. Plus, as though it wouldn't already be difficult enough, her precious strength—the sinner Oriana Thomson—had been captured.

"Ufu-fu." Nevertheless, she laughed at it. "How pitiful...Ah, how pitiful you are, Oriana Thomson. Fu...fu-fu. You must be saved, sinner lost and taken prisoner by them, you must be saved by my hands..."

Lidvia Lorenzetti twisted the misfortune and adversity around her, transforming it into a driving force to spur herself forward.

"To set foot inside Academy City, to fight against 2.3 million people, to safely rescue Oriana, to end everything without bloodshed..."

Everything coming from her mouth was a wish that could be called incredibly reckless.

Besides, if she returned to the Vatican now, she would surely be scolded for her selfish actions and her failure. Her own life could be put in danger before even suggesting that she would rescue Oriana.

But.

The more difficult the situation before her was...

The higher her final destination ascended...

Lidvia Lorenzetti thought about defeating all those obstacles herself, and she found the greatest happiness within those thoughts. It was like how an athlete felt when meeting a lifelong rival.

Shrove Tuesday, also known as the Mardi Gras.

It was the name of an exuberant festival the Crossists held just before Lent. The Rio Carnival and the Fasching in Germany were other celebrations of it.

There was one reason Lidvia had been given such a name.

"Fu...fu-fu. Ah-ha-ha-ha-ha!! I will go on. Fortune and misfortune, smooth waves and rough—I will hold back all of it! I will do my name proud, the name of that festival of mastication! I will dine on all reality and live on it as one would bread!!"

Give her candy or give her the cane. Her reaction would be the same.

It meant that ultimately, no matter what kind of person you were, you would never be able to stop her from doing. One who feels nothing but happiness no matter what was given to her would accept it all with a smile and keep on going. The very act of standing in her way spurred Lidvia's feet onward, making blocking her path a suicidal, futile act.

"First comes dealing with the aftermath within the Roman Orthodox Church. Then comes drawing up a plan to recover Oriana, and finally a second attack against Academy City! Ha-ha! The walls are high!! And how sweet they are!!"

She could tell the pilot in the cockpit jumped a little, startled at her creepy monologue. But even his attitude of suspicion converted into a burning fighting spirit within her.

And then it happened.

"Ah, hello? May I have your attention please?"

Suddenly, she heard a woman's voice.

Lidvia's shoulders jumped in surprise. There were no flight attendants here. It was a private jet. She could hear sounds of panic coming from the opened cockpit hatch. The pilot didn't seem to know anything.

But Lidvia did.

She knew this voice.

"I am Laura Stuart, archbishop of the English Puritan Church. I shan't allow any cold plays of ignorance, yes? **Little Miss** *Lidvia! ♪"*

The voice was amused.

She had a much more important nickname than the Mardi Gras. Any modern religious history book couldn't be written without speaking of her. The rumors went that she was a monster who held at least as much influence as the queen herself.

Lidvia sucked in her breath—both in terror and joy.

For her, such strong enemies were the most captivating of lambs.

"…Why this private jet?"

"Hm-hm-hmm! You seem to have transferred its ownership and

are trying to land now in France instead of Italy on purpose. Did you think me naive enough to fool with such a parlor trick? I had a little subordinate stuck right to the wall of the plane at the time. ♪"

"…"

Something was on the outside of the plane—likely a Soul Arm of some sort.

Still, she couldn't very well remove it now. It would be impossible to cling to the wall of a craft flying at supersonic speed. Besides, just opening the door would create a difference in air pressure, and all the air inside would go rushing out into the wild blue yonder.

Had she found this plane through the efforts of only the English Puritan Church?

If she had, she would have instigated something when she first brought the Croce di Pietro to Japan. But she hadn't, which probably meant she'd figured out which plane it was only after Lidvia landed.

Which meant there was only one possibility.

Academy City cooperated with her…

Whatever the case, her situation was hopeless.

If she'd placed a communication Soul Arm on the outside, then the United Kingdom knew where this plane was at all times. Lidvia could land right now and change airports, but there would easily be people waiting for her when she got there.

In spite of that, though, she let out a laugh.

"*…Unamiable as always, I should say,*" came back Laura. "*You cackle ever louder the more cornered you become. Can you not possibly do something about that personality of yours?*"

"It's the same as long-distance swimming or diving. The farther the distance, the more pain it gives—and the more happiness you feel when you overcome it all."

"*Your ascetic practice has earned you delight, you filthy freaking masochist. Or, no. You say you delight in making difficulty bow before you, so does that make you a sadist? Speaking of naive. Are you going to drag those feelings to Academy City and attack it again?*"

"…" Lidvia fell quiet for a moment at Laura's exasperated tone. "I have a debt to pay Academy City."

"*I wonder, who was it who said if someone strikes your right cheek, to show them your left? Besides, Oriana Thomson's custody is to be transferred to London. Even if you return to the Vatican and plot your next move, your beloved little Oriana won't be in the city anymore.*"

"No. What has real meaning is getting Oriana returned by taking over Academy City. The conquest of that land will pave the way for a Roman Orthodox victory. And on that day, the English Puritans will no longer be able to disobey even the simplest of my commands."

Her face was pulled back—into a smile.

A dark, zealous, beast-like one, filled with the hunger for victory. An expression unbefitting a sister.

"I will forgive. I believe that if Academy City had not resisted so much, *everybody would be happier right now.* Those inferior sorcerers and that boy who helped them…If not for them, Oriana would be with me on this plane right now!"

Her voice was filled with ardor as it grew even louder.

When she said she would not allow it, her expression slowly became even more ambitious.

"So I will never forgive them. But I am also happy to have encountered a new wall in my path! The more difficult the struggle, the more joyful it will be when I overcome it! Overcome it—and trample it under my feet!!"

Tears even formed in her eyes as she shouted.

Her eyes were wide and unblinking with the immense feeling of competition.

"By not aiming directly for England, and instead going the long way to destroy *them*, the difficulty of rescuing Oriana will be just as I like it!! I must thank the Lord for His kind preparation of such a feast! The thickest, hardest meat is the sort most worthwhile to eat!! I truly look forward to the next time we meet each other!! Ah-ha-ha, ufu-ah-ha-ha-ha!!"

Given a few more minutes of talking, Lidvia wore an expression that indicated she might actually bite into a thick steel plate.

Her voice had clearly gone off the rails.

"*Hm!*" Laura giggled. "*Heh-heh!*"

"…? What is it? This may be a joyful occasion for me, but I don't understand why you would laugh at this time."

"*Oh, come on. It's truly simple, you see. The higher the wall, the more difficult the struggle, the more joy it gives when you trample it under your feet, is it?*"

The communication spell fell meaningfully silent for a moment.

"*I was just thinking you might have a point, you freaking cliff-lover.*"

What? Lidvia took a moment to understand what she said.

Then there was a huge *bang!!*

It came from the side. She quickly turned to look and saw the private jet's entrance hatch gone, leaving a squared-off window to the outside. And she saw the orange glow of metal being melted by scorching heat.

This…this archbishop…Did she put the Soul Arm on the hatch…?!

It was too late now that she realized it.

The hatch plate had been blown off as though by an explosion, out into the night skies. At the same time, like a hole in a balloon, the air inside the craft all began to rush outside because of the difference in air pressure. It was less of a wind and more of a roaring tempest as the energy stormed out of the plane. Even the sofas and tables, bolted to the floor, were mercilessly torn away and flung into the sky at an altitude of eight thousand meters.

"‼"

Lidvia frantically tried to dig her fingers into a protrusion in the wall, but she wouldn't last two seconds. Like dust blown up by a breath, her body left the floor—and was immediately flung out of the plane.

She didn't even have time to squeal.

The sky eight thousand meters above sea level only intensified the darkness of the night. No clouds, a brightly shining moon, and countless stars around it. The cloud layers were below, so there was nothing to hide the heavenly bodies.

Grhghh, ahh…!! I can't breathe…!!

She kept sucking in the super-high-altitude air, but she couldn't feel any oxygen being absorbed into her body. Only a below-zero chill seared her chest. She was far too high up; she couldn't even feel herself falling. It was more like she was being held up by an immensely powerful blast from below.

As her face contorted into sheer surprise and terror, something whizzed past her.

It stopped abruptly in the air in front of her, matching her downward velocity—a single card. It was made of a thin, plastic-like material, with just a few letters written on it in black marker. A Soul Arm to fool children; it had no history, no *character*. But the magic circle within it was as exquisite as any Persian rug.

"Ha-ha! Lidvia, I do admit it is a darn shame to lose that power you have. You could have just abandoned your Roman teachings and licked my feet. I would have saved you."

Lidvia knew she must have already had something planned for that. She could have an English Puritan force positioned at her landing point, preparing to capture her and retreat as soon as she got down there.

But Lidvia pushed aside all that. "What…You're mad!!"

*"I see. Then why don't you and that **thing** make a nice big crater for me?"*

Lidvia saw what she meant.

Only the private jet above her growing smaller was correcting her sense of distance in this world without scale. From the open door of the aircraft, the shape of a cross wrapped in white fabric shot out.

The Croce di Pietro.

The Soul Arm had great magical effects, but its durability was no different from a regular antique. If it dove out of a plane from eight thousand meters up, it would shatter when it got to the bottom, even if it hit water.

"…!! I will not allow it!!" shouted Lidvia, gasping for what little oxygen she could find.

She spread her arms then muttered an incantation. Her body slowed to a gentle, feather-like fall. This was supposed to be a defensive spell, one to slow the acceleration of any object, but when used to cancel gravity, it was like having a parachute.

"If I calculate the Croce di Pietro's trajectory and face it, with my current speed...I will likely make it. No, I will surely make it! There is barely any time, *but that's why it's so much fun*!!" she yelled, her voice ripe with rebelliousness as she awaited the falling cross.

"Approximately four hundred meters from here to the plane. You have jammed on the brakes, so even if you catch the marble object in free fall, you will be minced meat, Lidvia."

"Like I said, that's why it's fun, Archbishop!! You are correct—at my level of spell casting, catching the Croce di Pietro will be difficult even if I use all my power. But that is why! Standing one step away from such a tight situation—it is the joy of tribulation! Fu-fu-fu-ha-ha!!"

The Mardi Gras would extend her arms to accept even the most desperate of situations.

"Hmm!" murmured the card joyfully as it stopped next to her face. *"If you use that spell, you will have your hands full simply catching yourself and the marble cross."*

"Yes, and...?"

"Then how might you be planning to handle that?"

Lidvia's eyes shot back above her.

A new figure burst out of the destroyed private-jet door.

The pilot.

He was waving his arms and legs violently. It didn't look like he had a parachute. Flung out of a plane eight thousand meters in the air without preparation—the fact that he hadn't passed out yet was evidence of his constitution, but he might as well have been completely naked.

The moonlight illuminated his body.

On his face as he fell in a violent path, as though being kneaded by the air, was a scrambled mess of tears and fear at the irrational situation.

Yes.

Exactly as the sinners she had met in the past, estranged from society and civilization, had done.

"‼"

"Now, Lidvia. You can only hold so much. Which will you choose? One of the most powerful Soul Arms in the world, or a lost, pitiful lamb? Ku-ku. If you promise to bury your hands in the dirt and pray for forgiveness, I will gladly lend you a hand, y'know?"

"Y…You…! This is all your doing to begin with!!"

"No time for idle chitchat! Look, the first one is falling to you."

"Guh!!"

The cloth-wrapped cross hurtled toward her without mercy. The marble object was 150 centimeters tall, 70 wide, and over 10 thick. It had been falling for four hundred meters, so it was essentially a cannonball, capable of taking out a sailboat.

Creating forward defense, with thickness at the maximum amount! If I can slow its fall by having it break through a thick wall first…

A moment later, the marble object fell right down at her.

She thought her shield was thick, but it was crushed instantly. The cross had lost some speed, but it still slammed straight into Lidvia's chest. She heard dreadful creaking and cracking noises in her brain, from inside her. She coughed, sticky liquid that smelled of iron coming from deep in her throat and out her mouth.

"Grhh, urf! Ahhhrrrgh!!"

As blood spurted from between her teeth, she still grabbed the heavy cross with both hands. She dug ten fingers into the white cloth it was wrapped in with all her might.

"Oh, but look. The second one is coming."

The voice from the card sounded genuinely entertained.

Her consciousness was fleeing her, hazy with pain, blood loss, oxygen deprivation, and a whole host of other factors. But she shook herself out of it and looked up.

The pilot of the private jet was plunging toward her, the same way the cross had. With Lidvia in her injured state, it was practically a boulder fired from a ballista, meant to break down a castle wall.

*I…won't be able to…catch him like…this…*She gripped the cross tighter. *If I assume too much burden…we will all fall to the ground and die…If I want to save the Soul Arm, I need to abandon the pilot… But if I discard this, I can save a precious human life…*

Lidvia watched.

Watched the pilot's face, sullied with tears, snot, and anger at the absurd act of violence, as he drew near her.

"Oh? Lidvia, you did say you saved sinners, didn't you? Are simple victims below you, jerk?"

"How…dare you…?!" She tried to say more, but not much was getting out of her lungs.

She couldn't possibly catch them both. If she tried, they would all fall. Abandoning what she could would pose the least difficulty.

But that wouldn't be right.

The more difficult the situation got for her…

N-no…I can't think…about it! If I do…I will really die…but…but no…urgh…I must endure it! That…that sweet, sweet feeling…I need to discard it…!!

The more she thought, the more the flames of defiance smoldered in her back. As she sweat, there was something, something not pain or tension, something more *primal* beginning to mix in with it.

She grated her teeth, trying to endure something. Then she heard a voice from next to her.

A slipping voice.

Like water seeping into a wasteland.

Just like the temptation of the bewitching devil himself.

*"What's this? Lidvia, I thought you would say something ridiculous like you'd catch both of them at once or something. The higher the wall, the bigger the obstacles…**the bigger the delight when you over-come them and trample over me, the one who made them, right?**"*

Grrk.

Something inside Lidvia snapped.

Trample…over…?

The only thing she was aware of right then was the taste of blood. She could barely think.

That...arrogance...of yours...Archbishop...I will...trample...

The far-too-primal feeling that came after accomplishing *that*.

Without realizing her conceited speech was all part of Laura's plan, Lidvia laughed.

"Ha...ha-ha..."

Her lips parted wide, blood mixed with drool trickling out of her mouth. The pilot, whom she was supposed to be catching, gave a terrified cry. All her defiance, all her ambition was on her face now as she gripped the cross, once again stretching her arms out far.

Like a woman welcoming a lover returned from a distant land.

As if to say how happy she was with the intense pain that came after the direct hit.

"Ha-ha-ha! Ah-ha-ha-ufu-fu-ha-ha-ha-ha-ha-ha-ha-ha-ha!!"

With blood, sweat, tears, drool, and snot hanging from her face, Lidvia Lorenzetti beamed.

Then, a moment later...

The pilot's body slammed into hers, and with the immense impact came an indescribably primal feeling shooting through her entire body.

In Academy City, there was a building with no windows and no doors.

It was the sturdiest fortress in Academy City, made with special materials that could absorb and diffuse the pure heat and shock waves yielded from nuclear blasts. There were no hallways, staircases, or even ventilation inside it, which meant going in and out required the assistance of an esper skilled with teleportation. One "human" was there now, waiting silently.

The chairperson of the Academy City General Board.

The "human," Aleister Crowley.

"Hmm."

Aleister was in a dimly lit room. The room was large and chilly to the skin. In the center sat a giant enshrined glass cylinder, and a liquid of bright red filled it. Countless cables and tubes, big and small, connected to the cylindrical container, coiled about the entire floor and connected to the instruments and displays covering the walls on every side. In this room without any real illumination, the red and green lights on the instruments looked like a night sky filled with starlight.

Aleister floated upside down inside that cylinder.

The person's green surgical garments silently billowed inside the liquid as his long, long silvery hair, perhaps absent of pigment, coiled around.

Aleister could only be described as human: None could tell whether the person was male or female, adult or child, saint or sinner.

"To gain control of Academy City and secure authority over the world by using the Croce di Pietro…," Aleister muttered.

Whatever Oriana's and Lidvia's personal goals had been, it would have been impossible to carry out without the support of the Roman Orthodox Church itself. It was more natural to think the Church had planned the operation and Oriana and Lidvia had insisted on being the ones to do it, in an attempt to use it for their own benefit.

Behind Oriana Thomson and Lidvia Lorenzetti…

…was the Roman Orthodox Church.

"…They certainly have rocked the boat, so to speak."

Aleister sounded less threatened and more fed up with it.

The Roman Orthodox Church had been shady for a long time. Going back, it had probably begun during the age in which Galileo Galilei lived. When they were unable to stop the world's foundation shifting away from Crossism and toward natural science, their authority over all the lands had started to waver, subtly but certainly.

On the surface, the Church named itself the largest religious group on the planet, but there was another problem with that.

Right now, the Crossist faction—purely in terms of the sorcery world—was said to consist of three main pillars: the Roman, Russian, and English Churches. Of them, people generally said that Roman Orthodoxy was the largest in scale, embracing two billion followers…but having gathered two billion also meant it was actually in balance with the United Kingdom and its total population of ninety million. *And not every citizen of the United Kingdom was part of the English Puritan Church, either.*

In the future, if the English Puritan Church were to rise to power and scrape up one or two billion more disciples, what would happen to the Roman Orthodox Church? The problem had always been placed to the side. There was no actual population of that size for them to gain, as had been pointed out many times. Recently, though, the issue was showing other openings.

The first was that the Roman Orthodox Church's main combat forces had either been destroyed or exiled, with the Gregorian Choir and Agnes's forces being chief among that list.

The second was that other combat potential, such as Orsola Aquinas and the Amakusa-Style Crossist Church, had been incorporated into the English Puritan Church.

The scales in the magic world were just barely holding their balance, and now these events were about to make everything tip over. The Roman Orthodox Church wanted to protect their seats at the top of the world. They were being extremely cautious of how those scales were moving.

Those things had probably colored the recent events as well.

The pope and his cardinals, leading the Roman Orthodox Church—what would their faces look like right now?

As somebody who had abandoned sorcery, and as someone who now sat at the center of managing its polar opposite—the science side—with perfection, Aleister watched the state of affairs with contempt.

"But now…," Aleister said, exasperated.

They clung to it in such an unsightly way, so *how* they clung to it was not likely a consideration for them. They had brought out a Soul Arm on the Croce di Pietro's level this time, after all. It certainly didn't seem like they were going to stop attacking because of what happened, either. There was still the possibility, however slim, that they would again use a Soul Arm on the same level.

Despite a certain boy having settled the Croce di Pietro incident, frankly speaking, it hadn't seemed to be a very good plan. There was no proof the same idea would work in the future.

Which means I may need to accelerate my plans. I swear. This project was not originally supposed to be used for something so trivial…

As Aleister thought, a square screen appeared in the empty void.

On it was a detailed world map, with 9,969 locations marked in red. They showed the world locations of certain mass-produced espers. Aleister would use them, along with School District i, or the Five Elements Society, sleeping in Academy City. They were all carrying out this plan: to put a stop to all magical activity in the world.

However…

The Imagine Breaker is the key, but its growth is still unstable. I wonder if it will be really usable.

Originally, Aleister hadn't thought to be pressed to implement the project so soon. *If I had known then what I know now*, thought Aleister. *But I didn't. So…*

A new screen appeared as he thought, overlaying itself onto the locations of the mass-produced espers.

The square window showed a rectangular case made of glass.

And the twisting silver staff inside it.

I may need to begin considering the possibility of riding out myself. Hmm. Heh-heh.

The "human" laughed in the darkness.

Was that the laugh of the world's greatest scientist?

Or was it the laugh of the world's strongest sorcerer?

What was in the mind of this "human," who appeared both male and female, both adult and child, both saint and sinner, would never be illuminated by another—but it did make this "human" laugh.

Aisa Himegami awoke in a hospital room in the early morning.

Her room wasn't a private one like Kamijou's but one made for six people, with each person's space cordoned off by curtains. All the patients here were, of course, female, but they were of all ages. One was the same age as she was, too.

"..."

Himegami's idle gaze wandered to the ceiling, then she abruptly sat up in bed.

"It's early. What are you doing here?"

She directed her monotone voice toward the edge of the bed. A sister wearing a pure-white habit was sitting on the floor, with her upper body slumped over the bed railing, hovering there mostly limp.

Himegami had just woken up, so she was sleepy, too. But this sister's eyes looked absolutely exhausted. Her housemate (or, possibly more accurately, the owner of the place she freeloaded at) was injured and brought to the hospital very often, so this girl in white seemed used to staying up all night at hospitals. Apparently the nurses had begun talking about how she would fall asleep in chairs in single-patient rooms and on benches in the waiting room. It had ended with her being thought of as a mysterious girl who showed up at the hospital without rhyme or reason, one who liked TV and snacks and toys.

The eyes of the sister from the United Kingdom, Index, were narrowed into small slits as she yawned. "...They said I can't use the benches when morning came, so I had to evacuate to your room, Aisa. What a nice, soft bed..."

Her primal instincts seemed to be urging her to find a warm place to sleep.

Unfortunately...

"Stop that. Beds are not for chewing on. They're for lying on. Also. If you keep drooling on it for no reason. I will be the one they look at coldly."

"So warm..."

Index didn't seem to be in the mood for listening as she rubbed her face against the comforter. Her cheek was hitting Himegami's thigh, so she was feeling impatient with the girl. She was 70 or 80 percent asleep, like she was struggling through an afternoon class in the beginning of spring. Himegami thought for a moment, then he opened the door of the mini fridge beside the bed, about one meter tall.

"I will use the ice in the freezer. To get you to wake up. Take this."

"It's cold!!"

Tossing an ice cube against the sister's forehead made her cry out, which in turn made all the other patients in the room wake up as well. Himegami shrank back in bed and bowed her head in apology to them, then pressed a button on the remote control to automatically close her space's curtains. She couldn't bear the others staring at her.

After the ice cube bounced off her forehead, Index skillfully caught it in midair. Then, painfully unaware of Himegami's state of mind, she plopped it into her mouth and said, "Aisa, are you okay now? I got a report that our sorcerer did some dangerous healing magic just by imitation."

"I don't actually know what happened. I was unconscious at the time. I don't think I understood. But. The frog-faced doctor said. My examination went well. I should be back to normal soon." Himegami pulled at the collar of her pajamas as she spoke and looked down. Her cross sparkled. Her body was covered in professionally wrapped bandages from her chest to her waist, but apparently all the organs necessary to sustain life had been repaired, without a single blood vessel lost.

For Aisa Himegami, who was still a girl no matter how she acted, the question of whether this would scar her had unsettled her greatly. The frog-faced doctor, though, had smiled creepily (or happily, from his point of view) and said, "Heh-heh, who exactly do you think I am? I may not look like much, but I make it a rule to prepare anything and everything my patients need. Heh-heh-heh. How wonderful it is to have patients relying on you." So everything seemed all right. And come to think of it, despite a certain boy having had his right arm sliced off, he didn't have a single mark on him, either.

Himegami stared at the bandages underneath her pajamas and thought, *But the wound was so bad you could see bones.*

That red-haired priest had only done something hasty that would extend her life for a little longer, but that "spell" had easily repaired a wound that had clearly been beyond saving. She'd given up on the matter as hopeless, but now it had again turned into little thorns prickling her heart.

But...

Right now, more importantly...

"I can leave today or tomorrow. The frog doctor told me. But with my body right now. I don't think I can be in the events."

"??? Aisa, you look kind of lonely. Why?" Index asked with a blank look.

Himegami silently shook her head, but that obviously wasn't enough to make her thoughts disappear. So she told her—about the matter she'd decided to keep quiet about.

"Did he. Do something reckless again?"

"Yeah. Right! I forgot!" Index said in a bright voice, finally looking awake. "He didn't tell me the details yet, but some Roman Orthodox sorcerers attacked the city using the Dai-ha-sei Festival or whatever as an excuse! And then Touma ran off by himself without talking to me first, and then he did some crazy things, and then he came crawling to me with a report!!"

Index was shouting by the end, and in her anger she'd begun to chew on the end of the comforter.

Himegami didn't care about her nibbling.

Actually, she wasn't even paying attention to it.

Sorcerers. From the Roman Orthodox Church.

In the end, that was the reason the boy had clenched his fist and fought.

It was so obvious. Of course that was it. It meant he had been fighting someone, alongside a sorcerer, since before Himegami collapsed. That, along with the boy crying out in anger—it had all been just part of the process, a piece of some bigger goal, and that he'd only just happened to be sidetracked by it.

...

She'd felt the same thing back in the alchemist's fortress. She started to think about why the boy had even saved her at all. The fact of the matter was that the two of them didn't have enough of a connection for him to risk his life for her.

Which meant it didn't matter *who* it was.

The boy hadn't saved Aisa Himegami in particular.

He would have saved anyone if they were in her position, wouldn't he?

If Aisa Himegami hadn't been there...

...then she wouldn't have even been in a corner of his mind, would she?

The act of risking his life to save her gave no benefit to Touma Kamijou. Doing so was just part of his daily life. Even during these past couple of months, she'd seen him pounding sense into other people in class and getting them to rethink their lives twice a week on average.

I'm...

Aisa Himegami, sitting up in bed, thought about it.

She didn't have the strength or knowledge to be of use to anyone, like this girl biting her comforter did. She wasn't the kind of person to treat everyone equally and worry about others just from being near them, either.

I'm...really...

Himegami's face fell a little bit as she slowly grasped the comforter near her knees.

She couldn't think of a single reason to be with him.

She was sure he'd save her whenever she was in trouble. But if Kamijou and Himegami had no good reason to be together, that act probably didn't mean anything. His taking one action for her sake was like wasting his money on something entirely pointless. Injury, usually.

Am I not really. Worth saving?

She knew those were chilling words.

But in reality, she knew she wasn't blessed with any special talents or abilities that would make her worth someone risking their life to save. The only power she had was to hurt others and make them fight, and that detestable ability was the only thing unique about her. It wasn't like she could dominate others in non-esper fields like studying or sports.

It was ridiculous.

So why?

If the fact that she'd been saved…

Why. Did he save me?

…was some sort of mistake or a misunderstanding…

Even back then…

The words they'd exchanged when she was lying in a pool of her own blood in the alley.

He said it very clearly…

The promise he couldn't keep—his words that he'd return to the hospital before the night parade.

Then what am I worth…?

If even those kind words put pressure on the man named Touma Kamijou…

Is there a point. To my being here…

"…Maybe I. Only cause problems. For everyone else."

She thought those words would be cold. But they echoed in her heart after she heard them.

Then the girl nibbling on the comforter stopped abruptly.

She probably had both special talents and knowledge that would make her worth saving. And she had a heart that made others happy just by being around her.

"That isn't true. Touma looks like he's having fun when he's with you."

"Huh?"

For a moment, she didn't understand what that meant.

And yet, the girl in white, who he was always protecting, puffed out her cheeks and started chewing on the comforter again. "Touma's right hand. He punched too many people and now the skin on his knuckles is torn."

Index began to sullenly explain it to Himegami.

"Basically Touma hates doing work. The reason he does all this is pretty obvious. He doesn't do it because it's a rule or to save the world. He can't get serious about that stuff. Anything that seems like work…Like if a bunch of people get in a fight, he'll run away. And he won't make me tofu hamburgers. And he doesn't listen to me when I yell at him. But…" She paused. "When Touma decides something, he does it no matter what. Even if he has to fight hundreds of nuns by himself, even if he has to go into an alchemist's fortress with thousands of his pawns, he'll never run away from what he decides. He decided he was going to protect you. I think what he really couldn't forgive was *you being dragged into silly things like Roman Orthodox sorcerers or their trying to conquer Academy City.*"

Himegami listened. Silently, she listened.

"Touma protects a lot of people, so it's kind of hard to understand. But he'll never hesitate to protect you, Aisa. He would never think you were causing him trouble. If he did, he wouldn't have all those people around him. He never says anything about that, and neither does anyone else, so it's sort of hard to figure out his relationships with them. If you did figure them all out, maybe it would seem really amazing."

Index stopped, allowing a light silence to descend on them.

Himegami tried to tell her something, but she realized she couldn't talk. Her jaws and her mouth were trembling. For a moment, she thought about where that trembling was coming from.

"Wait, Fukiyose! You walk in the door to visit me, and the first thing you do is freak out at me. If you're that energetic, why are you even in the hospital?!"

"Sh-shut up, you! Anyone would panic if they suddenly saw a man naked!"

"But you're the one who suddenly waltzed into the room while I was changing—"

"Touma Kamijou! Just…finish getting changed and if you're still half-asleep you need theanine to activate your brain cells and there's a lot of that in green tea so drink some of *this*!"

"Aghhh, that's hot!! Hey, idiot Fukiyose! Don't pour boiling-hot liquid down other people's throats just to hide your embarrassment!!"

They heard some pretty loud voices coming from the hallway.

Then a series of quick, stomping footsteps, not often heard in a hospital setting.

"So is this one Himegami's room? Wait, you're not going to be *bothering* her with a sudden visit, I hope!"

"Eh? You know, Himegami may not talk much, but she doesn't necessarily like things quiet. You just have to look closely. When she's happy she actually smiles a tiny bit. For someone who's secretly a caring person, you should have realized that."

"Caring…? Who are we talking about, exactly?"

"Pfft. I mean, you didn't know where Himegami's room was, so you came to mine to ask, and then you spent thirty minutes deciding what fruits and flowers to get at the shop, so you're obviously a heroic soul who cares about her friends and— Hot, *hot*! I told you to stop pouring that green tea down my throat! I don't need my brain energized any more, so let's grab Himegami and go to the rest of our class! We went through all the trouble of borrowing a wheelchair from the doctors!!"

"All the events today are extreme, and first on the list is the all-school boys' mock cavalry battle, group A competition. Next time, plan to bring injured people to events that they actually *want* to cheer for!"

Index stopped biting on the comforter and looked up toward the voices. A partition curtain was in the way. Himegami looked over as well, then picked up the remote control that opened it.

"Hey. Do you know why. He fights like that. Even when he gets so badly hurt?"

"Who knows? I don't think I do," answered Index, without really thinking about it.

*   *   *

"When I asked him before, he said he did it for himself. Maybe that's just what makes him happy."

Himegami pressed the open-close button on the remote.
The curtains opened.
And lying beyond there was the world Aisa Himegami had always wanted.

AFTERWORD

Hello, those of you who have been buying these novels one at a time.

Nice to meet you, those of you who bought all ten volumes at once. I'm Kazuma Kamachi.

I broke into the double digits amid all the work I've been doing. In-universe, even after the tenth volume, it's still September. When I think about how Volume 1 began at the end of July, it makes me feel like things are going at an incredibly slow place. Plus, as those of you who've already finished the book will know, the flow of time has just slowed to an all-time series low. I suppose it's still better than one volume ago, Volume 9, but…

The occult theme this time is basically the same as it was in Volume 9, but I suppose I did add the theme of constellations in Volume 10. This is magic incoporating constellations—essentially astrology, but the basic rules changed every time the science side figured something out, as different factions kept branching off. It has a very long and interesting history. When Uranus was discovered, people split over the decision of whether to include it in their readings. And when the geocentric theory and heliocentric theories switched positions, it would have completely changed common sense about stars and probably caused a huge stir.

Given this series' thematic clashing of science and magic, I couldn't possibly leave it out, so I snuck it into this book. The rules and effects of astrological divination were entirely different based on whether they accepted Uranus and Pluto or not. It seems a lot like quantum theory to me in that respect.

As always, I'd like to apologize to and thank my illustrator, Mr. Haimura, and my editor, Mr. Miki. I'm looking forward to your continued support in the future.

And to all you readers out there, as always, thank you so much. I will go on thanking you in the future—please do continue to support me.

Now then, as I turn the final page of this book,
and as I pray that you will turn to the first page of the next book,
today, at this hour, I lay down my pen.

…Come to think of it, October is when winter uniforms start, right?

Kazuma Kamachi

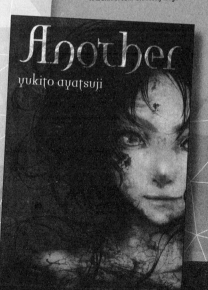